The Season of Sin
by Stacy-Deanne

Giving Your Soul a Rise...One Page at a Time

ISBN-13: 978-0-9850763-0-6
THE SEASON OF SIN © 2012 by Stacy-Deanne

Peace In The Storm Publishing, LLC.
P.O. Box 1152
Pocono Summit, PA 18346

Visit our Web site at www.PeaceInTheStormPublishing.com

Acknowledgments

Special thanks to my dad John for being so supportive of me. If not for you I wouldn't be able to pursue my dream of writing.

I'd like to thank my beautiful mother Elva who is resting in heaven. I think about you with every step I take and every move I make. It's like you're still here with me. I hope I've made you proud and I will continue to try to.

I'd like to thank Elissa Gabrielle and the Peace in the Storm family for showing unbelievable support. You guys have reminded me over and over what I love so much about this business. It's been an honor knowing all of you and I wish you all success in everything you do. We do it big at PITS!!!

Thanks to my favorite writing pals Ruth Ann Nordin and Sheila M. Goss for being that "shoulder" I lean on when I need to vent and rant about this crazy business. It's been wonderful knowing you both. It's hard to find people in this business that really cares about you and I cherish you both. We need more people in the world like you!

Thanks to all my fans, readers and supporters. I do this for you and I always will. I hope you enjoy The Season of Sin and keep a lookout for my future books!

Best Wishes!

Stacy-Deanne

Praise for
The Season of Sin

"A white knuckled hard hitting thriller. Stacy-Deanne could be dubbed the Princess of Plot. Twists and turns that keep you guessing…Witty and intelligently written. Incredibly moving and engaging story that draws you in from the start. The characters demand your attention. Be prepared to be affected by this story!"
~ *Treasure Books N' More*

The Season of Sin is a psychological fast-paced thriller. Readers will be enthralled within the pages at the cleverly done plot filled with multiple layers, twists and turns. While reading Stacy-Deanne's The Season of Sin, I felt like I got an inside view of a Lifetime suspense movie. I can't get enough of Detectives Brianna "Bree" Morris" and Steven Kemp. The chemistry between the two oozes off the pages. If you're looking for a captivating suspense novel, then you don't want to pass up adding The Season of Sin to your shelf.
~ *Shelia M Goss, National Best-selling author of Delilah, My Invisible Husband and Savannah's Curse*

"Stacy-Deanne is at her best! The Season of Sin is such a riveting page-turner of secrets, lies, sex, and yes sin. This best-selling crime novelist has done it again!"
~ *Serenity King*

CHAPTER ONE

"Ahh." Brianna awoke on Nadia Hollister's couch not remembering how she got there. Cops walked in and out of the front door. Someone barked orders among overlapping voices. Cameras snapped in the distance. People trudged through the halls.

An ice pack slid from underneath her when she lifted her head. A spasm traveled through her neck. Goosebumps covered her brown skin.

"Detective Morris?" A female officer bent over her. "You okay? Don't move too fast okay?"

The lady's high-pitched tone multiplied the agony in Brianna's head.

"*Mmm.* What the?"

"You're at Nadia Hollister's. Don't you remember? Are you in a lot of pain?"

"No." She touched her head. "Just, just dizzy."

"We'll get you to the hospital. We were gonna take you there when we first got here but Detective Kemp said it was best not to move you yet."

"Steve?" Brianna sat up. "Steve's here?" She focused on Nadia's computer desk.

"Yeah he's with Detective Matthews."

"Jayce is here?"

If Jayce is here something terrible has...

"Detective Kemp said you were supposed to meet him earlier after you left here and when you didn't show up he came looking for you. And that's when he saw what happened."

"What happened? Is something wrong?" Brianna grabbed the lady's shirt. "Where's Nadia?"

"Uh..."

"What happened?" Brianna shook her. "Where's Nadia? Where is she?"

"Let me get Detective Kemp." The lady pulled Brianna's fingers from her shirt. "I think it's best if he explains it to you." She ran out.

Officers drifted in to check on Brianna. She fanned them away, lying that she felt okay.

"Bree?"

Detective Steven Kemp squeezed between the forensics officers at the doorway. Humidity forced his short blond hair into small spikes. His turquoise-blue pupils zeroed in on Brianna as if he expected answers she couldn't give.

"Oh, Bree." He adjusted his gun belt and sat beside her.

"I'm fine." She massaged her temples. "Just tell me what's going on."

"I'm just so glad you're all right, baby." He kissed her forehead.

"I feel like someone ran over my head then came back, saw that wasn't good enough and decided to pound it with a brick."

"The medic checked it. There's no lump or anything." He combed his hands through her hair. "Just need to get you to the hospital for tests to make sure everything is okay."

Someone had taken down her ponytail. Her neat curls had dissolved into kinky ringlets.

"I don't need to go to the hospital."

"I don't care what you say you need. You got hit in the head with that thing." He pointed to the canister on the floor.

"I'm fine, Steven."

"Get up without wobbling then."

She got up. "Oh! Oooh." She fell back down.

"See, you're going to the hospital."

"What happened? Why is Jayce here?"

He lowered his head. "I'm so sorry, Bree."

"What?" She put the ice pack on her head. "Steve spit it out."

"Nadia was murdered."

6

"What?" She dropped the ice pack. "You...that's impossible."

"Bree."

"No wait a minute! We were just together tonight, *here*. We were gonna watch a movie." She felt her head. "This can't be true. It just can't be."

"It is. We believe whoever attacked you killed her."

"Just tell me how it happened please."

"She was stabbed." He lowered his voice. "Multiple times."

"Oh." She covered her mouth. "I don't believe this. Nadia's dead?"

Officers stacked boxes in the den.

Steven held her. "I'm so sorry, Bree."

"I don't believe this. Who would hurt Nadia? And I was here? I was right here and I didn't stop it!"

"It's not your fault."

"Oh god." She cried into her hands. "Steven this makes no sense. Who would want to kill Nadia?"

Homicide Detective Jayce Matthews sauntered in. The muscular, light-skinned black man passed a small plastic sack to an officer then approached the couch. He sunk his hands in the pockets of his coat. His hard face softened with sincerity and concern.

"Bree honey you all right?"

"I'm fine, Jayce."

"She's lying." Steven rested his foot on the coffee table. "She's in a lot of pain."

Jayce took her arm. "We need to get you to the hospital. You look good but we need to be cautious. Come on."

She snatched away. "I'm not going anywhere until I find out what exactly happened."

"Your health is more important right now," Steve said.

"Jayce?" Brianna rubbed her head. "You're on this case?"

"Yes."

"I want all the details."

"It was one of the most vicious murders I've seen since I started Homicide." Jayce scrunched his face. "She was stabbed everywhere. She had wounds on her arms, her legs and under her neck. I suspect the slice under the neck killed her instantly."

"I don't believe this."

Steven kissed Brianna's cheek. "It's okay."

She sobbed. "It's not okay. She was probably crying out for help and I couldn't help her. Oh god. I'll never forgive myself."

"Shh." Steven caressed her hair.

"But I don't understand. Why wouldn't he kill me too?"

"Maybe he thought he had," Steven said. "Either that or he didn't find you a threat. He obviously came up from behind you so he knew you couldn't identify him."

"Or maybe he didn't wanna kill Bree." Jayce dug in his pocket. "Maybe knocking her out was enough as long as she didn't see him. He was after Nadia and I think he knew her personally. A murder this brutal is rarely random." He knelt beside Brianna. "I know this is a lot for you to take."

"You got that right. Someone bopped me over the head then killed Nadia right under my nose and I couldn't stop it."

"How could you when you were knocked out?" Steven scoffed. "When are you gonna realize you're not superwoman?"

"I just don't believe this."

"I know it's hard but try to think." Jayce held her hand. "Did you get a look at the person who hit you?"

"No. I was down here waiting for Nadia to take her bath. She'd invited me over and we were gonna watch movies. She put on some tea and she was gonna be down in a little while. I got up to go...shit I can't even remember where I was going. I might have been going to the kitchen to check on the tea. I remember being hit and falling on the floor. After that I can't tell you anything."

"So you didn't see anything?"

"The only thing I remember was a smell."

"A smell?" He bounced on his knees.

"It was some kind of fragrance, cologne." She sniffed. "If I smelled it again, I'd know right off. I wanna see Nadia."

"They already took the body away. Besides I wouldn't have let you go in there anyway."

"*Let* me, Jayce? What about her daughter Dylan? Has anyone told her yet?"

"Were gonna notify her and the rest of her family. You and Nadia were close huh?"

"We'd become good friends. It started out as therapy for me but we had so much in common we started hanging out. Nadia was very lonely. She'd been depressed lately. She and Dylan had some kind of falling out and it really bothered her. She always seemed to need my opinion about something. I started feeling like *I* was the shrink you know?"

"How old is Dylan?" Jayce scratched over his thin mustache.

8

"Twenty-seven. Nadia adopted her."

"Hmm." Jayce nodded.

"She's an artist. She's really talented. Her work has been in the museum under the local artists section and she's even been profiled in the Albany paper."

"Guess I missed that." Jayce scratched his ear. "You said they had a falling out? Was this recently or..."

Brianna held onto the couch. "Don't go there, Jayce."

"What?"

"I know those gears are grinding in your brain but you're wrong. Dylan's a sweet girl and she loves her mother. She wouldn't have done anything like this. Back off."

"Well there weren't signs of forced entry." Steven bobbed his foot. "The person came in through the back patio door."

"So? Nadia probably forgot to lock it. Anyone could've walked through there right?"

"So you know Dylan well enough that you're certain she couldn't have done this?"

"Jayce if I thought Dylan was capable of murder I'd be the first one going to get her. Sure she and Nadia had friction but she adored her mother. Their relationship has been strained for a while. It started because of Dylan's ex-boyfriend, Bruce."

CHAPTER TWO

"Know a last name?" Jayce readied his pencil to write.

"McNamara."

"Ever met him?"

"No."

"What did Bruce have to do with Nadia and Dylan's friction?"

"Nadia couldn't stand Bruce."

"Why?" Steven asked.

"I don't know."

"Well wonder if he disliked her too?"

Jayce tapped his notepad. "Bruce McNamara huh?"

"I've heard that name before." Steven scooted to the edge of the couch. "McNamara. Isn't he in the system?"

Jayce shrugged. "He *could* have a record. I'll check it out."

"If he does then that's a reason Nadia wouldn't like him," Steven said. "Not too many people want their daughters with jailbirds."

"I don't know anything about all that." Brianna raised her hand. "I just know she didn't like him."

"Wonder if it went both ways," Jayce said. "Either way it's a little something to go on. I'm gonna check to see if McNamara has a record when I get back to the station."

"I wanna see the bathroom."

"Oh no, Bree." Jayce held her to the couch. "I couldn't forgive myself if I let you do that."

"I wanna see it." She stood. "I want to see what happened."

He put his hand on her shoulder. "What you need to do is go to the hospital, get checked out and rest."

"I don't need to go to the damn hospital! I can take care of myself! I only care about finding out who killed Nadia." She fixed the bottom of her turtleneck. "We at least know where to start looking."

"We?" Jayce shook his head.

Another officer laid boxes in the room.

"This is my case, Bree. You and Steven stay out of it. Besides this is homicide, my turf."

"What's with these boxes?" She looked through one filled with books, files and CD's.

"I told them to gather up some of Nadia's things and we're gonna look through them to see if we can get any answers. She had all these files and things."

"Course she was a psychiatrist, Jayce. Part of her job is research."

"Or maybe she's some collector," Steven said. "Look at all these old newspapers and clippings of famous events. Like decades of history before our eyes."

Brianna read a clipping. "Nadia loved newspapers. She said they captured memories. She liked to smell the paper you know? She said it signaled nostalgia."

Jayce stood behind her. "We found some fascinating things in her bedroom too. She has these chests full of stuff but some of them need a key to get into."

"Let's see what this is." Steven thumbed through a thick, college-ruled notebook.

Brianna peeked over his shoulder. "What's that?"

"A journal or something she wrote in."

"Jesus." Brianna leaned in the box. "Look at all these notebooks. Just stacks and stacks of 'em."

"They'll come in handy." Jayce took the journals from them. "If Nadia wrote in these regularly there might be clues." He put them back in the box. "At least we'll know more about her."

"She was hurting but you wouldn't know it by being with her." Brianna smiled. "She kept a smile on her face even when she was suffering."

"Wonder why she trusted you so much?" Steven pushed a

box out of his way. "You haven't known each other that long."

"I don't know. Sometimes you bond with people over things that only they can understand I guess. She always said she was comfortable with me. Maybe it's because I wasn't apart of her family." Brianna looked through another box. "I don't know."

"What about Nadia's family?" Jayce dug through a box.

"Her parents are dead. She has three sisters and two brothers. The brothers don't live in Albany but the sisters do. She's very close to Jasmine, her older sister. She hasn't spoken to her brothers in some years."

"Do they all get along?" Jayce watched her out of the corner of his eye.

"She didn't tell me *all* her business."

Steven read clippings. "For someone who didn't tell you "all her business", she sure told you enough didn't she?"

"We talked about normal things okay? You act like I'm hiding something that Nadia might have told me."

"I didn't say that I just think she might have told you something important, that at the time you didn't *think* was important. Get it?"

"No." She wobbled. "Ooh. Oh, my head's pounding."

"That's it." Steven put his arms around her. "You're going to the hospital."

"I don't need a damn hospital."

"No, Steve's right. We'll talk more about this when you're feeling better."

"Jayce I want in on this."

"No."

"If you think I'm gonna just sit back until you spoon feed me answers then you don't know me as well as you think."

"Are you forgetting that your life is in danger too? The person who killed Nadia might come after you too."

"They know I didn't see them. Even if they did I don't care."

"Sttttuuuuubbbbbooorrrrnnn." Steven sang.

"Shut up, Steve. I knew Nadia and you didn't, Jayce. You need me whether you like it or not. Steve and I can help you out. Certainly you wouldn't turn down help right?"

Steven opened a box of camera film. "Jayce is right. We should stay the hell out of it. You forget we have cases of our own right now anyway?"

"Do I look like I give a shit right now, Steve?"

"All these years I've known you Bree and I still can't

understand what goes on in your head sometimes."

Steven tossed the film in a box. "Me neither."

An officer walked in. "Detective Matthews we need you for a sec, sir."

"I'll be right there." He turned to Brianna. "I'm just trying to protect you."

"I don't need your protection."

"Don't argue with her dude okay?" Steven searched another box. "It's better that way."

Jayce poked Brianna's chest. "Just remember I call the shots. You jeopardize this case and you'll regret it."

"I wouldn't do that. I just wanna help. I won't be a pain in your ass."

"Too late." He stomped out the room.

"I think you pissed him off." Steven put his wool cap on.

"I don't care. I'm gonna find out what happened whether you both agree or not."

"Come on. I'll drive you to the hospital. We'll tell one of the officers to get your car."

She got her coat. "I don't need a doctor, I need an *Advil*."

"Just come on. We're through with this discussion."

Brianna cut her eyes to the officers in the hall. She waited until they left then signaled to the box of journals.

"Steve?"

"Huh?"

"Wait."

"What? Come on. You know it'll take forever at the hospital."

"Get the box."

"What?"

"We're gonna take the journals."

"Are you nuts? I'm not touching that box. You wanna steal evidence then do it by yourself."

"It's a box of journals not the murder weapon. Might not be anything useful in them anyway."

"Then why the hell do you want 'em?"

"Just do what I say."

"I'm not taking those journals, Bree. And how will you explain them being gone?"

"Look at all the boxes over here. Jayce won't remember this one's gone."

"Yeah right." He scratched his nose.

"Steven I never ask anything of you but I'm asking you to

help me now, please."

"Shit." He picked up the box. "You better be glad I'm still in love with you."

She kissed his cheek.

CHAPTER THREE

"Just stop it, Aunt Jas!" Dylan stomped across Jasmine Hudson's upstairs hallway Monday morning.

"No I won't stop it!" Jasmine walked so close to Dylan she almost tripped her.

"Get out of my way!"

"Who do you think you're talking to?" Jasmine waved a tissue. "You just don't wanna face facts."

"No I can face facts." Dylan bumped into Jasmine when she turned around. "I face the fact that you're completely nuts!"

"Am I? Because I speak the truth?"

"No because you are just so determined to keep the feud going with Bruce that you won't see reason!" Dylan ran downstairs.

Jasmine chased her. "Get back here young lady!"

"I don't wanna hear it! I cannot believe that you can't be sensitive to what I'm going through. My mother was just murdered!"

"And she was my sister! I loved Nadia and I love you! I've always loved you like you were my own!"

"You coddle me just like Mom did. The point is you are dead wrong about Bruce. How dare you try to suggest he's a killer?"

"Oh did I only suggest?" Jasmine flung grayish-brown strands out of her eyes. "I'm saying it straight out. Yes, I think Bruce did it. So there."

"You stop it! That's a horrible thing to say! Bruce would

never kill anyone!"

"Oh yeah? He's a criminal."

"He *was* a criminal. He's paid for his mistakes."

"He could never pay enough in my opinion." Jasmine straightened books on her bookshelf.

"I wasn't even seeing Bruce when he got in trouble anyway. You're no one to judge, Aunt Jas. You never done nothing wrong?"

"Yes but I never murdered anybody."

"And Bruce didn't either."

"You know damn well he hated her enough to do it. Use your brain Dylan, that's what it's for."

Dylan held her waist and threw her chin into the air. "Bruce couldn't have done it because he's been out of town."

"You don't talk to Bruce anymore or so you claim. How the hell would you know where he's been?"

"His father died and he went out of town to see his family. Rhonda told me."

"Oh yeah?" Jasmine bent over to straighten another shelf. "I still think he did it and that's exactly what I'm gonna tell Detective Morris when she gets here."

"Oh no you're not. I don't even want you in the room when she comes."

"Well tough it's my house!"

"Stop it you two!" Zoë Peron came from the living room. "You two have been arguing all morning! How can you act like this after what's happened?"

They glanced at the gorgeous black woman but muttered instead of spoke.

Zoë stood between them. "You're family! You shouldn't be fighting right now but consoling each other. Detective Morris is going to be here any minute. You want her to see you two fighting like you got no common sense?"

"Aunt Jas I wish everyone would stop blaming Bruce for everything. That's all I ask."

"Well I'm sorry. Nothing you can tell me will ever convince me Bruce's changed."

Zoë turned from one to the other. "Wait how did this get about Bruce?"

"She thinks Bruce killed Mom."

"What?"

"Now isn't that the dumbest thing you ever heard, Zoë?"

"But doesn't it make sense too?" Jasmine pulled Zoë close. "We all know that Bruce hated Nadia and he's a very violent man."

"That doesn't make him a killer."

"He's even said he wanted her dead! Why don't you wake up?"

"He didn't mean it like that, Aunt Jas. Stop twisting things!"

"You keep on with that smart mouth and that's not the only thing I'll be twisting."

"Hold it! Hold it!" Zoë held Jasmine back. "Jas you got no cause to throw around accusations like that."

"I..."

"Thank you!" Dylan snapped her fingers.

"Come on, Zoë. You know Bruce could've done it."

"Leave me out of this. I'm not going to accuse an innocent man of murder."

"Innocent?" Jasmine guffawed. "Bruce and innocent are two words that never belong in the same sentence."

Ding! Dong!

Jasmine gestured. "Would you please get that, Zoë?"

She went to the door.

"Aunt Jas please cool it."

"No. If I feel there is anything the police should know, I'm gonna tell them. This is about your mother and not Bruce McNamara. Where the hell is your loyalty, Dylan?"

"I was just gonna ask *you* the same thing."

"Hello, I'm Zoë Peron."

Steven's mind went blank when he saw the gorgeous black lady at the door.

Brianna held out her hand. "Hello. Uh, I'm Detective Morris. This is..."

Zoë took Brianna's hand. "Yes I know who you are, Detective. Dylan's told me all about you."

Her eyes landed on Steven. He tightened in a rigid stance. His mind void of any thought except how this woman looked naked.

"You're Detective Kemp right?" Zoë put her hand out.

"Huh?"

"Steven." Brianna nudged him.

"Oh yes. Uh I'm Detective Steven Kemp." He shook her soft hand. "It's nice to meet you."

"You too."

His face ran hot.

"How are you connected to Jasmine and Dylan again?"

"Oh I'm Dylan's best friend. You two sure look young to be detectives."

Brianna smiled.

It wasn't everyday Steven saw a woman that looked like this. Sharp exotic features complimented her dark mahogany tone. She radiated, boasting a chic style that hypnotized.

Dylan walked through the front hallway. "You're crazy, Aunt Jas! Nuts, nuts, nuts!"

"Me?" Jasmine waved fists. "Young lady, you could write a book on crazy!"

Steven stood on his tiptoes. "Let me guess, bad time?"

Zoë rocked with her hands on her hips. "It's always like this when these two get together."

Brianna peeked around Zoë. "Why are they fighting?"

Zoë batted her thick lashes. "Same reason they always are. Dylan wants to run her own life and her family won't let her. They've been arguing like this since I got into town."

"Where are you from?" Sweat streamed down the back of Steven's neck.

Brianna glanced at him then back to Zoë.

"I live in NYC. I come down from time to time to spend time with Dylan."

"I think that's very considerate for you to help Dylan during this awful time."

"*Do* you?" Brianna whispered.

"Yes well she needs me. Anyone who really cared would do the same."

"May we come in?"

"Oh." Zoë felt her forehead. "I'm sorry, Detective Morris. Come on in. You can put your coats there." She pointed to the rack behind the door.

Brianna unbuttoned hers. "No thanks we won't be staying that long."

Zoë called for Dylan and Jasmine. Those skintight leather pants and turtleneck highlighted her fascinating physique. Her long brown hair fell down her back in a sleek ponytail that stopped at her luscious butt. That retro-style makeup illuminated her glamorous features. While other women got out of bed in the mornings she got off magazine covers.

Steven bumped into Brianna.

"Watch it."

"Sorry." He moved back.

She fixed her coat. "Maybe if your eyes weren't connected to Zoë's ass, you'd know where you were going."

"What? That's ridiculous." He pointed to the floor. "I tripped on that tile that's coming up."

"Right. Then why are you staring at her ass?"

"And why are you being such a bitch, Bree?"

"You think this is something I haven't shown you nothing yet."

Who could blame him? Being around Brianna everyday drove him crazy enough. You throw a woman like Zoë in his path and his hormones popped like guppies in bowling water.

Dylan walked in. She wore her short jet-black hair in pristine layers. The shaven sides accented her slender face. Long, uneven bangs were gelled across her pencil-thin brows. Not many women could pull off a cut like this but it flattered Dylan's sharp features and skinny neck.

The local artists of the underground culture scene had reincarnated this New-Wave style from the eighties into a modern phenomenon.

Of course Dylan's eccentric look wouldn't be complete without that zodiac choker, the studs crowding her ears and that mood ring.

Yep. This should be interesting.

Jasmine soared into the room with her arms stuffed in her robe. "Detective Morris I'm glad you're here. I got something I need to say."

"Shut up, Aunt Jas!"

"Don't tell me to shut up!"

"Whoa just hold on, ladies." Steven flapped his hand. "Is everything okay, Dylan?"

"No. I can't even grieve in peace around here."

"And to top it off Detective Matthews was here this morning. He grilled us like we were criminals. He asked me and Dylan if we had alibis. I've never been so insulted."

"That's standard procedure, Ms. Hudson."

"With all due respect Detective Kemp I don't take it lightly. I wanted to call Matthews' superiors. That's how upset I was."

"Wouldn't you prefer to be a little offended if it would get everyone closer to answers?" Brianna asked. "Jayce was just doing his job. It's normal to suspect the ones closest to the victim."

Jasmine gasped. "So we *are* suspects?"

"Not necessarily. That's why Jayce asked you questions, to check you out and eliminate you," Steven said.

"We're gonna do our best to get answers. We promise."

"You don't have to look far believe me, Detective Morris." Jasmine wiggled her finger in front of Brianna's face. "*I* got answers."

"Don't listen to my aunt she's warped as usual."

"If you guys want to know who killed Nadia then you can go talk to Bruce McNamara."

Dylan pulled Jasmine by her robe. "I've had it with you!"

"And I've had it with this trance that Bruce has you under!" Zoë exhaled.

"I'm not under a trance!"

"Uh..." Steven raised his hand.

"Bull!"

"Hold it!" Steven flung his arms. "What were you saying, Ms. Hudson?"

"Bruce killed my sister."

"You have no right to say that, Aunt Jas! You can't go accusing people just because you don't like them!"

"She's right. You can't accuse people without cause."

"Detective Morris with all due respect I know Bruce did it. He hated Nadia and he's a criminal. He's been to prison before."

"And he paid for his crime, Aunt Jas!"

"We know Bruce had a record. We checked it out."

"Detective Kemp it's not what you think. Aunt Jas is making it out as if he's this monster and he's not. Bruce made mistakes but he's trying to get his life back together."

"Oh please." Jasmine huffed. "He said that a hundred times before and he never changed."

"Aunt Jas you don't know enough to speak about it."

"I don't know enough? *I* don't know enough?"

"Ladies!" Steven clapped.

"Look Steven and I can't help if you two keep fussing. We came to see if Dylan might be able to tell us anything about people Nadia knows."

"Like what?" Dylan crossed her arms.

"Like men?" Steven put his hands in his pockets. "Was your mother seeing anyone?"

"Well we haven't been talking lately but it wouldn't have

been a man anyway. My mother was gay."

"She was?" Brianna gawked. "I...I never knew."

"Wait but she was married years ago," Steven said.

"Yeah well she was also confused and in denial for years." Dylan walked to the stairs. "Lots of people are married to the opposite sex but are gay. You get married for different reasons, not always love. Plus if you'd known Clay Hollister you wouldn't be surprised. Evil son of a bitch could turn any woman off to men."

"Nadia said he drank himself to death," Brianna said.

"With good riddance." Jasmine brushed lint off her shoulder. "He treated Nadia and Dylan horribly. Didn't deserve the affections of either one of them."

"Detective Morris I thought you knew Mom was gay."

"Bruce is the only person I know who'd hurt Nadia," Jasmine said. "You should see him when he gets mad. It's outrageous."

"Look I'll admit that Bruce has a really bad temper but he couldn't kill anyone. He just couldn't."

Jasmine shook her head. "I don't know what hold he has on you."

"Detective Morris he was out of town when Mom was killed."

Jasmine waved her finger in the detectives' faces. "I want Bruce arrested."

"I'm sorry Ms. Hudson but you can't just wave your finger and expect things to go your way."

"Don't bother explaining, Detective Kemp. Aunt Jas hates Bruce and that's all she's basing this on."

"Dylan is there anyone else that we should talk..."

Jasmine cut Brianna off. "Bruce suckered you in from the beginning, Dylan." Jasmine turned to Steven and Brianna. "When she met Bruce she was a virgin you know."

"That's my business, Aunt Jas!"

"He conned you out of your virginity and you were too blind to see it."

Brianna and Steven exchanged glances.

"Dylan wanted to wait until she got married but Bruce suckered her out of that like he did everything else."

"Bruce didn't make me do anything I didn't wanna do."

"He conned you. You met Bruce on a Tuesday and by Friday afternoon you had your dress over your head."

"Oh!" Dylan shrieked. "How *dare* you?"

Steven covered his grin.

Jasmine got in Dylan's face. "You didn't love Bruce. You only got with him because he was the bad boy and you were curious."

"That's not true!"

Zoë shook her head.

"You're a wreck because of Bruce! He came into your life and tore it upside down. He ruined your relationship with Nadia. How much more will you let him take from you? How much?"

"Just shut up! You've embarrassed me enough!"

Brianna whispered to Steven. "I've seen wars more peaceful than this."

Zoë leaned in. "Oh believe me this is mild compared to the fights they've had in the past."

"Bottom line is that I'm grown, Aunt Jas. It's not your business what I do."

"Oh yes it is! Nadia always told me to look after you if something happened to her and I intend to! You stay away from Bruce!"

"I am but it's not because you told me to! I'm so sick of this. I'm twenty-seven and you treat me like I'm two."

"He killed Nadia and I'm gonna make sure Matthews does something about it! If that doesn't work I'll go to the commissioner and the mayor! I'll go to the media until Bruce pays for what he's done!"

"I give up! I can't talk to you! You don't listen!"

Dylan ran upstairs.

"Hey!" Jasmine trekked upstairs with her index finger in the air. "Come back here! Don't walk away from me in my house! Dylan!"

A door slammed upstairs.

Zoë looked over her manicured nails. "I'm sorry about that. You guys came over to help and you had to get into this drama. Dylan's gonna be staying here with Jasmine for a while."

Brianna did a double take. "They'll kill each other."

Zoë chuckled. "I just hope I'm spared. I think I'm gonna invest in some earplugs."

Steven trembled from her radiating smile. "What do you know about Bruce?"

"He's still in love with Dylan and would do anything to get her back."

"Anything huh? Sounds kinda obsessive doesn't it?"

Zoë shrugged. "Bruce is a good guy at heart."

"So you don't think Bruce is capable of murder?"

"Of course I have no proof but I don't think he did it."

"I asked you if you thought he was *capable* of it. Not if you thought he did it."

Zoë even looked beautiful flustered. Steven bit his tongue for fear of saying that aloud.

"I don't know what you want me to say, Detective Morris."

Brianna winked. "Your expression says it all."

CHAPTER FOUR

"You wanna see Bruce?" Old Man Swaggert spit tobacco juice on the garage floor. He picked his teeth with his crusty pinky nail. He hobbled around the chaotic front counter. His oily suspenders hung off one shoulder and sagged in the back.

"Yes we would like to talk to Mr. McNamara." Brianna wiped oil off the bottom of her shoe. "Is he around?"

He scratched his armpit. "Dis 'bout Hollister ain't it?" He spit in the trash can.

Steven unbuttoned his coat. "It's between us and Bruce."

"Hey I know you." Swaggert looked Brianna up and down. "Yeah you said yo' name's Morris right? Saw ya' on the news. You're the cop that was with Nadia when she died."

"Yes I am."

He scratched his greasy neck. "Don't tell me y'all think Bruce killed the bitch."

"Detective Morris and I just need to clear some things up with Bruce that's all."

"Bruce is a good guy he just got a rotten temper." Swaggert swatted a mosquito. "He's a hothead." He spit. "Yeah ol' Bruce don't take no shit but he don't bother folks that don't bother him first. Know what I mean?"

"Oh I've had my experience with hotheads. Haven't I,

Steven?"

Steven rolled his eyes. "Where's Bruce?"

"He out there in da' back." Swaggert spit again. "Fixin' on that shit mobile. Come on. I'll show ya'."

They followed him through the junkyard packed with dilapidated cars and auto parts.

"Come on." Swaggert led them behind the garage. "He ova here!"

Swaggert's cell rang.

"Shit." He spit on the gravel. "Uh, just go on back there. I gotta take this call."

They went around back. A tall muscular guy with black hair leaned under the hood of a red Trans Am. Hard Rock bellowed from the cheap radio in the weeds.

Steven walked from behind Brianna. "Let me handle this. Say?" He stepped over the radio and tool kit. "Excuse me! Bruce?"

Bruce bobbed his head to the music.

"Hey!" Steven bumped him in the back.

"Whoa!" Bruce fell on the engine. "Yo, man!" He slapped grease out of his face. "Man what the hell you doing?"

"Well sorry but obviously you didn't hear me."

"Shit. Man you gave me a heart attack."

Brianna stepped in front of him. "Well you are Bruce aren't you?"

He nodded. His blue eyes flickered under his black brows.

"We aren't going to take up much of your time. We need to ask you some questions. This is Detective Steven Kemp and I'm..."

"I know who you are. You're Detective Morris. I saw you on the news."

"Yes I am."

"I'm sorry for what happened to you." He tinkered with something under the hood. "Are you all right?"

She touched her head. "I'd be better if I knew who killed Nadia."

"Well." Bruce yanked on a tube inside the car. "We all want something don't we?"

"You don't seem too upset about it." Brianna peeked under the hood.

"Come on, Detective. I'm not stupid. I know someone's told you how much I hated her right?" He cleaned his stained hands with a rag. "I'm not upset about her being dead and I'd be lying if I said I was. Nadia was a stone cold bitch and she made my life a living hell. If you ask me she didn't die soon enough."

Steven peeked under the hood. "That's a shitty thing to say."

"Look she wasn't this innocent great doctor who saved poor souls like she let on. The woman was fucked up. Probably ten times worse than her patients are. You guys don't know anything. You're just the cops coming to clean up the mess." He bent under the hood.

"Do you realize you could be a suspect?"

"Say what?" He laughed. "Lady you're outta your mind. I haven't done shit. If I had I would be shouting it from the rooftops with pride. I hope the bitch rots in hell but I feel sorry for the folks down there who gotta deal wit' her."

"I suggest you start taking this seriously very quick."

"I didn't do anything to Nadia, Detective Morris. Guess she'll haunt me now right?" He slammed the hood. "She didn't give me peace while she was alive so now she's gonna fuck with me from the grave too?"

Steven ran his hand down the side of the Trans Am. "She mentioned you in her journal."

"Journal?"

"Nadia kept journals and I'm reading them to see if they lead to any answers." Brianna leaned on the car. "She wrote you'd been threatening her. She seemed very scared."

"I told her to stay outta my business." He got a wrench from the ground. "If she took it as a threat, that's not my problem."

"Oh come on, Bruce." Brianna looked at his dirty fingers. "You're a big guy. I can't imagine anything you say that can't be a threat. The reason you guys fought was because of Dylan wasn't it? You were really in love with her weren't you? I bet you still are."

His jaws swelled. "I'm not gonna discuss Dylan with you. That's my business."

"A crime has been committed." Steven checked out the car's interior. "So it's our business too."

"Nadia tried to keep you two apart didn't she? Why would she not want you with Dylan? Is it because you're dangerous?"

"No it's because she couldn't stand me. She thought I wasn't good enough. She never even tried to get to know me. I didn't kill Nadia. She wasn't important enough for me to throw my life away on. I was in the pen for three years. You think I'd risk going back for someone I hated?"

"It can't be ignored that you had a motive," Steven said.

"I can prove I didn't kill her. I've been out of town for the last week. I just got back last night." He shuffled his feet in the grass. "My dad passed. He had lung cancer."

Steven nodded. "We know. We're very sorry."

"How did you know my dad died?"

"Not important." Brianna got off the car.

"Since you know I wasn't in town then you know I wasn't the killer. Case closed huh?" He got his radio and headed to the garage. "Go bother someone else."

"Hey!"

Bruce stopped but didn't turn around.

"Bruce it would be in your best interest to cooperate."

"Look I don't need to be dragged into this shit. I'm trying to keep my life straight, Detective Kemp. Next year I'll be thirty and look at me." He shook the radio. "I'm still right where I was at nineteen, doing the same shit I was doing then. I haven't accomplished a damn thing. I don't wanna be a fuck up my whole life. People around here treat me like shit and I wanna prove to them I'm not."

Brianna shielded her eyes from the sun. "I hope you really are trying to get your life straight."

"Look I lost the most important thing in my life because I didn't fight hard enough. I'm not losing anything else."

"You mean Dylan?" Steven stood beside Brianna.

"See I did everything to make her happy and it still didn't work out. Shit they say you gotta work for what you want, well I did and got screwed anyway."

Brianna watched him. "Fighting for someone you love is anything but easy."

"Just so much shit has happened you know?" He scratched his hair. A line of grease trailed down his forehead.

"Yeah well don't let anything stop you when you're in love." Steven glanced at Brianna. "Sometimes it's worth it to keep fighting for it."

Bruce swatted at a fly. "We're getting off point here. I didn't kill Nadia. I told Matthews that and now I'm telling you."

"Jayce's been here?" Brianna asked.

"Yeah and he was getting on my nerves more than you two are. There is no way you can put Nadia's death on me because I didn't do it. So please leave me alone."

The detectives gave Bruce their cards and went to Steven's car.

Bruce watched them leave then headed inside.

Swaggert tottered from behind the counter. "Dey gon'? They was tryin' to pin Hollister's murder on ya' huh?" He spit.

"You should know." Bruce put his radio on the bucket behind the counter and sat in Swag's chair. "I'm sure you were listening." He rested his feet by the computer.

Swaggert laid his scrawny arm on the counter. "Why you smiling like that? Oh hell. I know what you're thinking and if you had half a brain, you'd cut it out now."

Bruce popped in a piece of gum. "And what am I thinking since you know so much?"

"Don't be a bigger fool than you are, Bruce. You thinkin' now that the doc is outta the way it's free season on her daughter's pussy." He spit. "But cha' wrong."

"You're an old dirty, perverted dog, Swag."

"Shit you thinking with momma out the way you can start banging her daughter again with no hassles and problems. Well you forgot how much trouble all that shit caused? You been whining about changing things, moving on and having a better life." Swaggert got the broom from the corner. "And not to mention getting out of this hell hole. You keep your mind on that and off that girl you'd be better off."

"Why don't you just stay out of my business, old man?"

"Oh yeah I'm old when I ain't saying what you wanna hear right? But I ain't old when you need somebody to bail your ass outta jail. Or when you need rent money. I ain't old then."

"You think you know everything. It's not easy to just stop loving someone. I'm in love with her. I always will be."

"And what the hell's so special about that bony, weird-looking girl? Look how she dresses and acts. Wear all that scary black eye shadow. All them damn piercings." Swaggert motioned with his hands. "Girl got mo' holes in her than a sifter. Remember when you first met her she had that green hair." Swaggert shook his head. "I thought the bitch was on crack or something. It ain't normal."

"She's from the artistic crowd. They're different."

"Look at cha'. Got stars in ya' eyes already. Don't let your dick lead you into misery, Bruce. Forget her. She ain't worth it believe me. Go out and get you a tall sexy blond who's dumb as a brick and won't talk back." Swaggert swept dust. "You'll be better off believe me."

"Nah. I like my women with a brain."

"Why? The brainless ones are all right to me. Ha, ha!"

Bruce took off his oily shirt and got a clean one from under the counter.

"Can I knock off now for lunch?" Bruce took out his car keys.

"Oh, man. See I knew it."

"Can I?"

"You going to see that girl?"

"Maybe." Bruce swung the keys. "Maybe not. That's my business." He hopped from behind the counter. "I'll be back in an hour."

"Bullshit you got work to do!" Swaggert hobbled out of the garage behind him.

"And it'll be here when I get back."

"Don't be a damn fool, Bruce."

Bruce slammed the door of his white Mustang. Pearl Jam blasted from the radio when he revved the engine.

"Turn that mess down! You know I don't like all that loud music!"

He waved out the window. "I'll be back later!"

"Don't open up old wounds!"

Bruce sped toward the gate with a trail of dust behind him.

"Forget her!" Swaggert hollered in his hands. "Dylan Hollister ain't nothing but trouble!"

CHAPTER FIVE

Friday

Jasmine flung plates of Red Velvet cake and glasses of punch to her sisters, Donna and Sandra. They smiled at Brianna and scampered out of Jasmine's kitchen to serve the guests.

Jasmine carried a giant tuna casserole to the table that already spilled over with food. "Would you like another piece of pecan pie, Detective Morris?" She dumped globs of casserole on the antique plates.

"No I've already had two pieces." Brianna did a half-twirl in her snug dress. "That's my limit."

"Limit?" Jasmine grabbed plates from the cabinet. "I swear your waist is smaller than one of my thighs." They laughed. "Besides, we've gone through the worse part of the day so we can at least celebrate Nadia's memory by enjoying the food."

"The funeral was lovely. It's so nice that you invited Steven and me."

"It was Dylan's idea. I mean, I'm glad you came too of course." Jasmine got homemade sauce out of the refrigerator. "It meant a lot to Dylan that you came."

"Why?" Brianna moved out of Jasmine's way.

"Well she likes you. You also meant a lot to Nadia. She says that you guys are making this much easier for her to handle. You and Zoë."

"So they're real close huh?"

"Zoë's like a sister to Dylan."

Brianna bit into a peanut butter cookie. "Uh, she's very pretty."

"Zoë?" Jasmine chucked balled up napkins into the trashcan. "The girl's gorgeous."

"Yes she is." Brianna found the cookie harder to swallow. "She takes over a room. Can't help but notice her."

"And that body. Heck when I was in my twenties I had a great body but I didn't look like *that*."

Brianna faked a smile.

"Did you see how all the men were looking at her?" Jasmine licked vanilla frosting off the spatula. "Here we are trying to bury Nadia and those pigs are looking up and down Zoë's dress. Even Pastor Hill ought to be ashamed."

Brianna dusted cookie crumbs off her hands. "Boys will be boys I guess."

"But there's one man who wasn't looking." Jasmine filled glasses with juice. "Detective Kemp didn't seem to notice Zoë's dress, or lack of it."

"Oh please. Believe me he noticed big time. Did you see when he tripped coming out of the church? His eyes were glued to Zoë's behind the entire time."

Jasmine shrugged. "Okay well we can't blame him. He is a man. Still he seemed more interested in the lady standing beside him. I think we both know who that is."

Brianna flushed with warmth.

"I'm sorry." Jasmine put the juice away. "That isn't my business."

"No you didn't do anything wrong."

"I embarrassed you didn't I?"

"No I'm not embarrassed."

"I just can tell that there's more than business between you."

"So it's that obvious?" Brianna searched the cookie tray for an oatmeal and raisin. "Steven and I were together for a long time."

"You see I could tell." Jasmine sucked frosting off the spatula. "You two ever think of rekindling the fire?"

Brianna went to the other side of the kitchen. "Uh, everything, uh really was lovely."

Steven walked in. He'd devoured his bowl of chocolate pudding.

"Speak of the devil. Detective Kemp." Jasmine gestured to the snacks. "Feel free to have some more of anything you like."

He scraped the sides of his bowl to get the remainder of pudding. He'd combed his hair so neatly Brianna could see the teeth marks. His Indigo suit made his eyes stand out more than usual.

"Whoo, wee! Ms. Hudson that pudding hit the spot. I love anything chocolate."

Jasmine sucked in a chuckle. Brianna covered her grin.

"What's so funny? Did I miss something?"

"No. Would you like some tuna casserole, Detective Kemp?"

"Oh naw." He scrunched up his nose. "But I'll take a tuna sandwich on wheat."

"Uh, I don't have any tuna sandwiches but I can make you one."

He set his bowl in the sink. "That's cool."

"Steven." Brianna bumped him. "Instead of asking for a sandwich why don't you help out?"

"Oh and is you eating all the cookies a form of helping out?" He moved the cookie tray.

Jasmine laughed. "I must say you two are keeping my mind off Nadia and I appreciate that." She got two plates, winked at Brianna and left.

Steven stirred a fruit cup. "What the hell was that about?"

"Nothing." Brianna sipped juice. "It's a woman thing."

"Jayce left a message on my cell." Steven gobbled a spoonful of fruit. "Boy does he want your head on a stick 'cause of those journals. I hope you weren't blabbing info about the case to Jasmine."

"We weren't even talking about that."

"So what were you talking about then?"

"Nothing." She got a napkin.

"Didn't seem like nothing to me. I could tell you were talking about me."

"Jasmine said she could tell we'd been together that's all. She thought we were still a couple but I told her we weren't."

"And whose fault is that?"

She scooped onion dip on a chip. "Don't start."

"I'm not starting anything." He moved closer. "Jasmine's a smart lady."

"She said she could tell by how you were looking at me during the funeral."

"Oh?" He caressed her shoulder. "Did she notice how you were looking at *me*?"

"What?" She swallowed the rest of the chip. "I was not."

"You were."

"I wasn't."

He laughed. "Since you can't admit you're still in love with me then I'm not surprised you'd deny you were looking at me."

"Stop it." She washed her hands. "What have you been doing?"

"Checking out some of the guests and looking for clues. Where's Dylan?"

Brianna opened a jar of sweet pickles. "I think she's resting."

"We need to talk to her in private. Shit can't get a word in with Jasmine around."

"Let's give her space today out of respect."

Steven got a piece of pecan pie. "I'll look like Michael Moore by the time we leave here."

"A lot of tension at the funeral wasn't it?" Brianna lowered her voice when some of the church members passed the kitchen door.

Steven nodded and chewed. "I was talking to that skinny neck lady in the pink hat. She said when Nadia's parents died the siblings went at each other's throats."

"Really?"

"Mmm hmm." He sucked on a pecan.

"You think they could've been involved in her death?"

"I don't know but you said you read she had some secret in her journal right? Well the hat lady said that Nadia had been hiding something."

"No shit?"

"Nope. That secret might have something to do with her family."

"Well it definitely has to do with Dylan. Nadia kept writing she had something to tell Dylan but knew it would ruin both their lives. What kind of secret could be that powerful?"

Steven shrugged.

"Get out of my house now!" Jasmine yelled from the living room. "You're not welcomed here!"

"What the hell?" Brianna put the pickles down.

"Come on." Steven held the kitchen door for her.

When they got into the living room the guests were staring at the scene with their mouths opened and eyes wide. Donna and Sandra stood in the doorway like soldiers. Jasmine waved a spatula at the man in front of her.

"Get out, Bruce!"

"Go to hell, Jasmine. I'm not going anywhere." He looked at Brianna and Steven. "What are you guys doing here?"

Jasmine swung her hand. "They were invited unlike you."

"You are an ingrate, Bruce McNamara." Sandra flung her arm. "How dare you come here? You have no shame. You can't even respect our wishes on this day?"

"I came to pay my respects."

"Ha!" Donna jumped in his face. "Who the hell do you think you're kidding? We all know you hated Nadia. What do you want? For us to tell you where she's buried so you can break dance on her grave?"

"I don't give a damn what any of you think." He glanced at the guests. "I came to see Dylan and I'm not leaving until I do."

"The hell you're not." Jasmine snapped her fingers. "Detective Kemp please get him out of here."

"Gonna sic the cops on me now, Jasmine? Get off your damn high horse. You're a bigger fake than Nadia."

"You watch your mouth." She swung the spatula.

Bruce bucked up to her. "And you better get outta my face."

"Hey." Steven got between them. "Cool it, Bruce."

"So what now that Nadia's dead you're gonna step in as the designated pain in my ass, Jasmine?"

"Get out and don't ever come back here or I'll have you arrested."

"I'm not scared of the cops and I'm sure as hell not afraid of you."

"Get...out...now."

"Well." He sized up Jasmine. "I guess being a bitch runs in the family?"

"And being a bastard probably runs in yours."

"You bitch."

"Get out!"

"Okay you've had your fun, Bruce. Don't let your anger make you do something you'll regret."

"Oh believe me I won't regret it, Detective Kemp."

"You're an animal. My sister had every reason and right to keep you away from Dylan and you can bet I'll pick up where she left off."

"Oh yeah?" Bruce pushed up against Steven to get to Jasmine.

"Well Dylan and I belong together. No one can keep me away from her. She loves me."

"Get him out of here." Jasmine turned her back. "I can't stand to see his face."

"Come on go." Steven ushered him to the front door.

"You can't keep me away from her, Jasmine. She loves me no matter what you try to do."

"You stay away from my niece."

Bruce reached over Steven. "You can't understand the love Dylan and I have for each other because you don't know how good a love like that could feel."

"You're right I don't understand it because I can't figure out what she'd see in a lowlife like you."

Bruce balled fists. "Lowlife?"

"You're nothing." Jasmine looked him in the eyes. "You're less than something I'd scrape off the bottom of my shoes."

"I'll scrape your ass off this floor." He lunged at her. "Who you think you're talking to?"

"See?" Jasmine pointed and looked at the guests. "He's an animal just like I said he was! No self control."

"No one calls me a lowlife, lady."

"Well I did!" Jasmine headed for him. Donna pulled her back. "And you won't do a damn thing about it."

Steven pulled Bruce by his suit jacket. "Leave now or I'll arrest you!"

"This isn't over, Jasmine." Bruce fought Steven's hold. "You can't keep me from Dylan. None of you can!"

CHAPTER SIX

The guests milled off into separate directions. Pastor Hill turned his focus back to the television.

Brianna patted Jasmine's back. "You okay?"

Jasmine touched the bridge of her nose. "He just makes me so mad. I'm just glad Dylan didn't see him."

"Well I think he got the point."

"You don't know Bruce, Detective Kemp. Determination and being a pain in people's asses are two of his famous qualities."

Zoë came downstairs. "What happened?"

Steven lost breath for a second. One look at her sent him into convulsions. Her curves stretched the fabric of her dress to where he barely needed his imagination.

"It was just Bruce." Jasmine patted her chest. "He's gone thank goodness. Where's Dylan?"

"She's on the patio. I was coming down to check on her. She wanted to be alone."

"Oh please go check on her, Zoë." Jasmine took her hand. "I don't want her to be alone."

Zoë went down the hall. Steven watched the magnetic swing of her plump ass.

Brianna snapped her fingers. "Steve?"

"Huh? What?"

"You're staring."

"No I'm not." He tugged on his blazer. "At what?"

"Maybe that should be, at "whom"."

They followed the Hudson sisters into the kitchen. Jasmine stacked plates and bowls into the sink.

"You all right?" Donna asked her.

"No I'm not all right. The last face I needed to see today was Bruce's."

"Well he's gone now thank goodness." Sandra cleaned off the table. "Hopefully we'll have no more surprises." Jasmine threw a dishtowel on the table. "All we need is for Shannon to show up and we'd really have a day to remember."

"Who's Shannon?"

"Oh." Jasmine jerked at Steven's voice. "Oh uh, we didn't notice you two were in here."

Donna laid a plate in the sink. "Come on, Sandra. Let's see if the guests need anything else." They smiled at the officers on their way out.

"Some kind of scene that was, Jasmine. Damn you'd swear Bruce was the antichrist right, Bree?"

"You're telling me."

Steven chewed a chip. "So Jas what's so bad about Bruce?"

"Look I don't wanna waste my spit talking about Bruce." Jasmine rinsed out the casserole dish. "He's never been good enough for Dylan and never will be."

"Dylan's grown. Shouldn't that be her decision?"

"I know what's best for my niece, Detective Morris." She washed off the table.

"You gonna keep avoiding the question?" Steven bent down beside her. "What's up with Bruce? Why do you guys really hate him?"

"He's of no importance. Not even important enough to speak about."

Brianna wandered to the sink. "For someone so unimportant he sure does get under your skin. So who is Shannon?"

"Excuse me?"

"You mentioned someone named Shannon. Who is she?"

"Oh, she's nobody."

Steven sat at the table. "Nadia sure knew a lot of nobodies."

"Shannon is a friend of Nadia's." Jasmine scooped crumbs off the table and dumped them in the sink. "That's all." She squeezed out the rag. "It has nothing to do with the case."

Steven got a peanut butter cookie before Jasmine could move the tray. "Shannon was Nadia's lover wasn't she?"

"Shh." Jasmine closed the kitchen door. "We have the church members here. What would they think?"

"Don't they know she's gay? Anyway we don't care about Nadia's sexual orientation. All we want to know is who killed her and bopped me over the head and almost killed me."

"Look all that's important to me is Dylan and making sure she gets through this."

"We need more info about Shannon. We're gonna find out who she is whether you tell us or not."

"Okay you wanna know, Detective Kemp?" She tapped her fingers on the countertop. "She was Nadia's lover. The thing is Nadia wasn't as serious about Shannon as Shannon wanted her to be."

"What's Shannon like?" Brianna asked.

"Nadia liked the same qualities in women most men did. She liked 'em young and easy. Shannon's beautiful, blond and young enough to be Nadia's daughter. She treated Nadia like a queen."

"Why?" Steven broke his cookie in half.

"Shannon was bewitched with Nadia because of who she was. Shannon felt blessed to have someone like Nadia even be her friend let alone her lover."

"What makes you think Nadia wasn't serious?" Steven brushed crumbs off his chin.

"Because for Nadia it was purely sexual. She had her chance at this young, hot thing that's gone over her and Nadia took advantage of that." Jasmine fixed her apron. "Nadia liked to play the field and she found plenty of partners."

"I see." Steven gestured to Brianna with his eyes.

"Nadia was sick of Shannon period but she broke it off because of the drinking. Shannon's a hopeless drunk. She's pathetic."

"So how did Shannon feel about that?" Brianna asked. "The break up I mean?"

"Horrible. She'd depended on Nadia for so long. She flipped when Nadia broke it off. She was always short a few brain cells but when Nadia dumped her she went completely loco."

Brianna got a cupcake. "Why didn't anyone mention Shannon before?"

"Detective Morris I'm trying to protect my sister's reputation. She's well-respected for her practice and the good she did for people. She didn't want people to know she was gay and it would have killed her if it got out."

"You should've told Jayce or us about this Shannon. She might be involved."

"Detective Morris I'm drowning here." Jasmine leaned over the table. Strands of hair popped from her ball. "I don't know how to act or what to do. My sister's been murdered! Can't you both be sympathetic? The last thing on my mind was Shannon!"

"I'm sorry okay?" Brianna touched Jasmine's shoulder. "We know you loved your sister."

"We just can't afford to have any secrets. You need to tell us anything that would help. You owe it to Nadia and Dylan."

"I'm sorry, Detective Kemp. I didn't mean to hide anything." Steven nodded.

"Here." Brianna handed her a napkin. "Your mascara's running."

Jasmine dabbed her face. "I hope I look better than I feel."

∞ ∞ ∞ ∞

Dylan lifted her head from Zoë's shoulder. "I'm sorry."

"You go on and cry all you need to." Zoë kissed her forehead.

"I'm just so confused." Dylan reclined in the patio chair. "I'm sad, hurt, angry, and scared."

"Why are you scared?"

"How do I know that whoever killed my mother won't come after me? I might know something that I don't know I know."

"What?"

"I told you Mom had a secret. She kept hinting she needed to tell me something but never did. That secret could be what got her killed. I gotta find out what it is." She sat up. "If I hadn't been arguing with her about Bruce then she'd have told me."

"And what if she had told you?"

"I could've saved her."

"Saved her? It wasn't your job to save her."

"I'll never forgive myself if I don't find out who did this and why. Don't you understand that?"

"Of course I do." Zoë moved the small saucer of pecan pie from her lap. "I just don't want you doing something you'll regret. You got a habit of sticking your nose in things then ending up in trouble."

"I don't care how dangerous or silly it might be, I'm gonna find out what she knew. She had to tell someone." Dylan chewed her thumbnail. "Someone she was close to. Someone she could trust as much as she trusted me."

"Your aunts?"

"No she wouldn't tell them anything. They found out from one of the church ladies that Mom was a lesbian remember?"

"Well do you think she told someone else in your family?"

"You know she didn't trust the family. Ever since grandma and grandpa died and that mess happened over the will." Dylan put her hands on the armrests. "Oh no."

"What?"

"I'll have to deal with Mom's will. I'm not looking forward to that."

"Would she tell Detective Morris this secret you think?"

"She doesn't know anymore than we do."

"I say just leave it alone. Maybe that's best."

"I can't live without trying to find out." Dylan walked to Jasmine's rosebushes. "She told someone." She snapped a rose. "Hold on."

"What? You think you know who she might have told?"

"Why didn't I think of her before?"

"Who?"

"Shannon."

Zoë brushed the back of her dress down. "Shannon's a drunk. Why would Nadia tell her something that she couldn't even tell you?"

"People tell lovers things they wouldn't tell others. I've told Bruce things I haven't told you and you're my best friend. Once you've been intimate with someone, there's a bond there you can't explain. You feel you can trust that person more than anyone else."

"Why wouldn't Shannon come forward then? Do the police even know about her?"

"She *could* be speaking to the police for all I know. If someone's told them information, you think the cops are gonna tell me? That's why I'm gonna do some investigating of my own."

"I'm gonna go put this plate up. You wanna come inside?"

"Nah I wanna be alone." She played with a rose.

Zoë hugged her. "Want me to bring you anything? You hardly ate."

"Could you bring me a piece of that coconut cake?"

"Sure." Zoë waved on her way around the house. "If they have some left."

CHAPTER SEVEN

Dylan lifted the rose to her cheek. She and Nadia had been happy together once. Close during her childhood. Nadia did her best to make Dylan's dreams come true. No matter what happened between them, there hadn't been a day that Dylan doubted her mother's love.

But something had been obsessive about Nadia's attention. She'd based her existence on Dylan. Claimed Dylan had been her only reason for living. A lot of parents didn't want their children to grow up but Nadia wanted to prevent it.

It scared Dylan to be someone's entire universe.

Nadia didn't like sharing Dylan with anyone but especially not Bruce McNamara. Dylan finally realized why Nadia held on so tightly. She'd been afraid she'd lose her.

Dylan picked the petals off the rose. The naked bud reminded her of her life.

Why did Nadia think she could lose her? Did it have something to do with that secret?

Someone walked up behind her.

"That was fast." Dylan plucked another rose. "You get my cake?"

"No but I'd get you anything in the world you want."

She turned around.

"Or I'd sure try to if you asked." Bruce smiled with a rose in his hand. He wasn't the type to dress up so she thought her eyes played tricks on her at first. His thick hair lay in smooth waves. The gray blazer ignited the glow in his blue eyes. His looks outranked any movie star in her book. That wasn't anything new. If Bruce's looks were all it took he'd be perfect. She'd missed his charming eyes. She got lost in them every time he looked at her.

She couldn't do this again. No. She'd finally gotten Bruce out of her system. She wouldn't let him draw her in this time.

She closed her eyes. Maybe if she didn't look at him she could forget how much she still cared.

"Hi." He extended the rose.

"What are you doing here?"

"You look so beautiful."

"What are you doing here, Bruce?"

"I just..." He looked at the garden. "I just came to say I'm very sorry for your loss."

"Is this a joke?"

"I am sorry. Please take the rose."

She did. "So you just go around snatching roses out of people's garden's now?"

"It's the thought that counts."

"I want you to leave." She blocked the sun with her hand. "Now."

"Don't do this." He touched her arm.

"Get out or I'll get my family to throw you out."

"They already did that but I came back. I wasn't leaving without seeing you."

"Always has to be your way with things doesn't it?" She moved her hand across the rose bush.

"Careful." He held her wrist. "You'll stick yourself on the thorns."

"The only thorn I need to stay away from is you. Leave."

"No. You know you don't really want me to."

"I don't know where you get that from. I told you I didn't wanna see you the other day when you showed up unannounced. Now you pop up here after Mom's funeral? How dare you? You're the last person anyone wants to see here. And you can take this rose." She threw it at him. "You didn't care about my mother."

"But I care about *you* and I wouldn't wish anything like this on you."

He reached for her.

"Get away from me."

"Let me hold you."

"No. That's where it all started, with you holding me. Everything was fine before I met you. I wish I never had."

"You don't mean that. You're talking like that because you're feeling guilty about Nadia. You still love me. I can tell."

"I don't have time for you. I just buried my mother. Do you know how that feels?"

"I think I do."

She cursed under her breath. "I shouldn't have said that. I'm sorry about your dad."

"Dylan. I don't know why but I can't stop loving you. I've tried so many times. I can't stay away." He kissed her hand.

"I won't. You know I've never loved anyone like I have you."

"Stop it." She pushed his hand from her waist. "It's over. Let it stay that way."

"It'll never be over between us. Something keeps bringing us together for a reason."

"And that same thing keeps breaking us apart. Anyway I got enough to deal with. How can you expect me to think about us right now?"

He stroked her shoulders and sniffed her hair. "Don't turn me away." He lifted her chin. "I need you now more than I ever did. I'm so alone."

"Bruce."

"I was never happy before you came into my life. I had nobody. I was nothing without you."

"We don't belong together." She fought the urge to kiss him. "We gotta realize that."

"I'll never accept that because it isn't true." He held her. "We can make it work this time, Dylan. We just gotta keep others out of our way."

She put her hands on his. "Let go."

"I want you back."

"Let...go."

"And you want me too."

"Just leave me alone. I never want to see you again."

"Well you're going to. I'm not giving up until we're together."

"It's always about what you want, Bruce. You don't care what else is going on or that I got more important things to think about than you right now."

"You can make time for me." He stood so close her nose touched his chest. "You could always see the true me even when others tried to tell you what I was. You know I'd never do anything to hurt you. Give me the chance to prove it."

"I'm going back in now."

He stooped over her.

"What are you doing?"

"Give me a kiss first."

"No." She turned her face to the side.

"Come on." His hand went down the back of her dress. "You know you want to."

She didn't stop him because she *didn't* want to kiss him. She wanted to *too* much.

"My family's right in there." She perched her hands on his wide shoulders. "I don't need the drama if they catch you out here. Please respect my wishes on this day."

He let go. "Okay but we need to talk alone. I'm tired of you avoiding me. I'll be at the garage tonight."

"So?"

"I want you to come by."

"If you plan to wait on me then don't waste your time."

He kissed her forehead. "I would never consider it a waste of time."

∞ ∞ ∞ ∞

"Ohh!" Zoë bumped face-to-chest into Steven in Jasmine's upstairs hallway.

"Whoa!" Steven fell against the wall.

"I'm so sorry!" She helped him up. "I didn't see you."

"Yeah well. Ahh." He dusted his pants. "You need headlights when you come down the hall. Fast as you were flying."

"Ha, ha, ha! I'm sorry, Detective."

Staring into her eyes made up for her clumsiness. After all, having a beautiful woman fall on top of him was a luxury he didn't mind one bit. She seemed to welcome his attention. A woman like her had to be use to it from any man.

"So." He let go of her hand when he realized he'd been caressing her fingers.

"I'm sorry again. I've been running all over the place."

"Yeah you have. No one can keep up with you. Every time I look for you, you're in another room."

"You've been looking for me?"

"Uh." He fidgeted. "I meant, every time *someone* looks for

you. You uh, seem to be gone."

"Uh huh." She walked past him with a furtive smirk. "I think you meant what you said the first time, Detective."

"I wasn't looking for you. Why would I be looking for you?"

"Whatever you say." She headed downstairs.

"Hey I did need to ask you something." He checked out her "backdoor" as he followed.

He bumped into her when they got off the stairs. "Sorry."

"It's okay. Oh god it's hot." She fanned. "Must be all this runnin' I'm doing." She stuck her fingers down her cleavage, leading his eyes to the lines of sweat on her breasts.

"Uh..." He wobbled.

"Detective? You okay?"

"Uh. Yeah uh it's just hot. Like you said."

"I think we need to turn the heat down."

You got that right.

"What did you need to ask me?"

"Well since you're close to Dylan you might know something about Nadia that could help."

"I'm sure I don't know anything more than Dylan does."

"You might know something that you don't know, you know."

Her tits bounced when she laughed. "What?"

Steven rubbed the back of his neck. "Just wondering if you need to uh..."

She stood against him. "What is it you're trying to say exactly?"

"If you need to talk about Nadia or something you feel might help, please call me okay?"

"Yeah." She licked her lips. "I think I understand."

One of Dylan's cousins bumped into Zoë as he turned the corner.

"Whoa!" The man's hands landed all over her.

"Oh!" She laughed. "Easy, there."

Steven's blood burned. Surely he wasn't jealous. Could you be jealous over a woman you barely knew? If so why?

The man apologized and ran upstairs.

"I uh do appreciate the offer, Detective Kemp. I might need to talk to you about some things. I usually talk to Dylan but I don't wanna burden her, especially if it's something about Nadia. It would be awkward."

"I understand."

She smiled.

"You can trust me all right?" He gave her his card. "You can call the station or my cell anytime. Don't worry it doesn't have to be official."

"No?"

"No if you just need a friend you can call me."

Lame ass line.

She stuck the card between her breasts. "Get out your phone."

"Uh okay." He got it out of his side pocket. She recited her number and he saved it.

"Detective?"

"Yeah?" He read over the number.

"The same thing applies to you. Call me anytime you want to."

She twisted away with her sumptuous ass pinned underneath that rigid dress.

CHAPTER EIGHT

The sound of footsteps threw Bruce off count that night. He laid the bolts by the tool chest. Soft perfume overtook the smell of gas and sweat.

"You came."

CRRRRAAAAACCCCK!

He spun around on his knees. She stooped inside the garage. Rain seeped down her long coat. The bottom of her pants and boots were soaked in mud and rain. Dirty-blond ringlets sheltered her face. Pieces of the broken *Jim Beam* bottle sprinkled her feet.

"Bruuuuucccccceeeee!" She drooled down her chin. "Damn you, Bruce!"

"Shannon?" He stood.

"Don't come near me." She slipped on glass and oil. "You motherfucker."

Mascara ran down her face. More lipstick was on her chin than mouth.

"I don't have time for your shit. Get your drunk ass outta here."

"You asshole. I *know*." She punched the wall. "I know!"

"Get outta here!"

"You killed her. Ahhhh!" She swung her fists. "I know you did. You can lie about it all you want but I know you did it. I knew you hated her but I didn't think you'd actually kill her. I loved her."

"I didn't kill Nadia."

"Bullshit." She spit on the floor.

"I was out of town when she was killed."

"No you weren't!" She sucked in tears. "You'd come back."

"No I didn't. What are you talking about?"

She stumbled. "Antwan told me he saw you buying beer by your house the night Nadia was killed. You were back in town."

"Antwan doesn't know what the fuck he's talking about. I hadn't made it back in town until the next day. You can ask Swag."

"Fuck Swag. He ain't nothing but your puppet. He do all you tell him to."

"If I killed someone you think Swag would hide that? Huh? Antwan made a mistake. He didn't see me."

Her head rolled to the side. "Ya' think I'm stupid, Bruce? You think I don't know how much you hated her? And you just walkin' around..." She danced with her arms spread. "Just walkin' around like you own the place. Like you gon' get away with it like you got away with everything else."

"What have I gotten away with huh?" He beat his chest. "I'm sick of you fuck ups throwing my past up in my face. I'm sick of all of you." He reached the counter.

"You stay away from me!"

"You only know the lies Nadia told you."

"No I know the truth. Everybody else is scared of you but I'm not."

"Listen, Shannon."

"Nadia wasn't scared of you either. But I bet you made sure she was when she died didn't you?"

"I didn't kill her."

"Get on the phone and call nine-one-one."

"What?"

"Get on the goddamn phone! You're gonna turn yourself in."

"Shannon how much you been drinking?"

"Do it!"

"Fuck you, bitch. I'm not calling anyone."

"Oh yes you will." She pulled out a gun.

Bruce stood back with his hands up. "I knew you were crazy but I didn't know you'd be this crazy."

"It ain't like you never seen a gun before. Now get on that fuckin' phone. I'm not playing with you."

"You ever shoot a gun before huh?"

"Does it matter?"

"If you kill me, where you think you'll end up? You'd throw away your freedom and future for me, Shannon? You're making a big mistake."

"My mistake was not protecting Nadia from you. She told me everything. Things she didn't tell anyone else. She loved Dylan so much. She'd do anything to keep her from you because she knew you'd ruin her life."

"Yeah well it sure is funny that Nadia was the one Dylan had the falling out with isn't it?"

"Nadia was just so desperate. Secrets can change everything."

"Do you know why Nadia was killed?"

"Stop fucking with me. *You* killed her because you hated her. Get on the phone or I'll shoot. I swear I will, Bruce!"

"You don't wanna do this."

"Yeah, yeah beg me just like I bet Nadia did when you stabbed her. What did she say? What did she do?"

"Shannon you are dead wrong."

"When you were slicing Nadia up did you think about Dylan at all huh? Did you?" She caressed the gun. "What would Dylan think if she ever found out what happened hmm? When she visited New York City last year."

"Shut up!" He raised his hand. "She won't ever find out. The worse mistake I made in my life."

She wobbled when she turned. The counter broke her fall. "You weren't saying that then were you? You enjoyed every minute of it."

"Dylan's never gonna find out about that. You understand me?"

"I'll tell her. Let's see how much she thinks you love her then."

"And who would believe some pathetic ass drunk like you?"

"Bet it made you hard to kill Nadia didn't it? Bet you got off on it. Come on, tough guy. Admit it. It had to feel good."

"Why not just go to the police yourself and tell them your warped theory? Why come here and do this?"

She cocked the gun. "I want you to confess."

"Bullshit. You didn't go to the cops because you're afraid they might think you did it."

"I'd never hurt Nadia."

"It's the perfect motive isn't it? I mean who would blame

you, Shannon? You had to be hurt and embarrassed to put so much love into Nadia, give her your all only to have her turn around and drop you like the sack of worthless shit you are."

"Shut up!"

"Man you must be dumber than I thought. You actually thought Nadia loved you? All she wanted was sex. Everyone knew it but you."

"Motherfucker!" She smacked his nose with the gun.

"Ahh!" He bent over. Blood dribbled on his shirt. "You, bitch! Aww!"

She steadied the gun on him. "Call the police."

"And tell them a crazy whore is holding me at gun point and making stupid accusations? Gladly!"

"You tell them the truth, Bruce."

"Fuck you!" He grabbed the gun and pushed her over.

"Stay away from me!" She got up and ran into the yard.

"Come back here, Shannon!"

∞ ∞ ∞ ∞

"Oh." She stumbled on gravel. Her foot caught in a tire. She fell over scattered car parts in the grass.

"Shannon!" Bruce ran out of the garage.

She ducked behind a rusted yellow car. She couldn't see him but heard his footsteps crunching the weeds in the distance.

"Shannon!"

She zipped behind another car.

"Shannon! Get out here!"

Her head felt hollow. Her stomach spun from nausea. She got dizzy. She tried to stand but fell back into the weeds. She got on all fours. She threw up before she could stop herself.

"Shannon!"

"Ahh." Vomit dripped from her mouth. "Ooh." She leaned against the car to steady herself.

How would she see Bruce when she couldn't see inches in front of her? Each car had a twin or triplet.

She stared at the light from the garage entrance. The crickets' singing resembled a base drum in her head. Every image multiplied. Every sound seemed a million decibels higher than normal.

She raced to her truck and ripped her keys from her coat pocket. She stumbled on the uneven payment, kicking up loose pebbles.

She pushed her key into the truck door.

A hand gripped her waist and another covered her mouth.

"Mmm! Mmmm!" She flapped her arms.

"Can't let you go, Shannon!"

She felt the gun in her back.

"Mmm! No!" She gurgled under his hand. "Let me go!" Bruce pulled her up the driveway from behind. His arm felt like a metal gate. If he squeezed any tighter he'd crush her guts.

"Mmm!"

"Shut up!"

He flung her side to side like a rag doll. Her heel broke off her boot. "I can't let you go to the police, Shannon."

She rammed her elbow into his side.

"Ahh!" He dropped the gun when he stooped over.

She snatched it up. "Get out of my way."

"Settle down!" He limped, reaching for her. "Can't let you leave."

"You stay away from me!" She bent down from nausea. "Just..." She saw ten of him.

"Give me the gun!"

"Leave me alone!" She swung. "Let me leave!"

"Give me that gun!" He snatched it.

"No!"

"Listen to me all right? Just listen to me."

"Leave me alone!" She ran behind the garage. "Someone help me!"

"Shannon!"

She slipped on an oily patch. "Oh!" Her face hit the gravel. "Uh!"

Pain rippled through her. Her ankle throbbed. Perhaps she'd twisted or broken it.

"I can't let you go to the police." His shadow loomed over her. Gun in hand.

She'd never felt this sick in her life. Never been in this much pain.

But that didn't concern her as much as the man standing over her.

And what he intended to do.

CHAPTER NINE

"*Drowning. I feel like I'm drowning. I can take the ones I love down with me or I can lie to them forever. I feel so selfish. I don't know what to do. Being right isn't always best. If it weren't for Dylan, I could just go away. But I couldn't live a day without her.*

I do everything in my power to make her happy but I only cause her pain these days. If only we didn't fight every time we saw each other. She's so angry. Why can't she see no one will love her the way I do? After all that's happened, this is the first time I regret what I did. The first time in my life I wished it never happened."

"Regret what you did?" Brianna closed Nadia's journal with her thumb still inside the pages. Davis meowed beside her. She laid the brownish-tan cat on her chest. "What the hell were you hiding, Nadia?"

∞ ∞ ∞ ∞

"Excuse me. Excuse me please!" Dylan pushed her way around the men at the junkyard the next day. They grazed in and out the garage checking out anything they could find. Swaggert sweated behind the computer at the counter. He could've eliminated some of the crowd who needed to check out if he could push more than one key at a time.

"Ah, shit!" He turned and spit.

"What now?" The first customer griped.

"I pushed the wrong button."

The sixth man in line stepped out of place. "Yo' Swag don't you know how to use the computer yet?"

They laughed.

"Shut up! I just made a mistake. You in such a hurry then do it ya' self!"

"Maybe we all should." The eighth man bundled up inside his coat. "Then we'd at least get outta here before next week."

"Excuse me." Dylan squeezed between the men.

"Well hello, sweet thang." A gap tooth man winked.

"Hey lady can you use a computer?" Another joked.

"I hope she can so we can get outta here."

"Shut up." Swaggert punched the monitor. "You guys throwin' me off!"

"Mr. Swaggert?" Dylan put her purse on the counter. "Mr. Swaggert?"

"Oh who the hell let you in? Get outta the way, girl. I'm busy."

"Have you seen Bruce?"

"Bruce? Don't even mention his name." Swaggert plucked keys. "I'm trying not to blow my top as it is."

A skinny black guy hauled a tire from the back area.

"Roy?" Dylan ran to him.

"Oh hey, D. You okay? I'm sorry about your mother."

"Thanks. I see you guys are very busy today."

"You don't know the half of it." He balanced the tire on his shoulder.

"I'm looking for Bruce."

"He didn't even show up today. That's why we in the mess we in. I was off today. The first Saturday in months I got off and Swag come callin' me in before I got a chance to wake up good."

He propped the tire over to the side then went to the back for another. Dylan jumped out of his way when he returned.

"I don't mean to bother you Roy but I needed to talk to Bruce about Mom. I'm grasping at straws but I think he could help me."

"We haven't heard from him. Swag's been calling his cell all morning. He's not answering. He didn't even clean up last night."

"What do you mean clean up?"

"He broke a liquor bottle over there by the door. Glass was

all over the place. I don't know what's wrong with Bruce's head. He know Swag don't allow nobody drinking at the junkyard."

"Bruce wouldn't do that. He takes this job very seriously. You know that."

"Well someone was here drinking last night. Unless it was a ghost than it had to be Bruce." Roy took the tire outside.

"Mr. Swaggert?" Dylan marched back to the counter.

"Here." Swaggert handed an Asian man his merchandise. "Next."

"Mr. Swaggert?"

"Get from ova here." He shoved Dylan from behind the counter.

"Look I know you don't like me."

"Damn straight." He punched buttons.

"What's up with Bruce? I called his cell and he's not even answering."

"I don't know, shit. Do I look like Bruce is in my damn pocket? Shit I know his ass was suppose to be working and he was in here drinking. I had to sweep up all that damn glass. I've had it with Bruce and his shit." Swaggert gave a man his change. The next customer stepped up.

"But this isn't like Bruce at all. Something's not adding up."

"One thing's for sure..." Swaggert took the customer's money. "I've given Bruce his last damn chance. If he's gonna piss all over me than he can go work somewhere else."

"Something could've happened to him."

"Why do you care?" He spit in the trash can. "It's because of you his life is a mess to begin with. He was doing all right until he hooked up with you and your crazy mother."

"How dare you? My mother is dead!"

"Good riddance."

"Oh!" Dylan snatched her purse. "You are the meanest and nastiest man I've ever met. No wonder no one likes to be around you!" She pushed her way through the men. "Go to hell!"

Swag spit. "You ain't got a hell to vanish me into, sista. And I ain't the only one in this room that'll be going."

"If you see Bruce tell him to call me. Could you at least do that?"

"I could but I won't. People got their own problems. The whole world doesn't revolve around you. That's your problem, ya' so damn spoiled. I don't know what Bruce sees in ya'."

"Oh yeah?" Dylan slapped her hand on the counter. "I'd say

the same thing about you. I see now why he's your only friend but I sure don't see why he'd wanna be!"

"Get the hell outta here!" Swaggert shot her the bird.

Dylan bumped into Roy on her way out the garage.

"You okay, D?"

"I just can't believe someone can be so nasty."

He tied a bandanna around his head. "Swag? Yep he's something else."

"If you see Bruce can you tell him to call me?"

"Sure. If *you* see Bruce tell him to stay away 'cause Swag wants his head on a stick." He went inside.

Dylan caught a glare off the ground as she walked down the driveway. She bent over. A gold hoop earring with a ruby in the center laid turned to the side in the gravel.

She traced her finger over the broken clasp.

She'd seen this earring somewhere before.

If only she could remember where.

CHAPTER TEN

Dylan made her way to Bruce's hallway.

Tkk...tkk...tkk...tkk...

His faucet always dripped.

Memories overwhelmed her as soon as she walked in. She missed that scent of oil and grime mixed with Bruce's natural smell. Gasoline made most women gag but she loved it. A vision of them making love hit her. How Bruce could control her body beyond comprehension. How his hands left tiny streaks of oil on her pale breasts. How she loved making love with him more when he'd been sweaty and musty instead of fresh from the shower.

Nadia had been right. Dylan changed when she met Bruce. The things Nadia disliked about him the most had been the things Dylan treasured. She admired his temper but hated how it got him into trouble. She liked how he worked his fingers numb just to suit his pride. How he ate with his elbows on the table, drove with a heavy foot, threw beer cans on the floor and cursed out anyone who gave him shit.

She loved everything about him.

Her body stiffened at the sound of footsteps. She couldn't see anything in the dark hallway. She'd found her way from memory.

What was she doing here anyway?

"Bruce?"

Someone wrapped their arms around her.

"Mmm! Let me go!"

"Quiet!" Bruce covered her mouth. "Shut up please."

"Bruce?"

He tossed her into his bedroom and turned on the light.

"Asshole!" She swatted him. "Scared me half to death!"

"You're the one in my house." He massaged his temples. "I'm the one that should be scared."

"Doesn't give you the right to sneak up on me!"

He covered his ears. "Just stop shouting please." His eyes were droopy and red with thick pillows.

"Bruce what the..."

He turned the lamp on by the bed. "Jesus." He flinched when he sat down.

"Are you all right?"

"I've been better." He stretched on the bed. He didn't have on a shirt or socks. His jeans were unfastened.

She crawled in beside him. "You look terrible."

"I feel like two trains are racing in my head."

"What's wrong with you?"

He buried his head in the pillow. "I feel horrible."

"You look it. What's wrong?" She touched his forehead. "You have a fever? Think you got the flu or something?"

"No I got a stomach virus or a touch of food poisoning. Woke up with a migraine and been throwing up. Got the runs too. Can't keep anything down. This morning I could hardly move."

"I'm sorry. How did you get food poisoning?"

He licked his dry lips. "Think I got it from that twenty-four hour deli I stopped at on the way home last night. Got an egg salad sandwich."

"Oooh." Dylan grimaced.

"I woke up feeling like this."

"You need to go to the hospital." She put her hands under his head.

"No I'm getting better. Besides you know I don't have insurance. My neighbor got me some stomach medicine. I've been in the restroom so much that I should have the bug out soon. I got a question."

"What?"

"What the fuck are you doing in my house?"

"I was worried about you."

He dragged his hand over his face. "Oh yeah?"

"Yeah. I went to the junkyard earlier. They said you hadn't shown up."

"I bet Swag's pissed huh?"

"Hmm, I think that's putting it mildly."

"Ahh, shit."

"Why didn't you just call in and say you were sick?"

"My cell needed charging. And the house phone got cut off."

"What?"

"Yeah I didn't have the money to pay the bill."

She had no idea he'd fallen on such hard times.

She caressed his hair. "I wanna be mad at you for making me worry but I can't."

"Oh?" He managed a tiny smile. "Why were you worried about me?"

"I wouldn't want anything bad to happen to you." He leaned up on his elbows. "Nah, it's more than that isn't it?"

"Just because we're not together doesn't mean I'm not concerned about you."

"Because you still love me right?"

"Don't start."

"How you get in here again?"

"I still have a key. You want it back?"

"No. I'm surprised you still have it. Still haven't told me what you want."

"I wondered if you might know something about Mom that could help me figure out why she was killed."

"What the hell would I know that you don't?" He put his hands over his eyes.

"I need to know what went on between you two. Why she hated you so much."

"Dylan."

"You don't hate someone like she hated you for no reason."

"She never liked me from the beginning. She thought I was some thug who was gonna ruin your life." He dipped a rag into the bowl of water on his end table. He held it on his forehead. "That's all."

"It's more than that. I know Mom never cared for you but it got worse after I'd gone to NYC for Zoë's party."

"It's old news now."

"I remember I was so sad that you couldn't be there. I never wanted anything more than to walk into the party being on your arm. Show everyone how much I loved you."

"You know I didn't belong there. That's why I didn't go. You were up there with Zoë's friends and all those models and artists and classy people. There was no way I fit in. I wasn't gonna embarrass myself and have to deal with the way your mother looked down at me."

"That shouldn't have mattered. What you should have cared about was how much it meant to me."

"You knew I loved you." He adjusted the rag on his face. "I didn't have to go to some damn party to prove it."

"The next day things were so tense. Mom told me she'd disown me before she'd let me be with you. What changed in that short of time?"

"I don't wanna hurt you." He stood. "I'd rather die than do anything to hurt you."

"Did you have an affair?"

He lowered his head.

She walked up behind him. "It's not *that* is it? You cheated on me didn't you?"

"Dylan."

"I remember how strange you acted when I got back into town. How funny it felt when you touched me, how you didn't wanna make love."

"I always wanted to make love to you. Every chance I got. I still do."

"It was like you were hiding something. You couldn't look me in the eyes. It was like you felt guilty about something."

He looked at her.

"You slept with another woman and Mom found out."

"Dylan."

"Oh god. That's why she wanted me to break up with you." She grasped her head. "Here I was thinking you were innocent and she was picking on you but she had a reason. You cheated on me! You slept with someone else. How could you do that, Bruce?"

"I never meant to hurt you. It was a mistake. It meant nothing to me."

"I don't believe this."

He reached for her. "Dylan."

"Don't touch me. Don't ever touch me again."

"I love you so much."

"You love me? I gave you everything. I chose you over my

family and it ruined my relationship with my mother."

"Listen to me okay? I'd never hurt you on purpose. Let me explain."

"You can't explain." She hit his chest. "Who was it? Who did you sleep with?"

"It doesn't matter."

"How did Mom find out?"

"Nadia was having me followed. She was relentless, waiting to catch me slipping up."

"What are you talking about? My mom wasn't following you."

"Yes she was but she never told you. See I'm not the only bad guy here. She had someone trailing me from the moment I came into your life."

"This is insane."

"It's the truth. She would have set me up even if I hadn't done anything wrong. Don't you see how fucked up she was?"

"Don't ever talk about my mom that way."

"She wasn't normal, Dylan. She only wanted you with her. She didn't want you having a life of your own, didn't want you sharing your love with anyone else. You know I'm telling the truth."

"You stop it! You're saying all this for me to forget what you did."

"Nadia wasn't right in the head when it came to you. You know that."

"I can't believe you'd sleep with someone else. I'd expect that from anyone but you."

He snatched her. "Let me make it up to you. Give me another chance, please."

"And I walked around missing you at that party like a damn fool and you're back here fucking someone else."

"It was only one time."

"It doesn't matter how many times!"

"I know it was stupid and I hated myself for doing it but I only loved you."

"Mom was right about you. You're nothing but trash and I should have never gotten involved with you."

"You don't mean that."

"You're a liar and I don't want to see you again." She ran to the front door.

"Wait!" He hobbled after her. He slumped over when he got

to the door.

"You make me sick."

"Listen! Your mother twisted things. Mmm." He clenched his stomach. "She even told me she was gonna get me out of your life no matter what. She loved you too much, Dylan. Way too much."

"I loved *you* too much. I hope your little fling was worth it because you've lost the best thing you'll ever have." She opened the door. "And to think I even considered giving it another chance."

"Dylan."

"Go to hell."

"Don't leave like this!"

She slammed the door.

CHAPTER ELEVEN

Tuesday Night (The following week)

So much for Dylan getting answers from the people in Shannon's apartment building. They hadn't seen or heard from her in days. Dylan wasn't sure if they lied to protect Shannon but she didn't pressure them.

She took the elevator to the first floor. She smiled at the maintenance man standing by the front office. She fastened her wool coat and pulled her collar up. She braced herself for the brutal chill and walked out the entrance.

She'd parked across the lot close to the bushes. A maroon Escalade blocked the view of her dark green Subaru. She ran down the lanes. Wind lashed at her coat and knocked her hat forward.

"Shit." She dropped her keys when she got to her car. Her knit gloves snagged on the pavement as she dug for them.

"Come on. Ah." She caught the key ring. "Got'cha." She brushed dirt off her coat and got in the car.

A man jumped from behind the bushes and ran to her window. "Hey, lady!"

She held onto the locked door.

"I need help!" He pinched at the door handle. "My baby! Please!"

"What?"

"My baby! Something's wrong with my baby! Can you help me?"

She parted her door but didn't get out.

He had bronze-colored skin and a body that could've been muscular or chunky but the bulky leather jacket made it hard to tell which. He towered over the car. His minuscule eyes suggested an Asian heritage. A crooked goatee outlined his purple lips. Breath smelled of cigarettes and jalapeno peppers.

He had a gold stud in one ear and a tiny gold crucifix hung from his beaded necklace.

She sheltered herself behind the door. "What's wrong?"

He rambled so fast she could only make out "baby".

"Calm down. I can't understand you. What's happening?"

He sobbed. "My baby!" He struggled with his accent. "My little baby! She's in my van! My van won't start." He caught his breath. "My daughter...she's not breathing!"

"Are you sure she's not breathing?"

"I live on the other side of town. I was on my way home when she started shaking real bad." He jiggled his arms. "Then she was kicking and then she just went still. Her eyes are up in the air! She's diabetic and I think she's having a seizure!"

"Oh my god. Uh..." Dylan twisted and turned. "Hold on okay?"

"My phone's not working." He pointed to the building. "I went to the apartments but the security guard didn't let me in." He pulled at his soiled sweats.

"Shh. Okay, wait." Dylan got her phone from her purse. "You can use my phone to call nine-one-one."

"I already did that! Please help. There's no time!"

"I thought your phone wasn't working. How did you call them?"

"Earlier it worked." He scratched his head. "They said an ambulance is coming or told me I could take her to the nearest hospital. That's all the way downtown. Please help me. She could die!"

"It's best to wait for the ambulance if..."

"She won't make it! Please just come help me. I don't know what to do. She might already be dead. Please."

"Look I wanna help you but it would be best if we tried nine-one-one again. They might already be at the van."

"I've been waiting forever. Please. You're the only person out here. I'll give you money." He dug in his pockets. "How much?"

"Put your money away."

"My van is not far from here. I just need someone to help me. Please. I beg you."

Something didn't seem right but she had to help him. If she were desperate she'd want someone to help her. What goes around comes around. She might be in the same situation one day. She couldn't let her fear stop her from helping his baby.

"Okay." She overlooked him and prayed in silence. "Get in."

He directed her from Shannon's apartment building to a homely area not far away with raggedy streets and abandoned apartment buildings. Her trembling hands made it difficult to drive but she didn't let on.

"Down there."

She went across the train tracks and ended up on a street with graffiti-stained houses and buildings with boards on the windows and doors.

"That's my van." He gestured to a crusty van parked on the street between dilapidated row houses.

He jumped out when she stopped. She almost choked on the stench of weed and mildew in the air.

She didn't do drugs but knew how weed smelled thanks to Bruce. Back in the day he'd done marijuana like a religion. She'd broken him of that. Too bad she couldn't change *all* his bad habits.

She got to the van.

"Come on." The man climbed inside. The van rocked from his weight. "Come on. She's in these blankets."

"Is she okay?" Dylan crawled in on her knees. "Is she breathing?"

He bundled a bunch of blankets in the corner of the van.

Dylan crawled past garden tools and pieces of metal. "Is she all right?"

"Yeah." He reached his hand back. "I need you to put your hand under her head. You know how to hold a baby right? Give me your hand."

She hesitated.

His voice seemed more relaxed than before. Calm as if he'd never been crying.

"Give me your hand." He wiggled his fingers.

She glanced over his shoulder. He'd piled blankets on top of each other.

Not a baby in sight.

She backed away. "What...what is this?"

He grabbed her arm. "You're not going anywhere."

"Let me go. What are you doing?"

"You and me are gonna have some fun. Hmm?"

"No." She crawled back. "Stay away from me."

"Come on." He pulled her to him. "We'll have tons of fun."

"Someone help me!" She jiggled the handle on the sliding side door.

"I'll help you." He bent her wrist back.

"Owww!"

He slid the door shut. "You're staying for this party whether you want to or not." He held her against him. "You're so pretty." He gripped her butt with one hand and her neck with the other.

"No!" She twisted in his arms. "Someone help me please!"

He flung her one way. She swung herself the other.

"No!" She reached for the shovel behind the driver's seat.

"Be still huh?" He sucked her neck and moved his hands inside her coat.

"No!" She struck his chest. "Help!"

"Don't bother yelling." He threw her down flat and got on top. "It's just you and me out here. We have plenty of time to have some fun."

"No! Noo!" She sobbed and kicked. "Nooo!"

"Come on." He tried to pull her coat off her shoulders but her movements stopped him from getting a good grip. "Settle down and you might like it."

His weight pinned her as if she were under bricks and steel.

"Help me!" Dylan swatted but he held her arms down. "Please! Stop! Don't do this!"

His stiff crotch poked her thighs.

"Settle down or I'll hit you!"

She almost choked from his rank breath.

"You wanted to be so helpful before didn't you? Ha, ha! You fell for it didn't you?"

"Stop! Get off me! Help!"

He stuck a small knife under her chin. "I said be quiet. I'm gonna do you so good, baby." He unzipped her pants.

"No!"

"I'll show you what a real man is all about."

"Get off!" She got one arm free. She swung it around. She didn't know what she hit but she kept reaching. The shovel fell over. The hoe plopped into the front seat. She knocked over a pail of old paintbrushes.

He pulled her pants and underwear down to her ankles with the look of pure malice in his eyes.

"I said cool it." He pierced her chin with the knife.

She'd have to kill him. It would be the only way she would get out of here.

He unfastened his belt.

She slammed her knee into his crotch.

"Ahhhh!" He rolled off of her.

Dylan snatched the knife. "Stay away!"

"You're not getting out of here alive."

CHAPTER TWELVE

"I'll bet..." The man's tongue ran across his yellow teeth. "You wouldn't know what to do with that would you?"

Dylan blinked to see through the tears. "I just wanna leave."

"And I want you to stay." He slid toward her. "Who do you think's gonna win?"

She swung the knife at his face. He grabbed it and knocked her down face first.

"No!" She reached for the door handle.

He pulled her arm back. "If this is the way you want it..." He rolled his hard center against her buttocks. "Hey it might even be better doing it this way huh?"

Dylan closed her eyes and prayed for a miracle or whatever came first.

The van door slid open. "Hey what are you doing?" A man with glasses asked.

"Get the fuck outta here." The attacker kicked at the man. "It's none of your business!"

"No don't leave! He's trying to rape me!"

"She's lying! Uh she's my wife. She's high see? Delusional you know? I'm trying to calm her down. She's having one of her spells."

"It's not true!" Dylan broke free and crawled to the corner of the van. "Please call the police!"

She stared at the middle-aged stranger. He was a handsome man with black hair and dark brown eyes that glowed from underneath his glasses.

"If she's your wife how come you have a knife?"

"I won't say it again!" The rapist raised the knife. "Get the fuck outta..."

The stranger snatched the attacker by his jacket. "Didn't anyone ever teach you how to treat a lady?" He put the rapist in a chokehold. "When a woman says no your ass better listen."

The stranger slung him down.

The rapist acted as if he'd put up a fight at first. Instead he climbed over to the front of the van.

The stranger grabbed the rapist's leg. "Hey get back here!"

The rapist knocked the stranger back with one kick. "Fuck both of you!" He hopped out the van through the driver's side.

The stranger tumbled over. "Hey!" He struggled to his knees. "Come back here!"

The rapist ran behind the row houses.

"Here's my phone." The stranger threw it to Dylan. "Call the police. I'm gonna see if I can find him."

"No!" Dylan reached for him. "Please don't leave me alone! Don't leave me please!"

"But he's getting away. I gotta..."

"I don't care if he gets away." She put her head between her knees. "Just don't leave me alone. Please. Please just stay with me."

He climbed in. "Are you all right?" He caressed her face. "Did he hurt you?"

"I prayed for you." She threw her arms around him. He covered her with one of the blankets. "I prayed and you came. You came."

"Shh. You're safe now."

She rested her head on his shoulder.

∞ ∞ ∞ ∞

"Dylan!" Jasmine jumped from the couch when Dylan walked in.

"Dylan where you been, girl?" Zoë set her coffee cup on the living room table and ran to her best friend. Brianna and Steven sat on the two-seater by the window.

Dylan nestled the man beside her. She'd already gotten use to his warm embrace.

"Dylan?" Jasmine looked her over. "What happened to you?"

"We've all been worried sick." Zoë hugged her. "We've been calling your phone and you hadn't gotten back with any of us."

Jasmine shook her. "You've been gone for hours. Where have you been?"

"Just let her catch her breath all right?"

Jasmine looked at the stranger from head to toe. "And who are you?"

"I'm a friend."

Jasmine flipped him off. "Dylan I want an explanation. And before you rant about being grown you can save it. A grown woman doesn't disappear without letting people know where she is."

"What happened to your clothes?" Zoë opened Dylan's coat.

Dylan closed her coat.

"Dylan what happened to you?" Steven asked.

"Are you all right?" Brianna walked to her.

"This is why I didn't wanna come home. People don't shut up long enough to listen. I just want someone to listen to me tonight. Just one person to hear what I say and know I mean it."

"What happened?" Steven pulled her from the others.

"She was attacked."

"Attacked?" Jasmine gaped at the stranger. "What are you talking about?"

"If you hadn't jumped down her throat and took the time to pay attention, you could've figured it out. You're the aunt right?"

"Yes I'm Jasmine Hudson."

"A man tried to rape your niece tonight."

"*What*?" Jasmine covered her mouth.

"I went with her to the police station. We've been there since eight something."

"Oh my baby." Jasmine held her. "I'm so sorry, honey." She kissed Dylan's tears. "I didn't mean to come down on you. I had no idea. I am so sorry. Please forgive me. I wouldn't ever want anything to happen to you."

"I know." Dylan stuffed her face in Jasmine's bosom.

"I love you so much, sweetie."

"I know."

"What exactly happened?" Zoë took Dylan's hand.

"I was so stupid. So stupid."

"No you weren't." The stranger put his arm around her

shoulders. "You did what any normal person would've done."

Dylan clenched her coat. "It happened by Shannon's neighborhood."

"That's a horrible area," Zoë said. "You shouldn't have gone there alone at night."

"I went to see if I could find answers. I wanted to talk to the people in her apartment building but apparently Shannon's missing or ran off or something."

"I told you to leave it alone."

"I can't just leave it alone, Zoë. Anyway I was in the parking lot."

Steven moved in front of Brianna. "Someone attacked you in the parking *lot*?"

"No. He came *up* to me in the parking lot. Damn it! I was a fool."

Jasmine hugged her. "Whatever happened, it's not your fault. You did nothing wrong."

"I was so stupid. I thought I was helping him."

Zoë put her arms around her. "What did he do?"

"He lured me to this van. Said his baby wasn't breathing and that his van didn't run." She closed her eyes. "He was so convincing, crying and everything. He was a very good actor."

"So he didn't rape you right?" Brianna asked. "You okay?"

"As okay as I can be. We called the police and they ended up acting like I'd done something wrong for being there at night."

"I'm sorry for that," Steven said. "It's definitely not your fault. A woman should be able to go anywhere any time of day without being attacked."

"They of course said they'll look into it but there wasn't any physical evidence or anything. I described how he looked and that's it."

"Dylan was too shaken to really go into a lot of detail. Plus it's very hard to prove attempted rape. She made a report, gave a description and we waited at the station for the cops to go check out the area."

"And you...were with her all this time?" Jasmine pointed a quivering finger to the man.

"Yes."

"Who are you?"

"He's my friend, Aunt Jas." Dylan took his hand. "If he hadn't been there I don't know what I would've done."

"Believe me I'm just glad I got there in time."

"Well you already know I'm Jasmine Hudson. I still don't know your name."

"Nick Sebastian."

"Nick." Jasmine shook his hand. "Nice to meet you."

"I wish it were under better circumstances."

"So the police knew nothing about this guy at all?"

Nick turned to Zoë. "No. They traced the license plate of the van and turns out it was stolen."

"Don't give up." Brianna got her coat from the two-seater. "They'll keep trying."

"Right. The police barely do things against suspects you *can* identify."

"Not for lack of trying, Jasmine."

"I'm sorry, Detective Morris. I didn't mean to offend. I'm just upset."

"I just wanna forget about tonight and go to bed."

Jasmine helped Dylan out of her coat. "Let's go upstairs. I'll bring you some tea and something to eat."

"Wait." Dylan stopped before she got to the stairs. "What are you guys doing here?"

Steven put on his coat. "We wanted to see if anyone had seen Shannon ourselves. Guess we got our answer."

"I know you want to do all you can to help but let us handle it, Dylan." Brianna fixed her coat collar. "This is nothing to play around with. The man who tried to rape you could have something to do with Nadia's murder."

CHAPTER THIRTEEN

"You really believe that, Detective Morris?"

"We can't take any chances, Zoë."

"I'm really glad you're all right, Dylan. Bree and I are gonna do all we can to help."

"Nick?" Dylan hugged him for the thousandth time. "I don't know how I can ever repay you."

"I'm glad I was there." He kissed her cheek. "I want you to get some rest. You got my number if you need it."

"Yes. Thank you so much." She hugged him again.

"Come on, sweetie." Jasmine pulled her away. "Go on upstairs and I'll be up in a minute."

She went upstairs.

"I hope she's gonna be okay." Zoë gathered the coffee cups. "I'm gonna take these to the kitchen."

"Good job I'm doing of protecting Dylan huh? I swore to Nadia I'd always look after her. I'm already screwing up."

"Jasmine it's not your fault," Brianna said. "Who could've known this would happen?"

"What's happening around here huh? Did we do something to deserve this? Is this payback for something?"

"Jasmine you gotta hold yourself together." Steven put on his gloves. "Call me and Bree if you need to all right?"

"You think Shannon ran off or do you think something

happened to her?"

"You know her better than we do," Brianna said. "What do you think?"

"No telling with Shannon. She's a master at disappearing."

Zoë came back in. "Who's a master at disappearing?"

"Oh we're just speculating about Shannon being gone," Jasmine said.

"Oh." Zoë patted her hair. "I'd put my money on her passed out somewhere dead drunk."

Steven hid his grin.

"The last person we need to be worrying about is Shannon. I don't know why Dylan thought she'd know something anyway."

Steven zipped up his coat. "It's not impossible to think she might have had something to do with Nadia's death. If you guys find out anything let us know."

"We will." Jasmine motioned to the door. "I appreciate the attention you're giving this case."

"Have a good night, everyone." Steven titled his head to the lovely woman beside Zoë. "It was nice seeing you again."

She put her arms behind her back. "You too."

Jasmine escorted them to the door. "Thank you so much."

"Bye." Brianna waved.

Jasmine went back into the living room.

Nick stuffed his scarf down his coat. "Well I guess I should be going huh? It was nice meeting you both."

"Nice meeting you too." Zoë went upstairs.

"Well." Nick tied his scarf. "Tell Dylan I hope she'll be okay."

"Wait, Mr. Sebastian."

"Call me Nick."

"I just wanted to thank you so much for what you did. I can't imagine what would have happened if you hadn't come along."

"I think your niece is much stronger than you give her credit for."

"Maybe so but I will always worry." She walked him to the door. "I owe you. If you need anything then let me know."

"That's not necessary."

She touched his hand. "There's nothing I could give you that would be worth what you did. You have no idea how much I care for Dylan."

He pulled his collar over his ears. "I probably understand more than you think."

∞ ∞ ∞ ∞

Brianna and Steven approached the front counter of the "Make a Deal" pawnshop the next day.

"Are you Antwan?" Brianna asked.

"I am." He escorted a customer to the furniture section then went back to the counter. "Is something wrong?"

"I'm Detective Brianna Morris with the Albany Police." She showed her badge. "This is my partner Steven Kemp."

Antwan dusted off a shelf of DVD players. "What's this about?"

"You're a friend of Shannon Kuriakis' aren't you?" Steven moved for a customer to pass.

"Look if this is about Dr. Hollister then you're on the wrong track. Shannon wouldn't hurt her. She wouldn't hurt anyone."

"That might be true but we need to find Shannon first. We believe she's missing. We heard you saw her Friday the fifth. It was the day of Nadia's funeral."

He straightened a bin of golf clubs. "Look I don't know where Shannon is. If I did I'd tell you."

Brianna stooped down to check out a computer scanner. "But you have to be concerned right?"

"We spoke to a young lady, Marley Blake." Steven checked out the televisions. "She said you're all close friends."

Antwan scratched under his hat.

"Marley told us you were all together the evening of the fifth. Marley said Shannon was very upset because she wasn't allowed at the funeral."

"I don't remember. She was rambling and everything."

Steven blocked him. "We're losing patience."

"Okay Shannon showed up at Marley's around one or two that afternoon. Marley called me over because Shannon was scaring her."

Steven glanced at Antwan then back to the televisions. "How was she scaring her?"

"She was talking crazy and yes, she was kinda drunk. Shannon's neurotic anyway but when she starts drinking she's out of control."

Brianna nodded. "What happened?"

"She was cursing and hollering about not being able to go to the funeral and how much she loved Nadia. Then she started talking about Bruce."

Steven played with a universal remote. "Bruce McNamara?"

"Yeah she kept saying she knew he killed Nadia."

The officers looked at each other.

"She said he wasn't gonna get away with it. Marley got scared because Shannon kept talking about getting her gun to go see Bruce."

Steven moved from the shelves. "Shannon has a gun?"

"Look she was just ranting and emotional. She didn't mean it."

Steven put the remote back on the shelf. "How do you know?"

"Shannon says things all the time when she's drunk. I told her to go to the police if she thought Bruce was involved. She cursed me out, left Marley's and I haven't seen her since."

"Do you think she saw Bruce that day?" Brianna asked.

He adjusted his cap. "I don't know. This isn't the first time Shannon's sprouted off and disappeared. You guys don't know how Shannon can be when she's drunk."

"Looks like we need to get back to Old Swaggert's junkyard huh, Steve?"

He gestured to the door. "I'm right ahead of you, Bree."

CHAPTER FOURTEEN

Steven and Brianna found Bruce underneath the hood of another car when they got to Swaggert's junkyard.

He turned the radio down and got a wrench from the pocket of his overalls.

"Well isn't this a lovely surprise huh? Let me guess. Wanna talk about the murder right?"

"You can say that," Steven said.

Bruce walked around Brianna to get to the other side of the car. "I thought we settled this before." He stooped back under the hood.

"You know Shannon Kuriakis is missing?" Brianna peeked over his shoulder.

"I heard something about that." He wiped his oily hands on his overalls. "Sure she's missing?"

Brianna stepped back. "What do you mean?"

"Well this isn't the first time Shannon's run off."

"We've heard." Steven stepped over a soda can in the grass.

"I suppose you've also heard she's a drunk?"

Brianna swatted a gnat. "We think it might be more than her just running off."

Bruce peeked over his shoulder at her. "Why?"

She shrugged. "Do you know Antwan Toussaint?"

He reached further into the car. "What did ole' big mouth Antwan say now? I swear he gossips more than a chick."

"Antwan saw Shannon Friday, the fifth. I'm sure you remember that day right?" Brianna stood next to Steven. "It was the day of Nadia's funeral."

"Get to the point if you don't mind."

"Antwan said that he and Marley Blake, another friend of Shannon's was with her that afternoon. She was upset about not being invited to the funeral and she was very drunk."

"When was Shannon not drunk?"

Steven bent down beside Bruce. "Antwan said Shannon planned to come see you and she was bringing her gun."

"Oh man this is total bullshit."

Steven rose. "Is it?"

"Yes. Now maybe she said she was coming to see me but she never did. I haven't seen Shannon in months. Ran into her at a bar last time I saw her."

Steven rocked on his tiptoes. "Kinda get the feeling you're lying there, ol' Bruce."

"Why would I lie about Shannon?" He cleaned his hands on his overalls. "She was no one in my world. I couldn't care less about her."

"It's just so funny that your name keeps popping up every time we turn a corner with this case."

"Well I don't know what to tell you guys, Detective Morris. If you really wanna find the killer I suggest you stop bothering me and go talk to someone else. I'm not taking more of this harassment. I'm getting sick of it and trying to control my temper."

Steven put his arm around Bruce's shoulders. "I think you're lying."

"For the last fuckin' time I didn't see Shannon that day and I don't know where she is. So you can run back and tell Jasmine that. She probably danced down the street when she found out Shannon claimed she was coming to see me so I'd look like the killer."

"We haven't even told her about Shannon coming to see you yet," Steven said. "Besides she's busy worrying about Dylan. I'm sure you're the last person on her mind."

"Dylan?" He tossed the wrench on the ground. "Is she okay?"

"I don't think it's your concern."

"Don't fuck with me, Detective Kemp. Is she okay?"

"She'll get better with time," Brianna said.

Bruce slammed the hood shut. "I'm losing my patience here."

"Dylan was attacked last night." Brianna glanced around the yard. "A man tried to rape her."

"What? You gotta be fuckin' kidding me."

"Steven and I were there when she got home. She was very shaken up and scared which is expected. So Jasmine isn't worrying about you right now."

"I don't believe this." Bruce leaned back on the car. "Who did it?"

"We don't know." Steven shrugged. "There's a detective over in Shannon's area that's handling the case. It happened over there."

Bruce lunged at them. "I want a name."

"We told you we don't know," Steven said. "Now you acting like a moron isn't helping anything."

"This is all Nadia's fault." Bruce marched to the front of the garage with his radio.

"How is it Nadia's fault?"

"Because if she hadn't stuck her nose in our business Detective Morris, Dylan and I would be together and I could've protected her from something like this."

"That's ridiculous. It was just something that happened."

"Detective Kemp you don't understand. Nadia did all she could to keep me out of Dylan's life and now all kinds of shit's happenin'. I gotta go. Swag!" He propped the radio on a paint can. "Swag!"

He hobbled out, scratching under his arm. "What?"

"I gotta go." Bruce got out his keys.

"The fuck you do." Swaggert smacked tobacco. "You get over there and finish that car. I've had it with yo' shit."

"This is serious." Bruce went inside and came out buttoning his jacket. "Something's happened to Dylan. Someone tried to rape her last night."

Swaggert spit brown juice by Brianna's foot. She jumped.

"You leave now then you don't ever need to come back!"

"What?"

"You get your ass over there and finish that car. If you don't then you're fired!"

"I don't care. Dylan's more important than any damn job."

"Ungrateful son of a bitch." Swag spit to the side. "You might think you run everything else but you don't run this. Now get your ass back there and get to work or kiss your job goodbye!" He wobbled inside.

Stacy-Deanne

"Fuck him. I'm going." Bruce trudged to his car.

"Wait." Brianna ran alongside him. "Isn't that why things got so messed up between you and Dylan in the first place? You and Nadia being too selfish to care about what Dylan wanted?"

He stopped at his car. "I know what she wants, Detective Morris."

"Listen." Steven blocked him. "I know what it's like to want to do all you can for the woman you love. Believe me. But you need to back off."

"Back off?"

"Put yourself in Dylan's place, man. She's embarrassed, frightened, confused, and even a little hopeless. The last thing she wants right now is to see you. Think about her and not yourself. Give her some space."

"How can I just sit back when she's in pain? I gotta show her I care about her."

"Then care for her the way she needs you to," Brianna said. "Not just how you want to."

CHAPTER FIFTEEN

That night Brianna and Steven made it to Jayson's restaurant to check up on a tip. Some guy who'd worked at the restaurant called Steven, claiming he might have info about Shannon. Something seemed fishy but Brianna didn't question it.

She couldn't remember the last time she'd gone out for fun. Her mother Beverly and stepfather Edgar always got on her for obsessing over work and ignoring time for play. They lived as if they were the ones in their prime and she the senior citizen.

Steven joked with the lazy greeter at the entrance.

Couples laughed as they toasted drinks and ate. Others delved into heavy conversations or danced.

She lost herself in the serene atmosphere and luscious aroma of entrees and sautéed vegetables.

A man whispered in his date's ear. She tickled him underneath the table with her foot.

Another woman gave her date a soft kiss on the cheek. In return his hand went down the back of her dress. Shit Brianna didn't have a man but she should've been doing the same damn thing right now not worrying about a case.

Steven suggested they grab something to eat while they waited for the guy to come out. He just so happened to choose Brianna's favorite table by the window.

"You all right?" He held her chair for her.

"Yeah just jealous as hell." She sat down. "I haven't eaten out in I can't tell when."

He danced to his chair. "Well you are now right?" He sat down and put the napkin in his lap. "Why you looking at me like that?"

"I just get the feeling something's up."

"I swear you're the most suspicious woman I've ever known."

"I'm a cop."

"You're suspicious for a cop." He lined up the salt and pepper shakers.

"And this guy said he knows where Shannon is?"

"He said he might have info that could help us. He should be out soon. Here comes the waitress."

Steven ordered the haddock and green beans. Brianna chose the Chef's salad with the baked chicken breast.

"Okay, your order will be out soon." The bouncy waitress jotted down the order. "Let me know if you need anything else."

"Uh excuse me?" Brianna touched the waitress' arm.

"Yes?"

"We need to speak to Mr. Luckett. He supposedly works in the kitchen."

Steven covered his eyes.

"Uh, there's no Mr. Luckett that works here, ma'am. You might have the wrong restaurant." She left.

"Okay, Steve. I'll give you a few minutes to explain then I'm leaving."

"Okay I lied."

"You lied about someone having important information for a case just to trick me to go out with you?"

"Yes." He laid his hand on the table. "What do you want me to say?"

"Say you're sorry."

"Well I'm not. If I'd asked you to go out with me would you have?"

She didn't answer.

A couple walked past the window on their way inside the restaurant.

"I rest my case." He dragged his hands over the tablecloth. "I just felt we needed to talk about us and every time I bring it up, you're not in the mood."

"That's not the point. You don't use something as important as a case to fix up a date."

"Well jeez, Bree. Aren't you at all flattered? When we were dating you always said I wasn't romantic enough."

"Oh I didn't say that." She crossed her legs.

"Please it's what you bitched about eighty percent of the time. I finally do something romantic and I get attitude?"

"But we're not together anymore, Steven."

A waiter brought them water.

"And why aren't we? We damn well should be."

"Steve."

"We belong together, Bree. I don't care how much you try to fight it. I know you still love me."

"Love isn't always enough."

"Bullshit. I don't know why people say that. I just want to know why you broke it off. What turned you off?"

"It's not that simple. I told you."

The waitress brought their meals and went on her way.

Steven untangled his fork and spoon. "I still haven't heard an answer."

Brianna cut up her chicken breast. "You haven't exactly been straight with me tonight either have you?"

"Not surprised to get that comment."

"And I've had it with your sarcasm. You think you have a right to me and you don't. Just because we were together once doesn't mean we belong together."

He stuck his head in the air. "That's true."

"Oh I hate it when you do that." She shook her glass.

"Do what?"

"You're pouting like a big baby."

"Since you won't give me a straight answer then I'll just come out and ask. Can we start over?"

A chunk of chicken fell out her mouth.

"I'm officially asking. I want us to be a couple again. What you say tonight will be the end. I won't pressure you anymore but just give me a straight answer."

"You can't put me on the spot like this."

"I'm sick of going around in circles. It would be different if we weren't so damn attracted to each other. It's been too many close calls. Too many times we've kissed and started to make love only to be stopped because you don't know what the hell you want."

"I..."

"But I think you do know what you want. You want me and

you need to tell me right now. I wanna move on and if it's gonna be with you I gotta know something now or else..."

"Oh I get it." She set her glass down. "You want me to let you off the hook. You wanna know where we stand so you can decide if you wanna see someone else or not."

"No, no." He coughed between chewing. "Now wait a minute."

"You're trying to bully me into telling you if we have a chance so you won't feel like the bad guy by dating someone else. Obviously there's someone else you wanna date right?"

A pain ran through her stomach and it wasn't from digestion.

"You gotta make it sound so piggish, Bree?"

"Oh you men are something else. You don't have the balls to admit you're attracted to someone else."

"I'm not."

"Oh please." She stirred her vegetables. "I know you, Steve. You got your eye on someone else. I can tell."

He threw his fork down. "That's crazy."

"I'm not stupid." She chewed croutons. "I know you like Zoë."

"Zoë?" He coughed and hit his chest. "Where are you getting this from?"

"Ray Charles is blind *and* dead and he could see you got the hots for Zoë. It's okay. I couldn't care less."

"Then how come that vein in your forehead's doing summersaults?"

"Oh please." She faked a laugh. "Honey if you want to get it on with Zoë Peron then it is *fine* with me."

"Stop it. You know no woman could ever take your place in my heart. I want you but I don't wanna be strung along."

"Well I don't see the damn point of you tricking me to dinner just to tell me you wanna be with someone else!"

People glanced at them from the nearest table.

"People are watching, Bree."

"I don't give a damn. You're trying to run game on me."

"Game?"

"How many times I gotta tell you I'm not a fool?"

He slammed his fists on the table. "There's nothing going on between me and Zoë."

The couple at the next table smiled at the detectives and continued eating.

"You admit it you dirty liar. I see how you look at her and how you run over to Jasmine's every five minutes."

"To talk about the case!"

"Oh yeah right."

"I don't have time to convince you, woman."

"Well don't." She slid her plate away. "In fact I don't care what you do. You can be with Zoë or whoever the hell else. It's your business."

"I don't wanna be with Zoë but even if I did I wouldn't need your permission."

She crossed her arms. "Well fine then."

"Fine here too!" He crossed his arms and turned to the side. His ringtone went off.

"Oh. Oh!" Brianna laughed. "Let me guess is that Miss Zoë? Do you have a date with her after you drop me off?"

"It's Jayce. Shut up." He spoke quickly then hung up.

"What was that about?"

"They found Shannon." He put his phone up. "She's dead."

"What?"

"She was found in a field with a gunshot wound to the head."

CHAPTER SIXTEEN

Nick rested on his hotel bed with the Albany paper the next morning.

Woman Who Had Lesbian Affair with Murdered Psychiatrist Found Dead.

He laid his fingertip on the victim's name.

Shannon Louise Kuriakis, 26 years old

A bystander found her fully clothed in a field with a gunshot wound to the face. Her clothes smelled of alcohol and human excrement. No weapon found at the scene. Police had no suspects or leads.

He stuffed a mini powered donut in his mouth. "What a surprise."

A soft knock startled him from the article.

He threw on his robe and answered the door.

Dylan walked in with that same terrified expression she had when he saved her. Her eyes revealed how lost she seemed. Losing someone you love could leave you hopeless and empty. No one understood that more than he did. He'd lived with the same pain for years.

If he hugged her again he probably wouldn't ever let go. The reality of her surpassed what he'd imagined when he got up close. Their meeting hadn't been blissful but at least it had happened.

"Am I interrupting you?"

He'd spend the rest of his life trying to make her happy if she gave him the chance.

"You could never interrupt me, Dylan. Is there something you wanted?"

"The last thing I want to do is bother you with my problems." She sat on the bed. "I mean you got your own life right?"

He sat beside her. "You're not bothering me okay? I want you to come to me if you need to."

"I appreciate that."

"Are you all right? How are you holding up?" He brushed her bangs out of her eye.

"Honestly I'm trying to push away what happened. I've always been like that. It makes it easier."

"You know that'll only help you temporarily." He took her hand and laid it on his lap. "You have to deal with what almost happened to you."

"I know. Maybe one day I'll be ready to face it but right now I got other things on my mind."

"So you're just gonna ignore what you went through and jump back into trying to find out who killed your mother?"

"I have to. I know it makes no sense but you don't know me." He looked at her.

"This is how I am, Nick. It's better for me to just put that behind me..." She covered her mouth. "I don't wanna think about it."

"Honey." He hugged her. "I'm sorry. I understand. The last thing I want to do is pressure you."

"I just wanna forget it. It'll make it easier you know?"

"Whatever you want, that's what we'll do. So what did you need to talk about?"

"You look different without your glasses."

"Better?"

"No, just different. You look good with them too. I don't understand this. You don't even know me but you seem to care about me as much as my family."

"I do."

"Why though? Why would you care so much? What's in it for you?"

"Do you think there's always a reason someone has to care about you?"

"When it's a stranger it makes it hard not to think so."

"You believe in fate, Dylan?" He opened his blinds.

"People always ask me that and I never know what to say."

He got two bottles of orange juice out of the fridge and passed her one. "Don't you know what you believe in?"

"I thought I did." She opened the juice. "How did you know I like orange juice?"

"Oh I didn't. Just figured you did. Don't most people like orange juice?"

"Just strange you'd hand me orange juice on a whim."

He smiled. "You make people feel like they're talking to the FBI sometimes."

She spit juice when she laughed. "I'm sorry. I didn't mean to make you feel like I was suspicious or something. It's just that even my family seems to know less about me than you do already. It's just a feeling I'm not used to."

"Is that so?"

"I feel so connected to you. I hated the way we met but I'm glad we did."

"That connection was brought on by fate. I think you do believe in it but just don't know it. I'd like to be your friend, Dylan. I don't want anything in return."

"Would you be angry if I said I didn't believe you?"

"No. I'm glad you're honest."

"How long you gonna stay in this hotel? You said you moved to Albany months ago. Can't you find a place you like yet?"

"I have my eye on this place on Avery Street. I'm still going over my options though."

"The houses on Avery are gorgeous. Not out of your reach?"

"No I got a good chunk of change."

"What do you do?"

"Uh I owned my own construction business. I've worked in construction all my life."

"Wow then you must be well off huh?"

"I wouldn't say all that." He loosened the curtains. "I owned a local company. I'd say my finances keep me comfortable but I'm far from rich."

"So you're staying in Albany then?" She smiled.

"Are you happy about that?"

"You said you lived in Baltimore?"

"Boston."

"Oh beautiful city."

"To me it was just home. You like Albany?"

"Yeah it's okay." She leaned back and swung her feet. "I've never lived anywhere else. I think I'd like to move though."

"Why?"

"Just want a change." She strolled around the room, picking up items as she did. "Zoë's been trying to get me up to New York City. She says my art would really fly if I moved there."

"She's right. Your work would reach a wider audience if you got in a museum up there. I'd give it serious thought. Your work deserves to be in museums everywhere, Dylan. Here and overseas."

She thumbed through the novel on his end table. "You've never even seen my work."

"I have." He pointed to his laptop on the back table. "Stayed up all night looking at your website. I know some of your work's in museums in the local artist section. You've had write ups in the paper. You donated several paintings to community centers and homeless shelters in the area. You were on Channel Five News last year."

"Okay how long have you been stalking me?"

He laughed. "You must be proud. You're very talented and one day the entire world will know it."

"Yeah well when my work is in Rome and Paris, or still raved about after I'm dead then I'll feel I've accomplished something worth bragging about." She shook up his snow globe.

"It'll happen but you gotta believe it will."

"Anyway I didn't come to talk about me." She put the snow globe on the dresser. "I need to talk to you about something very serious. I need some advice."

"Okay."

"What would you do if you knew something that might get someone that you cared about in trouble? And uh, you knew you should tell because it's the right thing to do. Also if you didn't say anything you might get in trouble too. What would you do?"

"Is this about your mother's death?"

"Did you catch the news or paper about Shannon Kuriakis?"

"Yes. She was seeing your mother wasn't she? They had a lesbian relationship."

"Right."

"Dylan this is making me nervous. What does this have to do with you getting someone into trouble?"

She breathed into her hands. "The paper left out some

things but the police told us that Shannon was wearing only one earring. They didn't see the earring anywhere in the field they found her in so they think she lost it where she was murdered."

"Okay now you're really making me nervous."

"I have her earring."

"The one that's missing?"

She nodded.

"You sure it's hers?"

"I'd seen Shannon wearing those earrings before. I remember how pretty they were but I couldn't remember it was Shannon's earring until the police told us she was missing one."

"Where did you find it?"

"Down at Old Swaggert's garage. My ex-boyfriend works there." She exhaled. "I think he might be involved."

"Isn't that a big jump? Just because you found an earring there?"

"People say Shannon was going to see Bruce the day of my mom's funeral. Now what's the chance that some woman who wore the same type of earrings happened to be where Bruce worked? And those earrings aren't the kind you just find off the rack."

"Well, wow." Nick took a deep breath. "That does sound suspicious."

"The cops said Bruce claims he didn't see Shannon that day at all."

"And you don't believe him?"

"I want to with all my heart but it's not adding up. Shannon's friends said she was going to see Bruce and she had a gun."

Nick sat on the chair by his ironing board. "Okay but maybe she never saw Bruce. Maybe he's telling the truth."

"Well she was very drunk supposedly. It's possible she was too wasted to make it. I'd hate to think Bruce was lying about this."

"You must still care about him."

"What do I do? If I take the earring to the police and tell them where I found it, do you think they'll arrest Bruce?"

"I don't know. I mean it depends on what they are already thinking about him. If Bruce is the prime suspect and they found out he lied then no telling what would happen. It doesn't look good but you really don't know if he lied. Shannon may not have made it to Bruce."

"You're right." She hooked her fingers. "She could've been

killed before she even got to see Bruce."

"The only way to try to find out what really happened is to..."

"I gotta talk to Bruce." She ran to the door. "See you later okay?"

"Be careful, sweetie."

CHAPTER SEVENTEEN

"Course I got time for you." Bruce cleaned oil off the thin tube and stuck it underneath the hood of the car. "What's up?"

"I'm sure you heard Shannon's been killed right?"

"Uh-huh." He leaned into the car until his foot lifted off the ground.

"You don't seem too surprised or concerned."

"I'm not a fake, Dylan. If I didn't like you when you were alive I'm not gonna pretend I'm upset when you're dead."

"She was still a person. Just the fact that you knew her should bring some pity."

"I doubt if something happened to me Shannon would crack a tear."

"Can you stop with that damn car and look at me please?"

"Hold on let me screw this in. Ah. There we go." He stood against the car. "You got my undivided attention."

"I gotta ask you something important and I don't want you jumping down my throat."

"I'd never do that. You can talk to me about anything."

"And you'll be honest?" She stepped over bolts and screws in the grass. "You promise?"

"Are you gonna be honest with me too?"

"About what?"

"About your feelings for me."

"Bruce please."

"I know it hurt you to find out I cheated but I always loved you and only you."

"Just stop it. I don't care about that now. This is important."

"And you're important to *me*. I just can't lose you." He touched her cheek. "I know what happened to you. Are you all right?"

"I...I'll be fine."

He banged his fists together. "If I find that guy I'll kill him with my bare hands. That's a promise I'll keep for the rest of my life."

"That's the last thing I need to hear from you. Is violence the only way you men can get your point across?"

"I can't help it." He held her waist. "I love you with every bone in my fuckin' body."

"Let go."

"You know I do." He moved his lips over hers but didn't kiss her.

"Let go." She turned her lips away. "Please."

He let go.

"I want you to be honest with me. Did you see Shannon before she disappeared? Before you lie I already know what Shannon's friends have been saying."

"Okay supposedly she told them she was coming to see me. That's the story."

"Did she?"

"No for the last time. Why can't folks believe what I say?"

"Why would Shannon's friends say she was coming for you if it weren't true?"

"I don't know. Okay maybe she planned to come and got killed before then." He raised his arms. "Is that not possible?"

"If you still love me you'd tell me the truth, Bruce."

"That is the truth. I'm sick of defending myself."

"And we both know you wouldn't be getting angry unless you had a reason."

"Why don't *you* be honest then huh? You think I had something to do with Shannon's murder don't you? Isn't that why you're here?"

"I didn't say that okay?"

"No you didn't say it out loud." He threw his rag down. "Why the hell you asking me all these questions anyway? Are you accusing me of killing Shannon?"

"No!"

He walked toward her. "Aren't you?"

She stepped over pieces of rubber and pebbles as she backed away. "I didn't say that, Bruce."

"I can read between the lines."

"Listen okay?" She held her hands out. "I just want the truth. That's all."

"I knew it. I fuckin' knew it."

"Knew what?"

"That you'd soon listen to all the horrible shit everyone's always said about me."

"This has nothing to do with anyone else."

"Bullshit. You've turned on me, Dylan. Just as judgmental as everyone else is huh?"

"I didn't turn on you. I only asked if..." He grabbed her. "Oh! Br...Bruce."

"I've had it with this shit!" He shook her. "I'm sick of people trying to ruin my life."

"Let me go!"

"I didn't kill Shannon."

"B...Bruce listen to me okay?" She put her hands on his chest.

"No you listen." He dug his fingers into her arms. "I don't need this shit from you or anyone else. I'm sick of living like I got a fuckin' sign over my head just because I've made some mistakes." Sweat dripped down his nose. "You understand me."

"Bruce. You're hurting me."

"I said do you understand?"

"Let me go." She sobbed. "Please!"

"Listen." His breath warmed her face. "I didn't see Shannon and I didn't kill her. You hear me?"

"Bruce you said you'd never hurt me. But you are now."

He thrust his tongue into her mouth. She suffocated from pain *and* rapture. Her fingers settled in his thick hair. She felt like a butterfly emerging from a cocoon when he kissed her. She'd missed this for so long.

But she shouldn't have.

She tore from his kiss. "We should stop. This isn't right."

"Nothing's been more right than us being together." He kissed her neck. "We both want it, Dylan." He caressed her backside. "Don't fight it. We deserve to be together. You know we do."

"No." She turned from his kisses. "Please let me go."

"I'll never let you go again. That's when things got messed up."

"Turn me loose."

"Dylan it's just you and me now. You can be honest." He forced his mouth on hers. "You don't have to pretend with me."

She drifted back to being in the rapist's van. How he blocked her movements and covered her mouth. How she fought until she couldn't breathe and it still hadn't been enough.

How his fingers tore at her clothes. How her throat ached from screaming.

How he wouldn't stop. He wouldn't stop.

"No!" She punched Bruce.

"Oww!"

"Get away!" She slapped and scratched. "Leave me alone!"

"Hold on!" Bruce seized her hands. "It's *me*, Dylan." He felt her cheek. "Shh. It's okay. You're safe now."

"Let me go. You had no right to grab me like that!"

"Oh honey I'm sorry. I didn't mean to scare you. I wasn't thinking."

"Just stay away from me."

"I'd never do anything to hurt you."

She ran to her car.

"Dylan!"

She sped off.

∞ ∞ ∞ ∞

"Don't protect him, Dylan." Jasmine sat in one of the chairs Brianna brought out at the station.

"Dylan what is it?" Steven sat on the edge of his desk.

"Tell them." Jasmine pushed her. "Tell them how Bruce attacked you."

"Aunt Jas please."

"Attacked her?"

"That's right, Detective Morris. She tried to give him a chance to explain and he lost his temper like he always did and scared her."

"It wasn't like that. He was angry because he thought I was accusing him of killing Shannon."

"I'm lost." Steven swung his leg.

"Me too." Brianna looked up something on her computer.

"I went to Swaggert's to talk to Bruce because..."

"He got rough with her. Can you believe that? After what she

94

just went through with that other creep?"

"Stop twisting things, Aunt Jas. He kissed me, yes but I started to think about the attack. I got scared on my own. Bruce would never hurt me."

"I don't mean to be rude." Brianna rocked in her chair. "But could you please tell us what you're here for?"

"I have Shannon's other earring." Dylan twisted her purse strap. "I found it before at Swaggert's garage."

"I see." Steven stopped swinging his leg. "And you're sure it's Shannon's?"

"I found it before she was thought to be missing. I didn't remember that it was hers at first."

Brianna chewed on her pen. "Uh-huh."

"I'm telling the truth. I wasn't trying to hide anything or protect Bruce. I didn't say anything because I had to make sure."

"And you thought Bruce would tell you the truth?" Jasmine laughed.

"So what did Bruce say?" Brianna put her pen down.

"The same thing he told you guys. He didn't see Shannon that night. But of course he has to be lying. I know this is Shannon's earring. It's too much of a coincidence."

"It could be someone else's earring."

"Oh come on, Detective Morris." Jasmine hit the edge of the desk. "We all know Bruce killed Nadia and Shannon and I don't know why he's still running around free. Who's it gonna be next, me?"

"Dare we dream?" Steven whispered.

Brianna grinned.

"Oh." Jasmine stood. "So this is funny to you? Our lives are a big game?"

"No." Steven cleared his throat. "I apologize. What do you think, Dylan? Is Bruce capable of these things?"

"Of course he is." Jasmine titled over. "We want him arrested!"

"I was asking *her*. Dylan?"

"I don't want to believe it. But why was the earring there? And why did people say

Shannon was going to confront him and now she's dead?"

"Where is the earring?"

Dylan passed a plastic sack to Brianna.

She held it up. "Well it definitely looks like the same earring."

"I want Bruce arrested."

Steven put the earring on the desk. "It's not that easy, Jasmine."

"Oh bull! Bruce McNamara is dangerous. You see how he treated Dylan today! He had no remorse for what she's gone through. He is violent, evil and cruel! He'll stop at nothing to get what he wants. He killed Nadia and Shannon. I feel it in my gut! Can you two deny that all this adds to Bruce? Why does his name keep popping up? I know you guys think he's guilty. I can see it in your faces. He's an animal. He needs to be locked up and stay there this time."

"What about the man who attacked me?" Dylan approached Brianna's desk. "You guys heard anything on that?"

Brianna leaned back in her chair. "No but we're keeping close contact with Detective Harris."

"What'll happen to Bruce?"

"We don't know," Brianna said.

Steven got off the desk. "It's not looking good for him. I think you knew that. That's why you were afraid to bring us the earring wasn't it?"

"Will you guys do me a favor? Please don't let Bruce know about this. Even if he's arrested, don't tell him it was me that found the earring."

Jasmine stuffed her purse under her arm. "Why would you care? What is *wrong* with you? Are you still in love with Bruce? You can't be after all he's done."

"I don't know what I am." Dylan put her purse on her shoulder. "I just know that doing this has been the hardest thing I've had to do. Only time will tell if it's right."

CHAPTER EIGHTEEN

Jayce ignored Bruce's denial of entrance and strutted into Bruce's living room that night. He got a Penthouse Magazine off Bruce's CD rack and relaxed on the couch. He met the burn of fury in Bruce's eyes when he looked up.

Tkk...tkk...tkk...tkk...tkk...

Supposedly Bruce scared everyone he knew. Some of what people said seemed blown out of proportion. They acted as if the spawn of hell would snatch them in the middle of the night if they dared to speak about him.

Tkk...tkk...tkk...tkk...tkk...tkk...

Underneath those angry blue eyes seemed to be a man misunderstood. At least Jayce wanted to give him the benefit of the doubt. Everyone deserved that.

Of course Bruce was lying but would Jayce be able to prove it? Should he listen to intuition or what people said about Bruce? Were those the eyes of a real monster or just a misguided man trying to get his life back on track?

Tkk...tkk...tkk...

Jayce turned the magazine sideways and ogled the breasts of a bikini model. "You should really get that faucet fixed."

"And I said you couldn't come in here." Bruce stood wide-legged with tight fists.

"Yeah well I understand why you might be a little tired of

me."

"A little tired of you? I'm sick of you, Morris and Kemp coming around hassling me. At least Detective Morris is better to look at."

Jayce flipped pages. "I'm sure she'd be flattered to know you thought that."

"You guys come to my job every damn day. Now you're at my home. Every time I turn around there's a fuckin' cop in my ass." He pointed. "Now I'm warning you."

"Warning me?" Jayce dropped his feet off the table.

"If you keep messing with me I'm gonna turn your ass in for harassment. Is this how you guys solve cases?"

Jayce switched magazines. "You should know right? Seeing how you were practically raised by the police department."

"Oh that's funny huh? You attracted to me or something, Detective? Maybe you keep popping up to check me out for more than the case."

"That's cute, Bruce. I'm not gay and even if I were, you wouldn't be my type."

"You think you're so tough don't you...brother?"

"*Brother*?" Jayce got up.

"But I don't give a shit you're a cop."

Jayce put his hands on his waist. "Brother?"

"I want you to leave me the fuck alone."

"I don't give a damn what you want me to do. Until your name stops coming up at every turn I'll be around."

"I'll report you."

"Report me then. I won't get in trouble for doing my job but you will if you try to stop me from doing it."

"So I'm supposed to respect your job but you don't respect mine? You've asked your questions and I've answered them so leave. And give me my magazine!" He snatched it. "If you really wanna do some good then go out there and find who really killed Nadia and Shannon and leave me the hell alone. Get out!"

"I'm giving you a chance to be honest."

"No matter what I say it's not good enough. You wanna come see me again then come with some kind of warrant."

"Hold on."

"Fuck you."

"You need to hear what I gotta say about Shannon."

Bruce threw the magazine. "I'm sick of hearing about fuckin' Shannon! What you got? You keep saying that she was coming to see me with a gun. Well she never did! I haven't seen Shannon in months!"

"I don't believe you."

"I don't give a damn what you believe."

"We know Shannon was at the garage before her disappearance."

"What?"

"Shannon's earring, the one that was missing, was found at the garage."

Bruce went pale.

"Oh what's the matter?" Jayce cocked his head to the side. "Was it something I said?"

"You're lying. You didn't find her earring at the junkyard because it wasn't there to find."

"Sure about that?"

"If there was an earring, which I doubt, how do you know it belonged to Shannon?"

"Because it's the exact same earring she was wearing when she was killed. It matches the other perfectly. Know what else?"

"I'm sure you can't wait to tell me."

"There was gravel underneath Shannon's boots. Looks like the gravel at Old Swaggert's junkyard."

"Bullshit."

"Course we can't be sure. We had some officers get a sample from the garage and we'll analyze it to make sure. We want all bases covered you know?"

"This is the last and I mean last time I am going to say this. I didn't see Shannon before she disappeared. I don't know shit about an earring."

"You know whoever shot her is not as smart as they think they are."

"Get the hell out of my house, Detective Matthews."

Jayce shuffled to the door. "Sleep well, Bruce."

"Fuck you."

∞ ∞ ∞ ∞

Marley Blake cleared trash off her couch and invited Brianna to have a seat. Brianna cringed at the rotting odor from the kitchen. She wouldn't embarrass Marley by asking what it was. She seemed embarrassed enough by just living here.

Brianna hadn't noticed how thin Marley was the last time. Did she eat at all? A plate with an apple core and half-eaten granola bar sat lopsided on the table.

"You on a diet or something?"

"No." Marley threw balled up tissues in the trash. "Just don't eat much. I don't get very hungry. Uh, please sit down."

The puke-green couch sat on bricks and took up half the tiny room. Grease and smudge tarnished the wallpaper. The carpet peeled up at the edges and bunched up around the wall. Dead roaches popped up every time Brianna walked.

Calling this place a dump would have been a compliment. What brought a woman like Marley who seemed intelligent and able to a state like this?

Brianna sat down. She wasn't here to figure out Marley's problems. She needed info about Shannon and Nadia's relationship.

Marley's blond hair fell like limp spaghetti around her pale face. Air filled out the shoulders of her sweatshirt. Even her petite-sized jeans seemed too big.

"You want something to eat or drink?"

I barely wanna inhale in this place.

"No. I'm sorry I popped up unannounced."

Marley's chapped lips spread into a smile. "I'm glad you came. If I can help you I want to."

"You cared about Shannon a lot didn't you?"

"We were very close. She was like a sis..." She covered her eyes.

"Oh, hey." Brianna moved Marley's hair out of her eyes. "Hey. I know. I'm so sorry."

"Nobody understands that Shannon wasn't a bad person. They've been saying all this shit in the papers about her being a drunk. Yeah so she had problems. Who's perfect? She was a good person and had a good heart. She was always there when you needed her. That's one thing you could always say."

"I'm sorry if you feel the media has been a little rough. I know how I'd feel if my friend was killed and berated for all to see."

"It just ain't right for them to be calling her a lush and drunk when they didn't even know her." Marley wiped her eyes with the bottom of her shirt. The skin on her stomach looked like a white sheet over train tracks. "Can't they understand that you can't help it if you're an alcoholic?"

"Meow!" A black and white cat jumped into Marley's lap and pressed its head in her chest.

"Aww. Well who's that huh?"

"This is Harmony. She's my other friend." Marley wiggled

Harmony's paw. "Say hi, Harmony."

"Hi, sweetie." Brianna scratched Harmony's ear. "Oh she's precious. I love cats I have one of my own. Davis. I've had him since he was a kitten. May I hold her?"

"Sure." Marley handed her the cat. Harmony settled in Brianna's arms as if she belonged there. "She likes you. I think cats can tell when someone is a cat person."

"Yeah I think so. Hi, baby." She stroked Harmony's head. "Remember I told you I've been reading Nadia's journals?"

"Uh-huh."

Harmony stretched her paws against Brianna's bosom.

"Well I found out something kinda surprising. Shannon got pregnant sometime last year didn't she? And Nadia wasn't too happy about that am I right?"

"Yes. Nadia made her get an abortion. Told Shannon there was no way she was gonna let her have that baby." Marley pushed her hands between her emaciated thighs. "What else did you find out?"

"Not enough." Brianna bounced Harmony on her lap. "Nadia didn't say who the father was in her entries."

"Why is that important?"

"It might not be but I wanna know."

CHAPTER NINETEEN

"Shannon only slept with the guy once," Marley said. "She wanted to make Nadia commit to her. She felt sleeping with someone else especially a man would make Nadia realize what she had."

"So Shannon planned to do this from the beginning?"

"Hard to tell with Shannon. Sometimes she just did things and thought about them later like a child. She slept with the guy when Nadia went to New York City with Dylan to her friend's birthday bash."

"Zoë Peron?"

"Yeah that's her. She was having some huge birthday bash up there with celebrities, artists and stuff." Marley rolled her eyes. "You know she use to model?"

Brianna groaned. "You don't say?"

"She's gorgeous. I've never met her in person but saw her in some photos. She probably doesn't even look that good in person."

"Oh she does." Brianna ignored the invisible stake in her heart. "She definitely does."

"Peron is her "stage" name she started using for modeling. Shannon says she picked it because of Eva Peron."

"I see."

"Anyway, she invited Dylan up there to meet some art people so Dylan could score a deal for her paintings. Shannon was upset because Nadia wouldn't take her. That was one of the main issues with their relationship. Nadia hid it from everybody."

"She wanted to hide she was gay?"

"No that's what her *family* thinks. Nadia didn't want people to know about how she manipulated Shannon into sex and all the freaky things they did. If people found out her career would've been ruined."

"Freaky?"

"Nadia would get on Shannon about drinking, but when *she* wanted to have sex, she'd buy Shannon all the liquor and dope she wanted just so Shannon would give it up."

"Wait a minute. I can't believe Nadia would buy someone dope just to get them into bed."

"A lot of people wouldn't but it's the truth. I've seen with my own eyes when Nadia gave Shannon pills and stuff. And I'd try to tell Shannon she was being used but she wouldn't listen. She lived and died for Nadia. Nadia only wanted to keep Shannon doing what she wanted in the bedroom. She didn't love her or anything. It was sick."

"Sick?"

"Oh man the stuff they did. They used to go to sex clubs and have sex in front of people. Nadia use to pimp Shannon out and video tape her having sex with other women."

"What?"

"They'd meet people online in chat rooms and have lesbian sex parties. Shannon invited me to one. Can you believe that? I almost smacked her for suggesting it. Shannon even said Nadia was into bestiality."

"You expect me to believe all this about Nadia?"

"It's true. Nadia was a pervert. Bet she didn't put that in her journals did she?"

"Why couldn't Shannon just give Nadia an ultimatum about their relationship?"

"That wasn't Shannon's way. She did things so you'd pay attention to her so she knew if she slept with a man, it would piss Nadia off. Nadia hated men. I guess you can't blame her."

"Why?"

"She was treated horribly by every man in her life. She was sexually abused by her oldest brother until she was a teenager."

"What?"

"Yeah and her other brother was horrible to her. The dad was a womanizer who was barely home and the momma a drunk. I don't know how her sisters did but Nadia had a terrible childhood. Then she got married to Clay Hollister, a sadist. He beat Nadia for years then died a drunk."

"She told me about her marriage but I had no idea she'd been abused when she was a kid."

"Shannon said that's why Nadia went into psychiatry. She wanted to help others." Marley got the cracker box off the table. "But Nadia hadn't dealt with her own demons." She chewed a cracker. "You can't heal someone if you haven't healed yourself."

"Meow." Harmony curled up in Brianna's lap.

"Who was the father of Shannon's baby?"

"Bruce McNamara."

∞ ∞ ∞ ∞

"Steven." Zoë walked from around Steven's car when he came out of the police station.

The wind blew her coat up. Her sweater dress accented the best parts while leaving wonders to the imagination.

"Hey." He got out his keys.

"Hey. Did I scare you?"

"No." He greeted some officers who passed. "Uh is something wrong?"

"Someone was following me home. I'd gone to NYC to check on something this afternoon. Well I just got back into town and when I was on my way to Jasmine's, I noticed a car behind me. I didn't think anything of it but I realized it was following me. I felt it was smart not to go to Jasmine's so I came here."

"Are you okay?"

"Yes. It's too dark to see who was driving. I think it was a man."

"Did you get the make of the car or anything?"

"No." She stroked her gloved hands. "I was just trying to get somewhere safe."

"You did the right thing."

"I know this might seem paranoid but every time something happens now, I can't help wondering if it has something to do with the murders. I mean this person is still out there." She shivered. "And we don't know what else they plan to do. What if they aren't done?"

"Shh." He touched her hand. "It's okay."

"I'm so wired up. I can't relax at all. I'm scared for Dylan. What if the killer comes after her?" She pushed her head in his chest.

"Shh. It's okay." He patted her head.

"I love her. If something happened to her I'd die."

"Shh. Look at me." He moved her ponytail off her shoulder. "Nothing else is gonna happen."

"How can you be so sure? I mean the killer's still out there. Every time we look around something horrible happens. I can't relax." She held up her hands. "See I'm shaking."

"Know what you need?" He unlocked his door. "You need to just relax. When's the last time you put your feet up and thought about something other than what's been going on?"

"I could use a break from all this drama. I sure as hell can't get peace at Jasmine's. She and Dylan fight about Bruce every ten minutes."

"You're spending so much time thinking about Dylan and not enough about yourself." He opened his door. "The offer stands if you wanna talk."

"I'd like that. Can we talk tonight?"

He winked. "We are talking."

"You know what I mean."

He got butterflies. "Well I'm not doing anything right now. You're welcome to follow me to my place if you want."

"I'd like that. I'm parked over there." She sashayed across the parking lot.

Steven looked at the night sky. "Oh you're slick, God."

∞ ∞ ∞ ∞

Steven brought two cups of coffee into his living room. Zoë checked out the stereo in his entertainment system.

"I like your place."

"Thank you."

She walked to the couch with her hands behind her back. Not many women made walking look like an art form. He tried to fight the burn in his center but he got hard just thinking of Zoë.

She batted her eyes at him while she sipped from her cup.

"Is it good?"

"It's delicious. I just didn't expect coffee. I thought you'd have some wine or something."

"Well honestly I thought of wine but I didn't wanna give the wrong impression."

They sat on the couch.

Her dresses never seemed to stay down on the sides.

"You mean you didn't want me to think you were trying to

get me loaded so you could take advantage of me?"

He brushed off his pants. "You can put it that way."

"Did you ever wonder if I would mind if you tried to take advantage of me?" She licked coffee from her succulent lips.

"Uh..."

"I'm sorry. Did that make you uncomfortable?"

"No." He put his hand over his crotch. "To answer your question I guess I wasn't thinking of it that way. I should've asked you if you wanted wine."

"Not really talking about the wine."

"I see." Steven unfastened his top button.

"I'll be staying in Albany for a while. Dylan asked me to. What do you think of that?"

He shrugged. "Is it my business?"

She crossed her legs. "I just hoped you'd be happy with the decision."

He smirked. "I'm not upset about it. Can I ask you a question?"

"You can ask me anything you want."

"How in the hell are you single?"

She laughed. "I was thinking the same about you. I don't know. I guess I haven't found the right man yet."

"I can't believe that. I know many have tried."

"A lot of men don't like women who like to be in control. Believe it or not I'm kinda bossy."

"Well when a woman is as beautiful as you being bossy becomes an attribute."

"That's very sweet."

"Uh, I don't mean to sour the mood but I wanted to ask something about Nadia. We found out that she had a bizarre sex life. Do you know anything about that?"

"I think there are a lot of things about Nadia that would shock you."

"Were you close to Nadia?"

"Yeah I guess. She was always very kind to me. She had issues with the opposite sex."

"Is that why she hated Bruce so much, because he was a man?"

"Nadia hated anyone who threatened her relationship with Dylan. I don't mean to talk bad about her but she did everything she could to run Bruce away. It's funny how a mother's love is huh? I mean if you don't have that, you don't have anything."

"You're adopted right?"

"I'm impressed. You've been doing your homework on me. Yes I was adopted. That's why Dylan and I click so well. We have a lot in common."

"Did you have a nice childhood? Sorry if I'm being nosey."

"No uh, my childhood was interesting. Uh, my mom and dad loved me a lot. My mother died."

"Your adoptive mother?"

"Yes but my dad's still living."

"You ever wanted to know your real parents?"

"No."

"Honestly?"

"Honestly."

"Do you think Bruce killed Nadia and Shannon?"

"I think Bruce gets picked on because he has a bad rep."

"But everything's beginning to point to him. You can't ignore that."

"I'm not a cop or psychic so I don't know. All I can say is what I think of Bruce and I do not believe he's capable of killing someone. He's a lot of hot air. He looks like a big bully on the outside but he has a very kind heart. He loves Dylan a lot. He wouldn't hurt her no matter what Jasmine or anyone else says. Can we talk about something else?"

"We can talk about your modeling career and why you don't do it anymore. Were you famous?"

"You ever heard of me before now?"

"Come on." He perched his elbow on the couch. "Must have been nice huh? Living such a glamorous lifestyle."

"It was just like any other career. It's worse on some levels."

"Why did you stop modeling?"

"It just wasn't the kind of life I wanted. I'd rather work behind the stage. I like designing clothes, dressing models and advising."

"You're too beautiful to be behind the stage."

"At least now I can make my own choices. I don't have to be what people think I should."

"Oh is this gonna be one of those no one-takes-me-seriously-because-I'm-so-beautiful speeches?"

"What?"

"Beautiful women always act like they have such a hard time being taken seriously because they're good looking. That's a crock. You got the world at your feet and men at your beck and call and you have the opportunity for all your dreams to come true."

"Is that what you think? That just because I'm attractive everything's easy for me?"

"I just don't get why beautiful women can't be honest and say they are glad they are pretty and stop trying to make people feel sorry for their nonexistent problems. It's like they feel guilty for being good looking."

"I could say the same about you. You're great-looking. But of course being a man it's different right?"

"Oh then here we go with the feminism. I knew that was coming."

"You're a jerk." She laughed. "Has anyone ever told you that?"

"Yes but I never enjoyed hearing it this much before."

She looked into her cup. "You've got beautiful eyes."

He scooted closer. "Can I be honest?"

She folded her legs underneath her. "Please do."

"I can't stop thinking about you. Ever since I first saw you, I can't get you out of my mind. I can't take my eyes off of you when I'm in a room with you and I keep telling myself to behave and concentrate on the case but it's getting so damn hard to when all I wanna do is grab you and kiss you."

"Then do it." She wrapped her arms around his shoulders.

He kissed her, embracing the damp heat of her mouth.

"Mmm." She lay flat.

He climbed on top of her and pushed his hand up her dress. He moved his fingers against her soft thighs and in between her legs.

"Oh that feels so good, Steven."

He leaned up on his knee and dug under her dress. He slipped her breast from its cup and flicked her nipple. He continued to fondle her nipple while punishing her mouth with his coarse kisses.

"Oh yes." She undid his belt. "Now, Steven. I want you inside me right now."

God must've been on Bree's side because as soon as Zoë unzipped his pants Brianna's face popped into his mind.

"Ah, wait." He lifted up.

"What's wrong?" He'd sucked off her lipstick. "It's okay. I want it."

"I do too but..."

"Then what's the matter?" She sat up. "We're both single so I don't see what the problem is."

He wiped her lipstick off his mouth.

"I get it. Is it someone else? You are single aren't you?"

"It's a funny situation."

"It's Detective Morris isn't it?"

"It's complicated. We're not together but..."

"You still have feelings for her?"

"I care about her yes."

She touched his hand. "That doesn't bother me. It's no big deal. We can still do this."

"I like you a lot but I need to think about this okay? If we end up getting together I want you to be the only woman on my mind at the time. Isn't that fair?"

She fixed her dress. "Well I couldn't confuse you with the guys I usually meet."

"I hope that's a compliment." He walked her to the door.

"It is. At least I know you're not the typical asshole." She put her coat on. "But rejection never feels good no matter the reason."

He kissed her. "I'm not rejecting you. I'm *respecting* you."

"Okay but I gotta warn you." She stepped on the porch. "It's gonna make it even harder for me to resist."

CHAPTER TWENTY

Monday Night (the following week)

Bruce tapped his feet on the grimy tile. He sat in the interrogation room of the downtown station going crazy until Jayce returned. Heat blew from a vent overhead yet he felt colder than when he first sat down.

Jayce claimed he only wanted to "ask questions". Police never put you in the interrogation room "just to ask questions".

He tried to block out his old foe, that deadening silence. He couldn't ever escape it.

In prison the silence forced him to reflect on his mistakes. Caused his regrets to manifest and made him endure the mental torture of counting the days until he finished time. It always mocked him and reminded him what he'd lost and might not ever get back.

That's why he loved noise. He couldn't sit in silence without his nerves driving him bat shit. Any noise would do. It didn't have to be pleasurable, the louder the better. As long as it kept away the silence he could breathe again.

And people wondered why he didn't fix his faucet.

Jayce walked in. "Okay, Bruce." He unhooked a folder from underneath his arm and sat down. "Sorry for making you wait. If you cooperate without giving me trouble you can be gone before you know it."

"Go fuck yourself. I'm not saying shit. You think I'm stupid?"

"Forensics found traces of a foreign substance in the grass at Swaggert's junkyard."

Bruce twisted in the seat.

"It was vomit and it matched the dried vomit found on Shannon's clothes."

"And what the fuck does that mean to me?"

"Anyone putting two and two together can guess that Shannon threw up in that yard. Another thing proving she was there." Jayce leaned in. "If I were you I'd be nervous. Or are you too tough to get nervous?"

"No reason for me to be nervous. Say Shannon *was* at the garage, does that mean I saw her? Does that mean I killed her? You got nothing to tie me to this. You're just grabbing at shit."

"Oh we got something, Bruce. What we found is enough for me to arrest you for First Degree Murder."

"Well this has been fun." Bruce went to the door.

"You're not going anywhere."

"You got nothing on me. Stop wasting my time. I didn't kill Shannon so fuck you."

"But you haven't heard it all yet, Bruce. Surely you don't wanna miss this."

"If you think you're gonna trap me, you're wrong."

"I know you're lying about seeing Shannon. She was at Swag's on the fifth and I know she was with you."

Bruce's palm grew sweaty against the doorknob. "Who's been lying on me *now* huh?"

"Can we talk like men huh? Can we cut the bullshit? See I think you killed Shannon and Dr. Hollister."

"Oh you do?"

"You lied about being in town the night Nadia was killed."

"So what Antwan says is the truth and everything I say is a lie right?"

"You can call a lawyer now if you want." Jayce sat back. "I'll wait. But if you're so innocent then why don't you take the polygraph?"

"Because I'm telling the truth and I don't need to prove shit to you."

"Well let's see if you feel that way after I tell you this." Jayce raised the folder. "We found blood on Shannon's clothes that wasn't Shannon's. It was yours."

"Stick whatever's in that folder up your ass. I'm outta here."

"Not so fast." Jayce pulled him back inside.

"Get the fuck off me! If you weren't a cop your ass would be on that floor."

"Can't handle the truth?"

"It's not the truth! My blood wasn't on Shannon because I never saw her!"

"It's right here if you wanna read it." Jayce shook the folder. "We matched the DNA, Bruce. Did you forget we have that on file from when you were in prison?"

He gripped Jayce's shirt. "You're trying to set me up."

"Get your hands off me."

"I didn't kill anybody. I don't care what you got in that folder it's a lie."

Jayce tossed him the folder. "It speaks for itself."

∞ ∞ ∞ ∞

"Damn you slow, girl." Swaggert limped through the hallway at the police station. The shapely brunette trotted behind. Her briefcase swung back and forth in step with her pace.

Swaggert swung his arm. "Fuck, fuck, fuck, fuck! What else is the boy gonna do next, *what*?"

They turned at the corner stairwell. A small gathering of people sat outside the interrogation room.

"Ahh shit." Swaggert shook his head.

The people broke from their conversations.

"What? You know these people?" The brunette asked.

"Hell I wish I didn't."

Brianna, Steven and Zoë sat on the bench by the door. Dylan stood beside Nick. Jasmine looked up from her *Better Homes and Garden* magazine.

"Well what the hell y'all lookin' at?" Swaggert dug in his butt. "I ain't studdin' none of ya'. Where's Matthews so we can get this shit over with?"

"He's talking to Bruce," Steven said.

Dylan checked out the brunette. "Oh god Aunt Jas they called an attorney. They're gonna arrest him."

"Good." Jasmine turned through the magazine.

"I should've kept my mouth shut."

"What do you mean you shudda kept yo' mouth shut?" Swaggert hobbled up to Dylan. "What'cha do, girl?"

"Nothing."

"Nothing my ass."

"Get away from my niece, Swaggert." Jasmine moved from

the window. "Can you just act like a human for once? I know it's hard but give it a try."

"Oh go dust off your cunt."

"Hey watch your mouth Mr. Swaggert," Steven said. "You don't talk like that in front of ladies."

"I don't see no ladies around here."

"Oh!" Jasmine threw the magazine down. "Swaggert you are the rudest and nastiest person I've ever met!"

"Get off my jock, lady. This ain't about me but yo' stupid niece." Bruce was doin' fine befo' her."

"Ha that's a laugh! Bruce was a loser before he met Dylan and he's a bigger loser now!"

"Stop it, Aunt Jas."

"And he should bend down and kiss the ground for her even looking at him twice!"

"Hey cut it out." Steven stood between them.

Swaggert reached over Steven's shoulder. "Better for him to kiss the flo' then yo' niece's ass!"

"Oh!" Jasmine swung fists.

"Why you here anyway?" Swaggert swung his hand in Dylan's face. "You already broke the man's heart. I can't understand the shit he puts himself through for you. Ha. I hope your pussy was worth it because the package it's carried in sure ain't."

"Hey!" Nick shoved Swaggert. "Watch your mouth."

Swaggert hid behind the brunette.

"Everyone stop it!" Brianna ordered. "Remember where you are!"

"Please everyone!" The brunette whistled.

Everyone froze.

"Please this isn't helping. Can we please keep this professional?"

"Tell that to him!" Jasmine kicked at Swaggert. "You old half-dead, wrinkled up crow!"

Zoë held her back. "Stop it, Jas!"

Swaggert spit into a tissue. "I don't care if none of ya' don't like me, lady. It don't make a damn difference to me. I'm telling the truth and you know it. Your niece is the reason he's in this mess. Guess she won't stop ruining Bruce's life until he's dead."

"I cared about Bruce. I loved him very much."

"Bullshit." Swaggert leapt in Dylan's face. "You sold him out you little brat."

"Oooh!" Jasmine fought Zoë's hold. "Nobody talks about my

niece like that, Swaggert! Nobody!"

"Yeah? You should have taught your niece to keep her legs closed and her mouth shut!"

"You bastard!" Jasmine reached for him.

Nick caught her. "Stop it! He's not worth it!"

"Get away from me, Nick." She tussled. "I'm gonna rip out his throat! We're already at the police station so they can lock me up after I kill him!"

Steven jumped in between everyone. "Stop it!"

Jayce popped out. "Hey! What the hell is going on out here? This is a police station not the damn street! Act like you got some home training."

Jasmine raised a fist at Swaggert. "He's gonna have a busted lip in about a second."

"Calm down, Aunt Jas. I don't care what Mr. Swaggert says or thinks about me and my relationship with Bruce is none of his business."

"Mr. Swaggert, I assume this is McNamara's attorney," Jayce said.

The doe-eyed brunette nodded. "I'm Annabelle Fontaine. You're Detective Matthews I presume?"

"Yes."

"May I speak with Mr. McNamara?"

"Let her, Matthews." Swaggert spit into his tissue. "No tellin' what you try'na do in there."

Jayce laid his hand on his chest. "Why Swaggert are you accusing me of trying to muddy the waters? I don't work like that. I've been telling Bruce what we know. He's smart enough that he hasn't said much of anything." Jayce bowed to Annabelle. "So counselor you should be happy about that."

"Thank you, Detective." Annabelle went inside the room.

Swaggert bucked up behind her.

Jayce stood at the door. "Hey where are you going?"

"I'm paying for her, I'm going in there." Swaggert slammed the door behind him.

"She sure is young-looking to be a lawyer," Nick said.

Jasmine fanned her hands. "The more inexperienced the better."

"What's going on, Detective Matthews?" Dylan asked. "Is Bruce gonna be all right?"

"I know you're concerned but what happens to Bruce is really none of your business. I thought you believed he had something to do with the murders."

"I didn't say for *sure*. I just said it wasn't adding up."

"What about him lying about not being in town when your mother was killed? What about him lying about seeing Shannon at the garage before her death? You can overlook that?"

"Please just tell me if he's okay. He must feel so alone."

"He's upset," Jayce said. "I think he realizes how much trouble he's in."

"I betrayed him. I was always the one Bruce could count on. I told him I'd always believe in him and I didn't."

Jasmine fanned with her magazine. "I'm at a loss for words."

"Since when?" Steven whispered.

Brianna and Nick grinned.

"If Bruce is innocent and if I've ruined things for him, I'll never forgive myself." Dylan sat beside Zoë. "Not in a hundred years."

Jayce walked to the bench. "I doubt you'll be so understanding once you hear what else we found out about Bruce."

CHAPTER TWENTY-ONE

"You gotta tell me the truth if I'm to help you, Bruce." Annabelle pulled out a small recorder. "You gotta be honest with me."

"I am. I didn't see Shannon before she disappeared."

"We both know that's not true. I'm on your side don't you understand that? Come on."

"Fuck." He kicked the chair when he got up. "What the hell does everyone want from me? I can't go back to prison for something I didn't do. If I'm supposed to trust you then I gotta know in my heart that you believe me."

"I believe you."

"Don't play with me."

"I'm not. I honestly don't think you did it."

He squinted. "Why?"

"I just don't. But Matthews has some damn good evidence on you. It didn't just drop out of the sky. I need you to admit what happened. Tell me the truth no matter how horrible you think it is."

"Okay I did see Shannon the night of Nadia's funeral." He walked around the table.

"How was she acting?"

"She was a complete mess. She was screaming my name. She had this bottle of Jim Beam and she dropped it at the door. She was so drunk it was amazing she could stand up let alone drive all the way to the garage. She accused me of killing Nadia and I told her to get out. She started ranting and raving and took out the gun. She told me she'd shoot me unless I called the police and turned myself in for killing Nadia."

Annabelle stooped over the back of her chair. "Did you get angry?"

"I admit Shannon had a way of pushing my buttons like you wouldn't believe. And she always loved to do it too."

"Well what happened after she told you to call the police?"

"I told her to fuck off and I grabbed the gun. She ran out the garage." He walked to the other side of the room. "I swear I just wanted to talk but she wouldn't listen. She hid from me. I caught her when she tried to leave. I grabbed her when she got to her truck and dragged her back to the garage. I swear I wasn't gonna hurt her."

"Did you still have the gun?"

"Yes but I dropped it when she kicked me."

"Why didn't you just let her leave?"

"I panicked. I didn't want her going to the police because I knew I'd lied."

"About being in town when Nadia was killed?"

"Yeah and they already had an eye on me. I just wanted to talk to her that's all. I also didn't want her going off as drunk as she was. She could've killed someone."

"So you were concerned?"

"Yes. I'm not the animal everyone says I am. Fuck me for being scared and confused but I'm human just like everyone else."

"How did your blood get on her clothes?"

"She hit me in the nose with the gun when we were inside the garage and I started bleeding. I guess some got on her when we tussled."

"What happened to Shannon?"

"I swear I have no idea. When I tried to talk to her she hit me again and drove away. I swear I'm telling the truth. I haven't heard from Shannon since."

"You should've come forward the minute she was found dead."

"I know but you think the cops would've let me walk away? They've been bothering me ever since this started. Hell I thought Shannon killed Nadia and maybe that's why she ran off. I don't know what happened but I didn't kill Shannon."

"*Someone* killed her."

"This might sound like bullshit but I think someone else was there at the garage. Maybe someone followed her and killed her. The same person probably killed Nadia."

"Speculation and guesses are useless, Bruce."

"Maybe the person did it to set me up. They saw the perfect opportunity and took it. All I know is I didn't kill Shannon. Besides Matthews' just blowing smoke out his ass. They don't even have a murder weapon."

"And do you realize how many people are convicted of murder with no murder weapon ever coming into the picture?"

"This is such bullshit. They don't give a shit about Shannon. They just wanna tie Nadia's murder to me. Well they never will because I didn't kill either one of them. I don't care what "evidence" Matthews comes up with."

She turned the recorder off. "We need to..."

Dylan charged in with Jasmine and the others behind her.

"Dylan?" Bruce ran to her. She held her hand up to stop him.

"Don't come near me you bastard." Tears ran down her face.

"Dylan what's wrong?"

"Just tell me this, Bruce. Was everything you said and did always a lie? Were you ever honest?"

"Dylan I'm sorry I lied about being in town when Nadia was killed but I did not kill anyone."

"I'm not talking about that. Shannon was the woman you cheated on me with when I was in NYC. Isn't she?"

Jasmine pulled her back. "Stop it, Dylan."

"Admit it you asshole!"

Bruce looked into the hungry eyes of the others. He could be back in prison for something he didn't even do yet he still cared about Dylan's broken heart.

"I...I love you, Dylan."

She punched at air with Jasmine fighting to hold her. "You are a disgusting liar and I hate you!"

"I'll explain it to you later. This just isn't the time."

"Don't bother explaining." She relaxed in Jasmine's hold. "Because from this point on I don't give a damn what happens to you. I think you did kill them and I hope you rot in prison for the rest of your life."

"You don't mean that. No matter what I've done you've always been the most important thing in my life. I fucked up but I need you on my side right now, Dylan. Please don't cut me out of your life now. I don't have anyone."

"I hid something from you too, Bruce. But I did it to spare your feelings. What a joke."

"What are you talking about?"

"Bruce." Swaggert moved from the others. "You got anything in yo' head that represents a brain?"

"Not now, Swag."

"Why the hell you even care what this twat thinks of you?"

"That's it, Swaggert!" Jasmine shoved him.

"Whoa." Steven blocked her. "Settle down, Jasmine!"

"You call my niece one more name and I'll pound your ass into ground meat."

"Stop it Ms. Hudson or you'll be spending the night!" Jayce warned.

She broke away from Steven.

"I want you to admit you did it." Dylan stared at Bruce. "Tell me to my face you slept with Shannon."

"Don't do this."

"Tell me!"

"Yes. I slept with Shannon."

"You slept with your girlfriend's mother's lesbian lover, Bruce? You have to be the sorriest excuse of a man to ever walk on this earth."

"Stay outta this, Aunt Jas."

"Hell." Swaggert stuffed chewing tobacco in his mouth. "This shit's just like a soap opera."

"And there's something else you're forgetting isn't there?" Dylan stood in front of Bruce. "Shannon got pregnant with your baby didn't she?"

"Don't do this. I've always only loved you."

"Well." Dylan chuckled. "Isn't this some kind of curveball? Once again I was worrying about you and didn't even know you'd been lying to me through most of our relationship."

"It wasn't like that."

"Oh? You slept with my mother's lesbian lover and got her pregnant and hid it from me! Do you see how fucked up that is, Bruce?"

"Please." He reached for her.

"Don't. Everyone was right about you."

"No. Listen to me, Dylan. I made a mistake but I couldn't tell you because I couldn't lose you."

"You didn't tell her because you're selfish and only cared

about yourself. She finally knows what you are."

"This is your fault, Jasmine."

"*Mine*?" She laughed. "I didn't put you in between Shannon's legs did I?"

"Jasmine if you were a man I'd kicked your ass years ago."

"Don't you dare talk to my aunt like that."

"Dylan. I love you so much, baby. I need you so much. You want me to beg?" He got on his knees. "Then I'll beg. Please forgive me, Dylan. You don't have to be with me if you don't want to but just don't abandon me now please. I'm scared. I'm truly scared because I didn't kill anyone."

"I don't believe you."

"You know it's true. I don't care who believes me as long as you do."

"I'll never believe anything that comes out of your mouth again."

"What did you mean when you said you hid something?"

"I was pregnant."

"What the hell did you just say?"

"I got pregnant back then too. I was gonna tell you but..."

"You were pregnant?" He fell into a chair. "What the fuck?"

"Dylan you don't have to do this in front of everyone."

"I want to, Aunt Jas. It's time we get all these secrets out once and for all."

"Let me guess." Bruce held his hands in front of his face. "You got rid of it huh?"

"Yes."

"What a surprise. I know you didn't do it on your own. I know you loved me too much to be pregnant and get rid of it without telling me."

"Just like you were supposed to love *her* enough to be honest with *her*?"

Swaggert bumped Jasmine. "Why don't you shut up?"

"You hear me, Dylan? I know you wouldn't get rid of our baby on your own would you?"

"What difference does it make?"

"It makes a hell of a lot of difference to me. Who made you get rid of it huh? Nadia or Jasmine?"

"I had nothing to do with it."

"Bullshit!" Bruce jumped up. Jayce held him back. "You and Nadia had everything to do with me and Dylan and that's why we're not together!"

"Don't blame me for you being stupid and not realizing what you had when you had it."

"So what happened huh, Jasmine? Did you and Nadia take Dylan to a clinic or did you hold her down while Nadia sliced the baby out herself?"

"You vile...ooh! I didn't even know she'd been pregnant until Nadia told me months after Dylan had the abortion."

"I don't believe a word that comes out of your mouth! You don't give a damn about Dylan only keeping her away from me!"

"I love my niece!"

"As long as she's doing what you want her to right?"

"It was my decision, Bruce."

"The fuck it was. I know you and you never would've gotten rid of our baby."

"We couldn't take care of a baby and you know it."

"I'd have made a way for us."

"How?"

"I'd have married you and done the best I could but you didn't give me the chance! How could you be pregnant and hide it from me?"

"Just like you hid everything else, Bruce? You forget where you are and why you're here?"

"I don't believe this." He walked around with his hands on his head. "What other surprise you got?"

"I could ask you the same thing."

"I don't care. We both made mistakes. We can get past them."

"Not this time."

"If your aunt wasn't standing here you'd be singing a different tune but you let her run your life and I'm sick of it."

"Don't blame it on me. Dylan's finally seen you for what you really are."

"You stay away from me, Bruce. I never wanna see you again."

"She's full of shit," Swaggert said. "She says that all the time. She'll be back next week."

"I mean it for good this time." Dylan went to the door.

Bruce followed her. "You're not getting away from me." Jayce stopped him at the door. "I won't lose you, Dylan. I will *not* lose you!"

"You already have."

"Bruce." Jayce took out his handcuffs. "You're under arrest for the murder of Shannon Kuriakis."

CHAPTER TWENTY-TWO

A Month Later

Jasmine, Nick, Dylan and Zoë were having lemonade on Jasmine's back patio when Jayce, Steven and Brianna arrived that evening.

The weather had been gorgeous for the last two weeks and Steven couldn't wait to take advantage of it. Unfortunately he hadn't a break since this case. The only pleasure he got was being around Zoë.

Dylan, Nick and Jasmine sat around the patio table while Zoë stretched out on a lawn chair. Brianna sat in the chair by the water hose. She looked at Zoë and then Steven like she always did when they came by. He kept denying he had feelings for Zoë but obviously they were harder to conceal than he thought.

Zoë wore a flimsy red summer dress and red flip flops with tiny bows on the top of them. The red sparkled against her dark skin. She propped her leg up, giving his eyes slight access to the silk panties underneath. He felt her gaze behind her shades. She wiggled her leg while sipping her lemonade through the straw.

Sweat beaded around his neck again. How could he want a woman so much so soon? For weeks he'd cursed himself for sending her out of his house without confronting this itch. Why the hell did he have to be such a good guy and respect her? Why didn't he just fuck her and maybe then she'd been out of his system.

"Steve?" Jayce spread the newspaper clippings in front of the others. "Man you okay? Look like you're about to faint."

"Do I?"

"Yes you're sweating." Brianna glared.

"Oh well it's kinda humid to me." He fanned.

"Maybe you need some lemonade too." Zoë plucked the end of her straw with her lips.

He wanted those lips wrapped around his...

"Detective Kemp would you like something to drink?" Jasmine asked.

"Uh no, I'm fine." He made sure to sit in the chair farthest away from Zoë. He hadn't any problems keeping his body away from her. It was his eyes that had a mind of their own.

Zoë slung her ponytail over her shoulder. She licked her lips between every sip.

God help me.

Jayce gestured to the clippings. "Think you can help us, Dylan? You might be the only one who can."

"Me?"

"These clippings were found in one of your mother's boxes we confiscated. She had many copies. They're about a woman, Elle Givens. Her baby was kidnapped almost thirty years ago. Know why your mother had these?"

Jasmine held a faded clipping. "I think I remember this from the papers. This lady killed herself didn't she?"

"Apparently she never dealt with the pain of the kidnapping," Jayce said. "She shot herself ten years ago."

Dylan went through the clippings.

Jayce continued. "It's been said that her baby was kidnapped in connection to a kidnapping ring. Elle sought out a private investigator but I don't know if it helped. A Jim Klein kept popping up as being involved. Some suspect he lead the ring." Jayce adjusted his belt. "But the police didn't have enough to go on."

"What happened to him?" Dylan asked.

Steven put his elbows on the table. "He disappeared."

"Without a trace," Jayce said.

Dylan flipped through more clippings. "How can someone just disappear?"

"Probably changed his name and took on a new life," Brianna said. "Might even be dead."

Dylan laid clippings in her lap. "Where did this happen?"

Nick read a clipping. "Newark."

Everyone looked at him.

"I remember when they first kidnapped the baby. It was a horrible story. The saddest I'd ever heard of. How could someone steal someone's baby and not give a damn?"

"Elle was married too wasn't she?" Jasmine brushed her dress down. "I remember them mentioning a husband or something back then."

"Yep." Jayce nodded. "Elle and her husband adopted another child not long after the other had been taken. A little girl I believe."

"Excuse me." Zoë hung her legs over the side of the chair. "I don't understand what this has to do with Dylan or Nadia?"

"Well that's what we hoped Dylan could tell us."

"I don't know what you expect me to say, Detective Matthews. I mean, I don't see how clippings would have anything to do with Mom being killed."

Zoë crossed her legs and looked at Steven. He turned and smiled at Brianna. She looked at him as if he had something hanging out of his nose.

"Ooh." Jasmine passed a clipping to Dylan. "The suicide scene."

"Oh, gross." Dylan covered her eyes.

Jasmine touched her chest. "God look at all that blood on the floor."

Zoë wriggled. "Do we have to look at these pictures?"

"I still don't understand what all this has to do with Mom's murder."

"I really think there's a connection between Elle's story and your mother."

Zoë swatted a fly. "Well it doesn't make sense to me, Detective Matthews."

"Me neither. Mom always read up on things and kept memorabilia from stuff that had nothing to do with her. She was the kind that was overly curious and so when something caught her attention, she focused on it. She'd do research, collect articles, and even write down things dealing with what interested her." Dylan shrugged. "This doesn't seem any different to me. I don't know why you feel it is."

Jayce leaned over. "These clippings are just a sample of what we found about Elle in Nadia's possessions. She had pictures of Elle that she'd blown up from the newspaper articles. She had articles where she'd outlined things about the baby's kidnapping. She had notes and passages about what had happened."

Dylan fidgeted. "I don't know why she had all this stuff. She never spoke to me about this. I think she was just collecting this story like everything else she collected."

"You don't look so sure," Brianna said.

"None of this makes any sense. What difference does it make why she had some clippings? Mom also has clippings of Charles Manson. Is he connected to this too?"

"Why are we even worrying about clippings when you already got Bruce in jail?" Jasmine asked. "He did it. You found Shannon's gun last week. You said Bruce's prints were on it. What more do you need?"

"We need to see if the bullet found in Shannon's head came from Shannon's gun."

"Well why the hell aren't you doing that, Detective Matthews?"

He titled his head. "Well I'm sorry if we aren't doing everything at a pace you're satisfied with Ms. Hudson, but things take time. Ballistics will do their thing and if the bullet matches that gun than we go from there."

"But you got his prints on the gun." She set her glass down. "You know he was at the garage with Shannon. He admitted it and you found his blood on her. I don't understand why you're wasting so much time."

"We have to identify the murder weapon. We can't be sure Shannon was killed with her gun can we?"

"What about my sister? You found anything substantial to link Bruce to Nadia's murder?"

"I don't need you to tell me how to do my job, Ms. Hudson."

"Which means you haven't done squat right?"

Dylan turned to Brianna. "Did you find anything about Elle in my mother's journals?"

"No. The first time I heard of this was when Jayce told us this morning."

"Could someone please just tell me how this all could possibly be connected?" Dylan looked around. "Please."

"Excuse me." Zoë got up. "I'll be right back."

She went around the side of the house. The way her ass moved in that dress stayed in Steven's mind. He broke from fantasizing to see Brianna's repulsed expression.

"Be honest with me, Detective Matthews. Do you believe Bruce is innocent?"

"It's not my job to decide that, Dylan."

"I asked what you *believed*."

"I uh…I think there are possibilities that he could be."

"Oh please." Jasmine threw her arms up. "If you believe that I have an invisible farm to sell you."

"Bruce is innocent until proven guilty."

Steven's phone buzzed in his pocket. He had a text from Zoë telling him to come inside the house.

"Something wrong, Steve?" Brianna rocked in her chair.

"Uh I have a call to make. I'll be right back."

CHAPTER TWENTY-THREE

Zoë stared at Steven from the top of the stairs. He could see out the patio door from where he stood. He turned before his vision reached Brianna. He loved her but even that wasn't strong enough to block this strangling desire he had for Zoë.

She slid her dress up on the side. She spoke with her eyes and body language, nothing else. She watched him with a bloodthirsty gaze that pierced his senses.

A tornado could tear through the living room and he wouldn't leave. His body *craved* Zoë so he had no choice in the matter. He couldn't leave. This yearning had become too big to fight and he didn't want to.

She slid the dress up higher. Her curves were more masterful than he'd dreamt. Turned out the tight clothing hadn't revealed too much after all.

Desire leapt off her and slammed into him with an intense heat that soothed and burned.

He walked up the stairs and stopped in front of her. They stared into each other's eyes. He'd dreamt of fucking this woman since he met her. He even masturbated in bed when he thought of her. He'd pretend her lovely body rested on top of him.

She pressed her firm breasts against him.

Her magnetism spread through him like a disease.

It had been easy to blame it on lust or an animalistic attraction. That would get him off the hook and he wouldn't have to feel guilty. Wouldn't have to think of how hurt Brianna might be if she knew how much he wanted Zoë.

She pulled her dress over her thighs and held it at her waist. From that moment nothing else mattered.

She placed his feverish hand between her legs. Just being this close made his cock leak.

She slipped his hand inside her panties. His fingers skated down her soft bush. He slid his finger inside her.

"You're so wet."

"Come on before someone comes inside." She held onto his shoulders.

"I don't have anything."

"I'm on the pill." She panted. "Come on shit." She kissed him. "Don't you wanna do this?"

He hoisted her up, sat her on the railing and tore her panties off. "Did this answer your question?"

"Yes come on." She wriggled. "Fuck me. I want you so bad."

He pulled down his pants and underwear. He hooked her leg over his arm.

"Yes. Oh yes come on. Fuck me, Steven." She closed her eyes.

"No, keep 'em open." He massaged his throbbing cock. "You're so beautiful." He licked the bridge of her nose. "So goddamn beautiful." He positioned her for his entrance. "I want you to watch me when I'm inside of you."

"Mmm yes." She licked her lips. "Come on. Now please. I'm about to come already."

He slid in deep with one thrust.

"Ohhh!" She dug her fingernails into his shoulders. "Yes... oh."

"Uh! Uh! Uh! Uh!" He drilled as much of his cock as he could into her. He wanted her to feel every inch. Feel it all the way up in her stomach.

"Oh! Oh!" She chewed her lip. "Oww!"

"Oh! Oh!" Steven pumped with such force he almost knocked her off the railing. He put his hands on her buttocks and spread her wider to get inside her more.

"Ooh! Yes!" She held onto his waist. "Deeper. Yes. Ohh!"

"Huh? You like that?" He squeezed her ass. "Ahh you feel so good. So wet I'm gonna bust."

"Oww! Oooh! Fuck me!" Her head bobbed with his movements. "Oh yeah...yeah...oh!"

Sweat burned his eyes. "God you feel so good. Didn't think you'd fuckin' feel this good."

"Oh! Yes!" Her buttocks slapped against the railing.

"Ah. Oh god you're so wet."

"Oh!" She laid her head on his shoulder. "Fuck me. Make me come all over you. Make me drown you."

"Ah...ooh!" He raised her leg higher.

"Fuck yeah! Ahh!" Zoë's clit contracted around his dick. "Oh...I'm coming! I'm coming!"

"Oh!" He became woozy but kept pumping. "Oh...Zoë ."

"Ooh...yes! Oh I'm coming." Her breasts slapped against him.

He delivered one final thrust. "Ahhh!"

"Ohhhhh! Uhhh!" She grabbed his head.

"Oh...oh...Jesus." He fell against her.

∞ ∞ ∞ ∞

Thirty Minutes Later

"It's weird how Nick's there all the time huh?" Steven stopped at a red light and turned the radio to his favorite classic rock station.

"I don't know." Brianna laid her head back. "He seems nice enough. I mean he obviously cares about her."

"She barely knows the guy and she acts like he's her best friend. I mean what makes her think she can trust him? Dylan seems like someone with so much sense but she just welcomes Nick into her life?"

Brianna turned the station to her favorite R&B channel. "It's not our concern."

"Yeah but how can Dylan be so sure he doesn't have something to do with the murders?"

"His alibi checked out for Nadia's murder." Brianna adjusted the volume. "And he didn't even know Shannon."

"How do we *know* he didn't know Shannon?"

"Jayce checked it out remember? There doesn't seem to be a link."

"Yeah well we still should keep an eye on him." Steven made a right.

"Who did you call?"

He wiggled in the seat. "What?"

"Who did you call at Jasmine's?"

"Oh uh, nobody."

"Sure was a long call for it to be nobody. You were gone a long time."

He drove toward Jayson's restaurant. "Wanna get something to eat?"

"No. I wasn't trying to pry but it just seemed like the call was very important."

"It was just a call." He fixed his seatbelt. "You look pretty. I like your blouse."

"I've had this for five years."

"I know."

"Then how come you complimented me like you've never seen it before?"

"Look I was complimenting *you*. Jesus." He crept over speed bumps. "What's wrong with you, Bree?"

"Nothing's wrong with me." She flipped through his CDs. "Nothing at all is wrong with me."

"Oh here we go huh? Here we go."

"What?"

"You know what." He made a left. "I heard that sarcastic tone. If you got something to say then say it."

"Okay." She set his CD's on the dashboard. "What happened between you and Zoë back there?"

"Uh...uh me and Zoë?"

"Uh yes. Uh...uh...you and Zoë."

"What about us?"

"Come on, Steven. I thought you respected me enough to not take me for a fool."

"I don't think you're a fool. Fuck, I'm sick of this." He skidded to the side of the street and turned the car off. "What are you talking about, me and Zoë?"

"If you really care about me then you can at least be honest."

"I don't know what the hell you're talking about!"

"Oh please you know exactly what I'm talking about. Like I didn't notice how you went into the house right after Zoë did."

"I had to make a call."

"Oh and is that why you came back all flushed, sweating and your hair sticking up?"

"Oh that's..." He twisted in the seat. "That's bullshit. I told you it was hot. I went into the restroom and put water on my face. I wasn't sweating. Why would I be sweating?"

"Why don't you tell *me*?" She crossed her arms and looked ahead.

"Whatever you think happened didn't okay? I care about you more than I've cared about any other woman. You know that."

"Are you attracted to Zoë?"

"Why the hell do all our conversations end up about Zoë lately?"

"I already know you are. It's more than obvious."

"Don't do this. This has nothing to do with Zoë."

"What am I to think? She's gorgeous and has a great body and you can't seem to keep your eyes off of her for a minute."

"Bree."

"And she seems to be more than willing to help you when you need a hand if you know what I mean."

"So because Zoë's attractive I gotta want her? You act like a nice pair of tits, great legs and a tight ass is all I care about. If so I wouldn't have been with you."

"Excuse *me*?"

"No wait, wait. I didn't mean it like that. You got a great body, ten times better than Zoë's."

"Yeah right. It doesn't matter anyway. I shouldn't have brought it up. It's not my business."

"No don't do that. Come on."

"I have no right to pry into your life."

"You *are* my life but you drive me crazy. Nothing's gonna change how I feel about you." He took her hand. "There is only one woman I love. After all we've been through you question that?"

"I see how you look at her."

"All right I am attracted to Zoë. But it doesn't mean anything. What I feel for Zoë couldn't compare to how much I love you."

"Steven."

"We belong together, Bree. I'm not gonna stop showing you that." He kissed her hand.

"Let me prove it to you."

"How?"

"Let me take you out."

Her hand went limp in his. "Steven."

"I won't pressure you. I won't make you commit to something you can't." He bounced against the leather seat. "I just want us to spend time together like we used to. I've missed it so much and we could both use some fun. We could go to the movies or

...ancing. How about that little salsa spot we used to hit?" He rocked in the seat. "I still got the moves."

"I don't know if going out is a good idea. It might lead to confusion."

"It'll just be as friends."

"Just as friends?"

"As buddies. How about Sunday night?"

"Ooh night would be dangerous." She took her hand away. "Too much like a date-date."

"Whatever time you want then."

"You're really serious aren't you?"

"You know I am."

"How about six then? We can go to that new Italian restaurant."

Steven started the car. "It's a date."

"If things get heated and I pull back, will you be able to handle it?"

He steered the car into the lane. "Will you?"

CHAPTER TWENTY-FOUR

Dylan came back to the patio after walking Jayce to his car. Zoë and Jasmine stared Nick down. Jasmine asked a thousand questions about his personal life again. He looked like a newborn puppy scrambling underneath headlights.

Dylan trusted Nick more than she trusted most of her family. Sure it didn't make sense but the best things in life often did. Shoot her and Bruce hadn't made sense but she'd spent some of her happiest times with him.

Nick filled the void in Dylan that Bruce left behind. Jasmine thought something romantic was going on. She couldn't have been more wrong. Dylan and Nick had a special bond, sort of like a father and a child. No matter whatever happened, she only had to look in his eyes and know he'd be there for her.

Nick dismissed another question and stood from the table.

Dylan rushed from the side of the house. "Everything okay?"

"Ask your aunt." He pushed the chair underneath the table. "She doesn't seem to like me very much."

"It's not that I don't like you, Nick. I don't know anything about you."

"I'm sure Dylan's told you things about me."

"But you won't share with anyone else."

"He doesn't have to share with you, Aunt Jas. Nick is my friend and it has nothing to do with you. As long as I trust him that's what matters."

"How many strangers off the street are you gonna bring around and expect us to accept without question? First Bruce and now Nick?"

"Jasmine I've been nothing but nice to you. I come over for dinners. I even helped you with your garden the other day." Nick pointed to the bushes. "I thought you liked me unless you've been faking it all this time."

"I do like you. But I can't understand how you popped up and now you and Dylan are inseparable."

"So?" Dylan peered.

"It's strange."

"To be friends with someone, Aunt Jas? A person who saved me from harm?"

"Let's be real here." Jasmine hit Zoë's shoulder. "Zoë you know what I'm talking about."

Zoë shrugged.

"Okay, Jasmine." Nick stood directly in front of her. "Be real with what?"

"Come on. Now isn't it a little strange for you two to be friends?"

"I don't see it that way and Dylan doesn't either."

"You know what I mean." Jasmine propped her hand on the chair. "You're way too old to be Dylan's friend."

"Aunt Jas you..."

"It is not normal for a twenty-seven year-old woman to be friends with a sixty-year old man."

"I'm in my fifties if you must know."

"Whatever! You're too damn old to be hanging around my niece and it ends today."

"Oh really? Well the last time I checked Dylan was a grown woman."

"Not grown enough obviously. She's still making childish decisions."

"Shut up, Aunt Jas! Just shut up and stop butting in!"

"Butting in? I'm trying to protect you because you still don't know how to be smart. I understand Nick saved you. I understand he's nice and charming and gives you attention but you're not looking beyond that, Dylan. You always do this with people."

"She has a point."

"Zoë you're supposed to be on my side."

"So just because I'm older than Dylan there has to be something going on?" Nick pushed up his glasses. "For your information Dylan invites me over when I come."

"You can refuse," Jasmine said.

"You're right but she needs someone right now and I do like being around her. But you know what? I don't need this. If our friendship is so much trouble maybe it shouldn't be."

"Don't listen to her. Aunt Jas always does this. She's as bad as Mom sometimes."

"No maybe she has a point."

"No. I need you, Nick." She laid her head on his chest.

"I meant what I said." He patted her back. "I will be there when you need me but I don't know if I'll be coming around here again anytime soon." He looked at Jasmine. "I don't like being somewhere I'm not welcomed."

"I never said you weren't welcomed."

"You never said I was either did you, Jasmine?" He left.

"Aunt Jas!"

"I don't wanna hear it, Dylan."

"Well you're gonna hear it. I am not letting you push Nick out of my life like you did Bruce."

"I didn't push Bruce out of your life. He's in jail."

"Maybe if I'd listened to my heart instead of being afraid to then none of this would've happened."

"This is about Nick. Now you can't see what others on the outside see but you guys being friends is ridiculous."

"I don't care what folks on the outside think and I don't care what you think."

"That doesn't surprise me because I always think with sense and you wanna do things without having consequences. See this is why people can't treat you like an adult, Dylan. You don't make adult decisions. Getting so attached to Nick is not sensible and you have to be careful. He could be involved in the murders."

"Oh? I thought Bruce was the killer."

"I don't feel like fighting with you today."

"I'm not fighting. I'm telling you off."

"Oh really?"

"Look Nick is gonna be in my life if I want him to be. If you got a problem with that then maybe we shouldn't be around each other as much."

"Hold on, Dylan." Zoë stood. "No one is trying to jump down your throat. We just don't understand how you two could be this close so fast. Do you have anything in common?"

"Zoë you and I have nothing in common except being adopted and we're friends."

"But I'm not a fifty-something year-old man either. It is a difference."

"So it is the age? We're all that narrow-minded around here?"

"Do you have a crush on Nick?"

"Oh!" She walked around with her arms up. "I knew your twisted mind was thinking that, Aunt Jas. It just has to be sexual doesn't it? Nick and I are closer in the mind than I have been with anyone except Bruce."

"Closer in the mind? You sound brainwashed."

"Wanna know why we're so close? I can talk to him and he listens. He respects my decisions. He lets me make my own decisions and doesn't try to live my life for me. I love you and I appreciate you being there for me but I can't keep going on like this. I feel like I'm suffocating."

"What do you want? Am I supposed to sit back and let you do something that might hurt you?"

"I just want you to trust me. If you really did you'd know I can make decent decisions and that I don't need you stepping in. How long is this gonna go on? I'm twenty-seven. What about when I'm thirty-seven, forty-seven? Will you still try to step in? When is my life gonna be mine? When will I be able to make decisions and not have to run them by your approval?"

"Just tell me this. Name one thing, one thing that you and Nick have in common."

Dylan breathed into her hands. "We understand each other. It's something I can't explain. And it's not romantic on either end. When I'm with him I get a feeling I've never gotten with another guy. He just makes me feel safe. I guess like a father."

"Is that why?" Zoë's voice cracked. "You see him as a father figure?"

"Lord knows I never had one. Clay Hollister was a joke. And let's not forget how he reminded me every minute that he didn't want me around. Aunt Jas remember how you felt when Uncle Charlie died? How lost you were afterwards? Well that's how I felt until Nick. He made all that pain better to deal with. It's as if I've known him all my life. Even the first night we met it wasn't like strangers. I know it sounds funny and maybe if I were looking in I'd feel the same as you two but I know Nick would never hurt me."

"You've said the same thing about Bruce and he did tons of times."

"Look it's my decision if I want Nick in my life. Either you accept it or you don't."

CHAPTER TWENTY-FIVE

Sunday

Steven turned around in the mirror for the hundredth time, impressed with the GQ centerfold in front of him. He'd thrown shirts and slacks around the room in search for the perfect outfit. He'd sampled ten different colognes. The room smelled like the JC Penney fragrance counter. He settled on *Stetson*, Brianna's favorite.

Smooth move. She'd be impressed that he remembered what cologne she liked.

He flattened the collar of his silk black shirt. He left the top buttons open. He pulled on his brand new black blazer. He examined the sharp creases in his slacks.

He slipped on his gold chain. The necklace lay on his chest where his shirt remained open. Damn. Funny how one little sparkle could turn an outfit into a creation.

Brianna wasn't ready for this.

His ring tone went off. He found his cell phone on the floor under two pairs of pants.

Brianna's name flashed.

"Hello?"

"Hey." She spoke over static. "Can you hear me? My signal's fading."

Why was her signal fading?

"Yeah I can hear you. Is everything all right? You sound like you're in a car."

"I am."

"Uh." He sat on the end of the bed. "I'm supposed to be picking you up remember? Did you have to run an errand or something?"

"No uh, I'm sorry but I can't make it tonight."

His heart fell on the floor and broke into a million pieces. "What?"

"I'm sorry. Something came up."

He squeezed the phone. "What came up?"

"Jayce asked me to ride up to Newark. He spoke to the investigator that worked for Elle Givens. She told Jayce he could come see her."

"What?"

"The investigator might know something that can help us with Nadia's murder. Jayce still thinks there is some connection between Elle and Nadia. It seems like a long shot but he found more clippings and I found some things in her journal that suggest that Nadia was doing more than keeping up with the story."

"I don't believe this."

"Look." Her signal broke. "I know you're disappointed. I'm very sorry."

"What about you?" He kicked shirts around. "Aren't you disappointed?"

"Yes. I was looking forward to it too but this is important."

"This date is important too, Bree." He stood against the dresser. "You have no idea how much this meant to me. I've been thinking about it since the other day."

"Believe me I wanted to go too but I can't now. Can't you understand that?"

"Why the hell can't Jayce wait huh? You don't have to go with him."

"He asked me."

"So? Tell him you have plans and that's the end of it."

"We're already on the road."

"You are something else, Bree."

"Steve."

"So you're calling me to break our date and you're already heading out of town?"

"This is important. I won't say it again but I'm sorry. We can do it another time."

"No forget it."

"Don't be like this, Steve. Come on."

"Damn it!" He punched the dresser. "I was looking forward to this. I'd been counting the days all week long and couldn't wait. This could've been the beginning for us, Bree. This could've been the night everything changed."

"I'm sorry."

He squeezed the phone until his wrist hurt. "Not sorry enough to stay and let Jayce go by himself right? Of course you wouldn't want to disappoint *him*."

"Steve."

"Your signal's breaking up."

"What? Wait."

He clicked off. His phone rang before he set it down. He answered without checking the ID.

"*What?*"

"Steve? It's me, Zoë."

"Oh hey." A tinge of anger disappeared.

"You all right?"

"I guess I could use some cheering up to be honest. As you women say, I'm all dressed up with no place to go."

"Oh. Had a hot date that cancelled or something?"

"Do you have any plans tonight?"

"Well not really but I'm in NYC. I came home to get a break from Jasmine and Dylan. They're driving me crazy."

"We all need breaks from time to time." Steven's crotch tingled.

"So if you wanna come to NYC you're welcome to."

"What's your address?" She recited and he jotted it down. "Ah so you live in one of those townhouses. Upscale." He got his keys off the dresser. "I'm on my way."

"You missed me?"

"I'll show you how much when I get there." He turned his bedroom light off.

CHAPTER TWENTY-SIX

Newark, New Jersey

"You can't blame Elle for wanting a friend. She said the lady seemed so kind. Trusting her had been Elle's biggest mistake." KC Styles pushed aside heaps of books. She sat down on an old plastic cart.

Brianna and Jayce sat arm-to-arm on KC's trashy couch. Piles of books, clothes and dirty dishes took up the living room and none of it seemed to faze KC. Junk had been stacked from the floors up to the ceiling. They'd climbed over boxes and years of trash to get into the living room.

"Elle's husband worked long hours and it was scary to be a new mom with all that responsibility. She met Kate when she took the baby to the park. From there they became quick friends. She said Kate had been so easy to talk to and Elle felt like she already knew her."

Jayce took another raisin oatmeal cookie off the tray and motioned to Brianna. She shook her head. She wasn't about to eat anything in this dump.

"So one rainy night Kate came to Elle's to have some fun. They were gonna watch movies until Elle's husband came home from work." KC wiggled her wrinkled fingers.

Brianna almost threw up from the stench of mildew and rotten food.

"Then what happened?" Jayce dropped crumbs on the floor. "Oops. I dropped crumbs on your floor."

Did it matter?

"Don't worry uh I'll get to it later."

"Please continue." Brianna propped her arm on the sofa. Boxes tumbled behind her. "Oh goodness. I'm so sorry."

"I'll get it later." KC moved the boxes she could reach. "Don't worry about it."

"Sorry." Brianna dusted off her hands. "Go on please."

"Well that night Kate claimed she got a bad headache. Elle offered her some aspirin but she said she was allergic. Elle offered to go to the store and get some painkillers for her. And to no surprise Kate was more than happy to watch the baby."

Jayce got another cookie.

"So Elle went to the grocery store. She'd been gone only a few minutes. When she came back the baby was gone." KC stared into space. "And Kate was nowhere in sight."

Jayce stopped eating for the first time since they'd sat down. "That's...that's..."

"Horrible," Brianna said. "I actually got chills listening. It felt just like I was there when it happened."

"That's how I felt when Elle first told me what happened. She said she searched that house over and over and over until she nearly passed out. She knew the baby was gone but couldn't bring herself to accept it. Of course she never saw Victoria again."

Though hearing the story had been fascinating, Brianna's mine stayed on KC's hoarding. She'd been in one of the most disciplined careers, law enforcement. Yet she'd fallen to a compulsive disorder that Brianna couldn't see anyone accepting let alone someone of KC's capability.

KC had been an amazing cop in her day. Awards and plaques covered her shelves, well the shelves you could actually see. She finished that fascinating career with an impressive stint as a private investigator.

The scattered photos told her life story. How long had she been living like this? What did she do to feed her life now? What happened to that man in KC's pictures? Why had that vibrant woman from the photos turned to a house of clutter for comfort? Why was she content with this dirty house and these dried up memories?

Brianna clenched her hands.

What happened to the man in KC's pictures?

"You okay, Bree?" Jayce bumped her with his cup.

"Huh? Oh yeah I'm fine. KC this entire thing is amazing."

Jayce dipped a cookie into his coffee. "What happened to Kate? Did anyone ever find her?"

"No." The wrinkles on KC's forehead deepened. "My guess is that Kate was just the middleman used to steal the baby. I suspect they killed her years ago, probably right after it happened. I don't think anyone will ever know what happened to her."

"Do you know why Elle and her husband decided to adopt a child instead of having another one?" Brianna balanced her cup in her palm.

"No I lost touch with Elle before they adopted the other baby."

Brianna exhaled. "I can't imagine how hard this was for her."

"One day she just stopped dealing with me. I think I reminded her of the pain as well. Not to mention that I couldn't help her."

Brianna straightened up. "You ever met the husband?"

"I met him at Elle's funeral." She scratched her forehead. "I forgot his name but he was very handsome. I remember he had coal black hair and I remember his eyes. They held such sadness. It was like I could feel what he and Elle had gone through just by looking in his eyes."

"You ever met the other daughter?" Jayce asked.

"Yes at the funeral." KC pulled at her plaid shirt. "She was a very beautiful girl. She was a teenager at that time. You could tell it was very hard for her to deal with Elle's death. After the funeral I heard they'd taken off. I guess they didn't even wanna stay in town anymore."

"And not one person knows what happened to Klein?" Brianna asked. "He just goes on with his life after what he caused?"

"A friend of mine with the FBI suspects that Klein has been living in Chicago for years as Kenneth Brockman. That's been the running rumor in the FBI but there's not enough to work with. Now it's my turn to ask questions. Why do you think Elle is connected to Dr. Hollister's death? Because of those clippings you told me about?"

"Apparently she collected stuff like this all the time but she had tons of news clippings on Elle's suicide, the kidnapping, everything. She put them away in this album as if they were keepsakes to her. It was too strange to ignore. I know I might be grasping at straws but right now any avenue to look into will do."

"Well that does sound weird, Detective Matthews. Why would Dr. Hollister have an album of clippings about Elle? Do you think she knew her?"

"We don't know," Brianna said. "But I've been reading Nadia's journals. Anyway, she kept mentioning that she had a big secret and so we assumed she might have been killed because of it."

KC nodded.

"But after Jayce told me about the clippings Nadia had of Elle, I did some more digging and Nadia mentioned a situation in her journals that sounded just like what Elle went through. We put two and two together and figured she might've been speaking about Elle."

Jayce scribbled something on his pad. "Do you ever wonder what happened to Victoria, Ms. Styles?"

"It's funny but I think about this all the time, even now. Out of all the cases I've worked on, Elle's haunted me. I guess I felt I let her down because she killed herself."

"Elle needed help that you couldn't give." Brianna patted KC's knee. "You did all you could do."

"I've told myself that for years but still I feel pain when I think that I could've done more. I knew Elle was hurting and I should've realized the depression would drive her to something drastic. I've prayed for Victoria. I just hope she ended up with a good life and people who love her so Elle didn't die for nothing."

CHAPTER TWENTY-SEVEN

New York City

Zoë poured a thin stream of Merlot on her thigh.

"Mmm." Steven's tongue slurped the wine as it drizzled down her leg.

She poured some into her belly button. Steven lapped it up like a dog drinking from a hose.

She spread her legs and put her ankles on his shoulders. She poured Merlot down her bush. His tongue dove straight for the bull's eye.

"Mmm!" Zoë clenched the sheet. "Ohh." Her legs bounced against Steven's back as his tongue poked her clit.

"Oh...oooh...yes." She dripped wine down his back and held his head to her crotch. "Mmm. Yes, oh! Mmm. Oh, Steven!"

His tongue prodded until she released a numbing orgasm that almost knocked her off the bed.

"Ohh!" She quivered. "Ohh! God yes!"

He held her hands to the bed to keep her from falling.

"Ahh!" She jerked. "Oooh!" She fell back. "Ah. Oh." She held onto the headboard." God that was great."

"You came hard." Steven poured Merlot over her nipple and sucked it. "Did I please you?"

"You know damn well you did." She gave him a slobbering

kiss. "Oh you felt so good. So fuckin'good."

He slipped his hands under her buttocks. "You pulled a couple of impressive tricks there yourself."

"So you noticed?" She combed her fingers through her extensions. "I bet my hair's a mess."

"Nothing about you could be a mess." He kissed her shoulder. "It's impossible for you to look bad."

"Well." She wrapped her legs around him. "That's because you've never seen me in the mornings."

"No there is no way you could ever be less than stunning. I don't care what you say." He licked the spot between her breasts. "Ready for round four?"

"Oh." She laughed. "I think you better let Momma rest a while."

"Well Papa's all revved up." He caressed her thighs. "Momma's gonna have to learn to keep up."

"I don't know if I can keep up with you, Steven." She kissed him. "But it sure is fun trying to."

He crossed his arms under his head and looked at the ceiling. "This feels so good you know? Like a breath of fresh air."

She played with his nipples. "I hope you don't think I do this all the time." She threw her leg across him. "I really like you."

"I like you too but I think you know that by now."

"This is so weird." She flicked her hair out of her face. "I've been attracted to men before but it never consumed me like this."

"You have no idea how much I wanted you. The first time I saw you..."

"Yeah?" She propped up to see his eyes.

"I wanted to tear your clothes off and have my way with you."

"Ha, ha, ha! You did not."

"Oh yes I did. Man I couldn't describe the perverted thoughts I had."

She kissed his stomach. "I felt something between us too but wasn't sure how you felt until you kept coming around Jasmine's. I just felt this heat every time I looked at you. I wanted you so much. My nipples get so hard just thinking of your name." She sat up on her knees. "I masturbate to you."

"What?"

"Yeah I close my eyes." She closed her eyes and touched her breasts. "And I touch myself and I imagine you inside me." She sucked her index finger. "And I stick my finger in my clit."

"Show me how you do it."

She circled her palm across her nipple and pushed her finger inside of her.

"And I rock so slowly." She panted. "And I imagine you kissing my neck and your breath on my ears."

He closed his eyes.

"And I go deeper." She leaned forward and rocked. "And deeper until I come. Oh." She bounced as she edged to orgasm.

"Does it feel good?" He sucked her neck. "Does it feel like I'm really inside you?"

"Oh god yes." She shuddered. "Ohh!"

He pulled her into his arms.

"Steven?"

"Yes."

"Why were you upset earlier? Before you came?"

"Huh? Oh it's not important."

"Look I'm not into sharing men."

"What?"

"So if there is something going on with someone else, Detective Morris, whoever then you need to let me know."

"Nothing is going on with anyone else."

"Are you sure? Because before you put on the brakes and now you wanna fuck me every time you see me. I don't wanna be used."

"Where is this coming from? We were having a wonderful time and you're flipping out now?"

"I'm not upset but telling you the deal. I really do like you and I don't mind playing with you because the sex is great. But I won't be the one you run to just because you can't have someone else. I am not anyone's substitute. You understand that?"

"I'm here because I wanna be."

She rested in his arms. "I just wanted to be clear."

"It's just funny to see someone so beautiful so insecure."

"No woman wants to be used."

"And I'm not using you. You invited me over here remember?"

"Yes." She rubbed his arm. "I'm sorry. I didn't mean to spoil the mood. Just hold me. Hold me all night."

"I wish I could but..." He checked his watch. "I gotta go."

"What?"

"Yeah I gotta get back to Albany. It's a two hour drive."

"You don't have to leave."

"I gotta go to work tomorrow."

She wrapped herself in the sheets. "To work or to Brianna?"

"Oh, man." He threw the covers off. "So it's starting already?"

"What?"

"You got the leash on me already huh?" He got his underwear from the side of the bed.

"Please no one has a leash around you but it won't hurt for you to miss one day of work."

"You gonna pay my bills if I get fired?" He got on his knees to find his socks.

"Oh please you won't get fired for calling in once." She hugged him. "Come on, baby. We can stay in bed all day and do whatever..." She marked his back with kisses. "We want to do." She turned him around to face her. "You can have me anyway you want me."

"And you don't know how much I wanna take you up on that offer but I can't." He flicked her chin. "You're not gonna get all clingy on me are you?"

"Clingy?" She walked around in the sheet. "I wasn't clingy when you fucked me was I?"

"I was joking. Lighten up." He turned in a circle. "Where the hell's my shirt?"

"I don't find it funny. I feel like now that you got what you wanted you're through."

"Oh come on, Zoë." He found his shirt behind the chair in the corner. "You know it's not like that."

"Do I?"

"What's up? We just had some of the most incredible sex of our lives and now we're arguing over bullshit. I'm going to work tomorrow because I have to. It has nothing to do with any woman okay?" He kissed her nose. "If you don't trust me now then how long can this possibly last?"

"So you do want this to become more than sex?"

"Sure." He put his arms around her. "But if it stays like this I won't complain."

She hugged him. "I'm sorry. Believe me I'm not usually like this but I really like you. I want this to be more than sex."

"Mind if I take a shower before I go? I'm all sweaty and stuff."

"Yeah go ahead." She put on her satin robe. He stared from the doorway. "I thought you were gonna go shower."

"Well uh, that robe's giving me other ideas."

"Get outta here." She threw a pillow at him.

"I'll be out in a few minutes." He hurried down the hall with his clothes under his arms.

Ding! Dong!

Zoë trotted across the checkered-tile hallway.

Knock! Knock! Knock!

She stopped at the front door.

The security guard always buzzed first to announce a visitor.

Knock! Knock! Knock!

She headed for the gun in her computer desk but remembered the cop in her shower.

Sometimes her nerves got the best of her.

Bang! Bang!

"Lisa!"

"Shit." She touched her chest.

"Lisa! I know you're there, baby! I smell that perfume all the way out here! Open the door!"

"Fuck! I don't believe this." Her chest throbbed. "Shit! Damn it."

"Lisa! I'm not leaving until we talk, baby doll!" He beat again. "Open the fuckin' door!"

She popped her head out. "Shh! What are you *doing* here?"

The green-eyed blond switched a toothpick around his mouth. His huge chest poked from under his muscle shirt. That deviant smile covered half his face.

"Hey, baby."

"What the fuck are you doing here?"

"Well I just missed you. What can I say?"

"I told you that what happened in Chicago stays in Chicago. I also told you I didn't wanna see you again."

He switched the toothpick to the other side of his mouth. "Yeah well I think we have unfinished business."

"We don't have anything. I can't believe you'd come here!" Her breast popped out of her robe. "Shit." She held it closed. "Get outta here, Billy. I'm warning you."

"But Lisa we got a bond remember?" He touched her hair. "You can't just erase me out of your life and pretend I don't exist. Not after all I've done for you."

"Leave."

"You don't know what that perfume does to me." He pushed his nose to her neck. "I always wondered if every part of you smelled this good."

"Get away from me." She shoved him. "Get out!"

"I'm not going anywhere until I get what you owe me."

"I don't owe you anything."

"I wouldn't be so sure. Come here."

"Let go of me." She struggled in his arms. "Billy!"

"Of course I could tell the cops what we had going and see if they thought you owed me. What do you think they'd say, Lisa?"

"Look." She swatted at him. "I'm not alone. We can talk about this another time. Get off me."

She tried to close the door. He blocked it with the toe of his boot.

"Uh-uh. I'm not going *anywhere*. You can't just sweep me under the rug and pretend I don't exist."

"Are you a complete idiot?" She pointed to the hall. "I said someone else is here."

"I don't care."

"He's a cop."

"Well looks like that could be bad news for you then. The faster you let me inside, the quicker I can leave before he comes out here."

CHAPTER TWENTY-EIGHT

Billy strolled around the living room. He checked out Zoë's China cabinet full of antiques.

"How did you get up here without security buzzing me?"

"Wasn't no guard down there." He turned a candy dish upside down. "I like your place. It's almost as sexy as you are." He touched the glass table.

"Get your ass away from that before you break it. Now you listen to me and don't ever forget what I'm about to tell you. You don't call the shots, I do. We meet when I say and not until then."

"Well I didn't like that rule too much, baby doll. I got sick of feeling like some whipped puppy. You owe me and you know what I want."

"I don't owe you a damn thing. You're lucky I had anything to do with you in the first place."

"The money's gone. I had things to do and the amount you gave didn't last."

"That's not my problem. I hope you remember how it felt to have it because it's more than you'll ever see in your pathetic life. I kept up my end of the bargain. I paid you. It's not my fault you ran through it."

"This ain't about money and you know it." He stared at her cleavage. "You know what I want."

"Go fuck yourself."

"I wanna fuck *you*."

"Let go of me!"

He stroked her thigh. "Give it a chance and you might not want me to."

"Get off! We had a deal and I'm not giving you anything else."

"I can't trust your ass." He fondled her buttocks. "And it is a beautiful, luscious ass."

"Get off me, Billy!"

"I keep thinking in the back of my mind that you're gonna turn everything around on me and I'll end up in prison."

"What the fuck you mean? No one knows about your sorry ass. You're in the clear now let me go."

"You're so beautiful." He pushed his hand up her robe. "I thought we had something going more than business."

"What do you want?" Her breasts sat on his chest. "*What?*"

"I want what you've been dangling in my face since we met."

"No." She punched his rigid chest. "Let me go!"

"You're not in the position to say no to me. I could tear your world apart. Now here's the deal. I won't tell what a bad girl you've been. I promise."

"Get your filthy hands off me."

"If you sleep with me."

"Fuck you." She broke loose.

"Ah come on." He cackled. "It's a great deal, baby! You sleep with me and I'll keep my mouth shut. I promise."

"It's not happening. I'd never be that desperate."

"I'm not bluffing. I'll ruin you and you know I can. Turn this fantasy you're living into the shithole of a life you been running from."

"You're disgusting. I shouldn't have ever gotten involved with you."

"Either you give me what I want or I'll go to the cops. I got you where I want you." He cornered her against the door. "I'm running the show now."

"Get off me."

"That's the deal, baby. You fuck me and then you never have to see me ever again. Now why don't you give me a sample right now?"

"Get away from me. Get away!"

"Hey!" Steven put on his blazer. "What the hell's going on?"

Billy let Zoë go. "And you are?"

Steven folded his collar down. "Detective Steven Kemp with the Albany Police."

"And I bet that makes you feel so important doesn't it?"

"Just go, Billy." Zoë opened the door. "You've caused enough trouble."

Steven fixed his sleeves. "If you don't understand what she means I think I can elaborate for you."

"I understand, Officer Kemp. I didn't mean to interrupt. Are you two fucking?"

"Miss Peron asked you to leave."

"Miss Peron? Lisa what the fuck is he talking about?"

"Lisa?" Steven looked at her.

"Just go." She jabbed Billy. "We can talk later."

"Mmm. Hope you wear that perfume the next time we meet because I love it."

She slammed the door.

"Who was that?"

"Nobody." She pushed her hair behind her ears.

"Why did he call you "Lisa"?"

"Because he thinks it's my name." She straightened the couch pillows.

"And why does he think it's your name?"

"I know him from outta town. He has a crush on me. He won't take "no" for an answer. When I first met him I told him my name was Lisa. I didn't want him to know my real name."

"Uh-huh." Steven twirled his keys. "Then how come he knows where you live?"

"I don't know. He just popped up outta nowhere."

"I don't like this. You know him well?"

"Just someone I met up with when I went out of town."

"Was he a boyfriend?"

"He wanted to be but I told him straight up I wasn't interested. He was just someone I had drinks with from time to time. But he made it clear he had feelings for me so I left it alone. I had no idea he was in New York and I certainly didn't know he knew where I lived. That's why I gave him a fake name so he wouldn't find me."

"Do you think he was the person who was following you that night?"

"Uh I don't know." She sat on the arm of the couch. "I didn't think of that. He might be."

"This guy could be a stalker, Zoë. There's too much crazy shit happening. Dylan's attacked, someone follows you and now this guy shows up. You gotta be careful. Promise me."

"I will. I never would've answered the door if I knew who it was. The security guard didn't buzz up." She fixed his collar. "Thank god you were here."

"Well I gotta go. I'll see you okay?"

"Hold on." She kissed him. "You can't just leave me like this."

He stumbled. "Come on. Zoë I gotta go."

She raised her robe. "Sure you don't want one for the road?"

"If I don't leave now I never will."

"You sure?" She slid her robe to the floor. "Are you really sure? Are you?"

"Shit. I can't get enough of you." He hoisted her against the wall and forced her legs around his waist.

"Oh yes." She helped him out of his blazer. "Fuck me, Steven." She unzipped his pants. "Make me come so hard it lasts until the next time."

∞ ∞ ∞ ∞

A Week Later

Zoë swirled her hand into the bubbly bath water. She dumped in perfumed salts she'd gotten free from her last trip at the spa. She threw in some rose petals. Nick had taken Jasmine and Dylan to dinner so she had Jasmine's all to herself. She wasn't about to tag along and be referee for another Hudson family spat. She took full advantage and decided to pamper herself.

She set out her favorite lotion, got the scrub brush and submerged herself in the suds.

She squeezed soapy heaven over her skin. Suds ran down her back and breasts. She thought of Steven. She slid the rag to her middle. She imagined those sexy blue eyes as she washed her tender center.

This man literally took her breath away. That was a switch seeing how she usually had that effect on men. She washed off her shoulder. At first he'd been a simple conquest to her. She became attracted the first time they met but she didn't seriously consider going after him until the day of the funeral. The sparks had flown on those stairs and her body would not let her ignore it.

She laid her head back and caressed her craving pussy.

Did he really think about her the same way? Hell she wasn't

expecting marriage. She'd just wanted to fuck him. But after that first time, she couldn't walk away. She'd never had a man who gave so much pleasure in such a short time. Not only was he gorgeous but he made love to her body as if he'd created it. He had the right moves, knew what made her weak and she always came before him. Now how many men could say that about their women? But was she completely out of her mind? Could this romp fest with the cop become something more? Did she really want it to? She had baggage to say the least. It became harder not to crack under the pressure.

She washed her red-painted toes. This wasn't the right time to fall in love.

"Fuck." Surely she wasn't falling in love with Steven. But if not, why did it make her angry when she saw him and Brianna together? Where did that jealousy come from?

"Focus, Zoë." She splashed water.

But what if she did love him and he felt the same way? Would he ever be able to love her? Like she craved a man to?

She laid back.

"Well." Billy walked in. "Looks like I came just in time."

CHAPTER TWENTY-NINE

"Ahh!" Zoë hid behind the shower curtain. "Oh my god. Billy! What the hell?"

"Well." He pulled the bottom of his T-shirt out his pants. "Isn't this poetic justice? How you doing, baby doll?"

"Get out of here!" She threw the scrub brush. "Get out of here right now!"

"Oh no, honey. I told you we got unfinished business. Now I'm gonna have to show you."

"I don't believe this! You've got to be the dumbest man I've ever met!"

"No you thought I was dumb but I'm not, Lisa. I bet you're wondering how I found you huh?" He picked up the lotion bottle. "You're no longer running this. I told you that the last time. I'm making the rules now."

"You're a fool, Billy. You're gonna get yourself caught for being stupid and it'll have nothing to do with me."

"I didn't like how you disrespected me when I showed up at your place. I figured with all I'd done for you, you'd be a little nicer."

"Pass me my robe."

"Why should I when my plan's for you to take it off again?" He raised his hands. "But I'll be a gentleman." He passed it to her and turned around. "Don't let that water out. We might start in the tub."

"You're insane." She put on her robe.

"I wasn't insane when you wanted me to do your dirty work was I?"

"Just leave. I can't believe this is even happening."

"Because you're not in control and you hate that."

"Look I told you we have nothing to talk about."

"Well that's fine because I didn't come here to talk."

"Well if you think anything else is gonna happen you can kiss my ass!" She marched to the guest bedroom. "Get out!"

"Oh come on, cutie pie." He ran in behind her. "You can't dance to the music and not pay the piper."

She turned on her bedroom light. "Look you did the job and I paid you. That's the end of it now get out!" She pushed him.

"Whoa." He held up a gun. "I don't think so."

"Oh? And I'm supposed to be scared of your sorry ass because you got a gun? You forget who you're talking to?"

"You think you're so tough don't you, bitch? But I've been waiting to teach you this lesson. Now take off that robe and get on the bed. Right now."

"Billy." Her robe slipped off one shoulder. "You don't wanna hurt me."

"Oh that's how you're playing the game now? What happened to all that big talk back in NYC? You think you can get men to do whatever the hell you want and not give anything?"

"I paid you."

"Fuck money!" He jiggled the gun. "You knew what I wanted from the beginning. I wanted you. It was never about the money. I love you, Lisa."

"Oh god this is pathetic."

"I do. I did what I did to get close to you don't you know that? Everyone told me you was using me and hell maybe I knew it but I wanted you so much I didn't care."

She faked a yawn. "Got a violin?"

"I'm not fucking with you, Lisa. Take that robe off and get in the bed."

"You're..."

"Do it!" He placed the tip of the gun on the side of her head. "I'm sick of going around in circles for your ungrateful ass. Now get that robe off, get it off!"

She got on the bed. "You stay the fuck away from me."

"Why is that robe still on huh?"

"Fuck you. If you're gonna rape me then do it but I damn sure won't help you."

"I'll tell the police everything."

"Oh?" She laughed. "Oh yeah that should be good. Yeah, *you* killed Jim Klein, Billy. Now tell me, Old Wise One, how you gonna put that on me? Besides I'll deny I ever knew you."

"People saw us together in Chicago. You forgot that?"

She wiggled her feet. "And they're all losers like you."

"I wasn't a loser when you begged me to kill Klein for you."

"I never begged. I asked." She leaned back on her elbows. "I offered you money to do a job. I didn't know you were attracted to me."

"Bullshit." Sweat ran down his nose. "You knew how much I wanted you. Then you think you can just walk around like you own every fuckin' thing? Klein paid for what he did. When will you?"

"If I go down, you can bet your ass you will too."

"Not worried. I've been to prison before. You couldn't survive a day."

"Oh honey you have no idea what I can survive."

"I might end up in prison for what I did, who knows? But you can believe I'm gonna get something for it. Now take that robe off and I'm not saying it again."

She spit at him. "Fuck you, limp dick."

"Shut up!" He climbed on top of her.

"Ooh, get off!" She snatched his hair.

"Aww!" He held her arms down. "It's happening so just enjoy it."

"Fuck you!" She kicked him off the bed.

"Ahhh!" He dropped the gun.

Zoë snatched it up and stood over him. "Get up."

"Wait." Billy clutched his middle.

"Oh what, didn't go as planned huh? Didn't I tell you before that you can't fuck with me, Billy?"

He stood with his hands raised. "I'll go okay? I won't bother you anymore. Just let me leave."

"So you can go to the cops?"

"I won't. I promise. I'm sorry okay? I wasn't gonna hurt you. I was just mad."

"Yet you still think I'm a fool huh? You men are so fuckin' stupid. You always thinking about pussy so much that you don't realize you're getting yourselves in trouble."

"What?" He panted.

"You actually helped me out by coming here, Billy."

"What the fuck are you talking about?"

"I'm talking about what I'm gonna tell the police. See, I was taking my bath when you broke into the house and tried to rape me."

"Wait a minute."

"And it turns out you're the same guy that's been stalking me."

"I wasn't stalking you!"

"You showed up at my place and Detective Kemp saw you. And now you showed up here and tried to attack me with a gun."

"Lisa."

"It's Zoë by the way."

"Whoever you are, listen! You can't do this, Lisa. Look at what I did for you! Look at that!"

"Oh I am very grateful. But see you made the mistake when you thought you could bully me. Baby no one bullies me especially not a piece of trash like you."

"If you think you gonna claim self-defense they won't buy it. They'll dig until they find a connection."

"Maybe so but until then at least I can rest knowing you can't tell them anything." She raised the gun.

"Please, Lisa. Please."

"Maybe next time when I tell someone not to fuck with me they'll listen."

"No!" He covered his face.

BANG!

Billy fell to the floor.

∞ ∞ ∞ ∞

Brianna watched the scene in Jasmine's hallway not knowing what she believed less, Zoë's story or how Jayce and Steven ate it up. Guess you had to be of the female persuasion to pick up on it.

Jayce wrote down everything Zoë said without question despite many inconsistences. Steven's lack of sense had been worse.

A gas bubble lodged in Brianna's chest. Was her jealousy taking over? Or was Zoë telling the truth about Billy Curtis? No way. Something about this just didn't make sense.

Brianna's stomach flip flopped but had it been the greasy

chicken fried steak sandwich or Steven's pathetic pampering of Zoë? She popped in a chewable antacid pill. She wanted to rip Zoë's weave out with tweezers.

"You all right, Bree?" Jayce looked up from jotting.

"I'm fine just a little indigestion pain."

"I told you that sandwich was too greasy." Steven glanced at her then went back to consoling Zoë.

Brianna almost popped him in the back of the head. He didn't get up to hold *her* hand.

"I just can't believe this is happening." Zoë gripped Steven's hands. "Will I get in trouble?"

"No it was self-defense." Steven stroked her hair. "It's okay now. Shh."

Oh please.

"Oh Steven I was so scared."

Please somebody get a clue.

Forensic officers roamed through every part of the house. Jayce had instructed Billy's body be taken out the back way for Zoë's protection.

Please.

"Oh." Zoë buried her face in Steven's chest. "I can't stop shaking."

"You sure you don't need to go to the hospital or anything?"

Zoë nodded at Jayce. "I'll be okay. I called Jasmine and Dylan before you guys got here. Traffic's probably holding them up."

"We'll stay here with you until they come."

"Thank you so much, Steven."

That sandwich went to town on Brianna's stomach *now*.

"You know you don't have to stay here tonight if you don't want to."

"She said she's fine, Steven."

"You got a problem, Bree? You act like you got an attitude."

"I'm not the one here with a problem."

"And what does that mean?"

So he can manage to tear his eyes off Zoë and look at someone else.

"It means just what I said, Steven."

He scoffed and went back to babying Zoë.

"Okay I'm gonna go over this again." Jayce turned to his notes. "You said you went to take a bath and Billy came into the bathroom while you were in the tub?"

"Yes." Zoë clenched the front of her robe.

"You told him to leave, he wouldn't. Then he dragged you into your bedroom and tried to force himself on you."

Zoë nodded with her hand over her mouth.

"He took out a gun, got on top of you and you kicked him off. Then he came toward you and you shot him."

"I didn't mean to kill him. I was just so scared. I just wanted him to leave."

"Shh." Steven kissed her hand.

What the hell was that?

"Just the look in his eyes you know?" Zoë sniffled. "I knew in my heart he was gonna kill me. He was crazy. I always had a feeling about him."

Brianna moved a curl out of her eye. "He was a drinking buddy when you'd visit out of town right?"

"He wasn't a drinking buddy." Zoë dabbed her eyes. "He was an acquaintance. I thought he was fun to hang out with at first but he became obsessive. I kept telling him I didn't wanna be more than friends and he wouldn't take no for an answer."

"Was that before or after you kept having drinks with him?"

She glared at Brianna. "What do you mean?"

"Well did you continue to have drinks with Billy after you knew he wanted more than friendship?"

"Bree."

"What, Steven? It's a fair question and one you should've asked when we first got here."

"I might've seen him a few times after I told him I wasn't interested because I thought we could still be friends."

"Zoë." Brianna looked at her own fingernails. "Most women who aren't interested in a man who has made it clear he's interested in them will not continue to hang out with him."

"It wasn't hanging out. Okay so I made a mistake. Is tonight my fault?"

"No." Steven hugged her. "Bree she's been through enough don't you think?"

"But how could he know you were in Albany when you don't live here? How would he know about Jasmine's place and that you'd be here alone?"

"I'm sure you know I was followed one night, Detective Morris. Billy was probably the person who followed me. He's probably been doing it all this time."

"I guess so if someone had been following you."

"Someone *was* following me. I didn't make it up."

"I didn't say you did, did I?"

CHAPTER THIRTY

Zoë smoothed her hair down. "I should've been more careful after Billy popped up at my place. Thank god Steven was there when he showed up."

Jayce glanced at Brianna.

Steven turned so red he could've shit ketchup.

"Excuse me?" Brianna poked her neck out. "Steven was at your place?"

"Yeah he came to NYC last Sunday to see me."

"Oh really?"

"Bree it's nothing. You got a big mouth, Zoë."

She smirked.

"Well if it was nothing Steven, why didn't you mention it?"

Zoë swept her hair over her shoulder. "Why does he have to mention it? It's no one's business is it?"

"Excuse me?"

"You act like you own Steven. What he does and with who is none of your business."

"Ooh." Jayce moved back.

"It might not be my business but Steven's my partner and my friend and I wanna make sure he doesn't get hurt."

"You mean like you hurt him?"

"Uh-oh." Jayce moved out of Brianna's path.

"Excuse me sweetie but you don't know what you're talking about so maybe you should keep your nose out of it."

"Jesus." Steven pulled the bridge of his nose.

"Oh I know what happened. I know he loved you and you broke his heart because you were too selfish to commit. I know more than that too thanks to Steven."

"Oh?" Brianna jumped in front of her. "So what else do you think you know?"

"Cool it." Steven pulled Brianna back. "Zoë's been through something terrible and I can't believe you're acting like this, Bree. You really wanna fight about me like a fool?"

"Enjoy it, Steve." Jayce popped in a stick of gum. "This opportunity doesn't come for a guy everyday."

"I'm serious, Jayce. Look this isn't the time for a catfight, ladies."

"No one's fighting!" Brianna flung Steven out of the way. "I just don't like what I see here."

"And what do you see?" Zoë swiveled her hips.

"I see manipulation and lies. I don't believe a word that came out of your mouth tonight, Zoë."

"So, you ain't nobody."

"Oh I got your nobody!" Brianna reached for Zoë's hair.

"Get away from me!" Zoë jumped back. "This bitch is crazy."

"Hey!" Jayce shielded Zoë. "Bree what the hell is wrong with you?"

"Excuse us, everyone." Steven grabbed Brianna. "We gotta talk about something." He dragged her down the hall.

"Let go of me, Steve!"

"Shut up." He shoved her into Jasmine's kitchen. "What the hell is your problem, Bree?"

"So you were at her place huh?"

"So it doesn't mean anything."

"Bullshit." She stomped around the table. "You two can't keep your hands off of each other. I'm not a fool."

"So that's what this is about? You're jealous?"

"No I just don't want anyone playing you for a fool and that's exactly what Zoë is trying to do. Drinking buddy? Please. She's lying about the whole thing."

"Oh this is pathetic."

"You and Jayce can sit there like saps while she bats her eyes and wiggles her ass all you want." She pointed to the door. "She knew Billy more than she lets on. If you could take your eyes off her tits long enough, you'd see that!"

"You are way outta line!"

"Am I?" She stopped by the refrigerator.

"He was stalking her, Bree."

"Bull."

"He was the one who followed her that night when she came back from NYC."

"And how do we know that? How do we know someone was even following her?"

"Why would she make it up?"

"I don't know but I think she did."

"Everything she says makes sense to me."

"Oh I bet."

"Billy tried to rape her!" He hit the counter. "Where's your compassion? You can't understand that she had to do all she could to protect herself? For god sakes you're a cop *and* a woman."

"Please listen. I'm not trying to be a bitch and I know you're enamored with her and wanna believe her..."

"I'm not enamored with her."

"Well you like her admit it. And I don't want you to end up regretting that. She is hiding something."

"You got proof of that?"

"No."

"Then don't bring it up again unless you do."

He left the kitchen.

∞ ∞ ∞ ∞

A few nights later Brianna paced around Steven's living room. Mr. Curtis, Billy's father had come to Albany for answers about his son's death. Brianna had taken it as an opportunity to question the man about Billy and the people he hung around. Steven didn't know what he found harder to digest, the overcooked meatball or Brianna's determination to "expose" Zoë. She went on about some friend of Billy's that his father mentioned and how he might be able to settle the mystery about Billy and Zoë's relationship.

Not that he believed there was a mystery.

She might have wanted answers but he knew why she really pushed the issue. Bullshit if she wasn't jealous. And she couldn't deny it.

God I want her so bad.

"Well?" She stood in front of him with her hands on her hips. He twirled his fork in the spaghetti. "Well what?"

"You're mad I spoke to Mr. Curtis aren't you?"

He moved his naked toes in the carpet. "I don't see what this has to do with Zoë."

"Mr. Curtis says it's all a lie. He says Billy wouldn't stalk or harass anyone."

"Of course he would. He's the guy's father."

"Steven." She sat on the couch. "You know you have questions about Billy and Zoë too. Things just aren't adding up. What hold is it that Zoë has on you? It's like anything I say about her, you'd dispute it."

"That's because you're targeting her and it's not fair."

"And why am I targeting her since you know so much?"

"Come on, Bree." He slurped pasta. "You're gonna pretend you're not at all jealous of her?"

"Okay I am." She put her arm on the back of the couch. "I'm only human, Steven."

"At least you admit it. But why are you jealous?"

"Huh?"

"You heard me." He scraped his fork on the plate.

"Steven." She cringed. "Don't do that."

"I forgot how much this pisses you off." He did it again.

"Don't." She took his fork.

"Tell me why you're jealous."

"You're a bastard." She twirled the fork. "I'm jealous of how you look at her. How your eyes light up whenever someone says her name."

"Bree."

"Jealous of the way you held her after the shooting. Should I go on or is that enough embarrassment for you?"

He took her hand. "I just had to hear it."

"It's true isn't it? You have genuine feelings for Zoë don't you? Not just infatuation or lust either. Am I right?"

"You listen to me." He curled his leg underneath him. "I've never felt for another woman the way I feel about you." He pressed his nose to hers. "I'm so in love with you, Bree. You know I am."

"She's so beautiful though."

He touched her face. "Not as beautiful as you. I could never care about Zoë the way I feel about you."

"Steven." She put her finger on his lips when he tried to kiss her. "I'm going to Chicago to talk to Billy's friend. I think it's the only way to find out the truth."

"There's nothing to find out." He cleaned his fork and continued eating.

"Steven."

"Okay so what if it turns out she knew Billy a little more than she says? Why is that our business?"

She scooted closer to him. "The point isn't what she lied about, but why she lied in the first place. I see it in your face that you don't completely buy her story anymore."

"I admit I would like to know more about her. But it feels like we're sneaking if we go asking questions behind her back."

"I doubt she'll be honest if we asked her to her face. If so she would have been from the beginning." She tugged on his T-shirt. "Think you could take a picture of her on your cell and send it to me? I want a picture to take to Chicago."

"I already have one."

"Oh. Guess I shouldn't be surprised."

"Well we need one right?"

"Wait, you're gonna come with me?"

"We're partners right?" He wiped his mouth. "I just hope for one thing."

"What?"

His mind reminisced about the softness of her tits and how her dark nipples tickled the roof of his mouth when he sucked them. He wanted to rip off her clothes, throw her down and suck her titties until he lost breath.

"Steve? What were you going to say?"

"I just hope that since you're searching for honesty, you'll finally be honest about the way you still feel about me." He touched the zipper of her jeans. "You have any idea how much I want you right now?"

"Oh yeah." She got up. "I think I do."

CHAPTER THIRTY-ONE

Chicago, Illinois

Steven and Brianna arrived at Billy's friend, Kael Thompson's place a few days later. This had been Steven's fifth trip to Chicago but she'd never been. The springtime weather hadn't hit Chicago yet so Brianna and Steven were back to turtlenecks and boots. Along with that came sinus problems and upper body cramps. Brianna's sniffles started on the plane and by the time they hit Kael's she couldn't smell and could hardly hear.

She should've stayed her ass at home.

Kael took the spot on the couch next to his girlfriend, Antoinette. Steven handed Kael his phone with Zoë's picture. Brianna breathed in the cinnamon smell of the hot toddy.

She had leg cramps from the heat going on and off on the plane. She thought she'd have to chisel her coat off when she first got to Kael's place. The fireplace seemed to burn everyone else up but hadn't done much for her.

Antoinette folded her legs Indian-style. "You warming up, Detective Morris?"

"Not really. I guess it's taking my body time to get use to this Chicago cold." She pulled the blanket over her sweater. "I hadn't realized how cold it still was here until we got ready to come."

"My family used to take vacations up here all the time," Steven said. "So I knew it was gonna be cold this time of year. But I guess I'm use to it."

Antoinette got up and fixed her sweater. "I'm gonna turn the heat up for you, Detective Morris."

"Yeah warm her up and fry the rest of us huh?" Kael didn't look away from Zoë's picture.

"She's a guest and you're not." Antoinette's socks caused her to slide a little across the hardwood floor. "Ooh." She held onto the shelf by the thermostat.

Steven blew into his cup. "You all right?"

"Yeah." She slid back to the couch. "I hate hardwood floors."

Steven blew into his hot toddy. "Is that the same woman Billy was with?"

Kael nodded. "That's Lisa Brewer or Zoë, or whoever you say she really is."

Brianna warmed up with that revelation.

Kael studied the photo. "I know one thing. If Billy attacked her, she deserved it. He was too into her you know? Usually I'd say Billy wouldn't have done what he did, but he wasn't himself after meeting her. She'd changed him."

"Come on." Steven sat back. "So Zoë supposedly corrupted Billy?"

"What was their relationship like then?" Brianna put her feet in Steven's lap. He looked at her but stayed quiet.

"Strange. I guess wild and maybe a little dangerous." Kael stroked his goatee. "I didn't like her from the beginning. Something wasn't right. I told Billy to stay away from her but his dick was controlling him. She was after something. I knew it and I told Billy that. He thought she really liked him. She came to my bar, looking for a sucker and she found the perfect fool in Billy."

Brianna stirred her toddy. "What made you think she wanted something?"

"I could tell she was trying to seduce him. She turned up the heat when Billy came around like she was trying to tempt him."

Steven twiddled his thumbs.

"Billy was so gone he took it as flattery. All she wanted was information, nothing more. She's a conniving bitch and you can't trust anything she says. I've known women like that before and they're always trouble. Billy didn't listen and look how he ended up."

Steven's face turned beet red. "Isn't that an unfair judgment?"

"No." Kael put his arm behind Antoinette. "She was looking to hook up with the first man who walked up to her and believe me she wasn't looking just for company. A woman that beautiful doesn't have to look for it. Okay I guess it's fair to say Billy became a little crazy over her."

"Obsessed?" Steven raised an eyebrow.

"It's not how Lisa paints it out to be. He fell in love with her. I mean, I couldn't believe he'd be that dumb but some women have that effect on men. When she came into the picture our friendship just went downhill."

"How?" Brianna asked.

Kael held onto the couch. "Billy was like a brother to me, man." Antoinette took his shivering hand. "We were always so close but when Lisa popped up that was all he cared about. It was like she put some spell on him. Billy didn't do the right things all the time but he had a heart. He never would've done anything wrong if it hadn't been for Lisa."

Antoinette laid her head on his shoulder.

"Billy had a lot of women in his life. I mean he loved women. But he didn't talk about anyone or look at anyone the way he did Lisa. He fell for her hard. They didn't even know each other long before he got hooked on her."

"Hooked enough to stalk her?"

"The point is even if he did stalk her or whatever, Lisa changed Billy into something he didn't even know he'd become. Women can do that you know? They really can. I don't care what she said about Billy. He wouldn't have done anything to her unless she pushed him to. She was like his drug."

Steven lowered his head.

"You okay?" Brianna asked Steven.

"You said something about Billy in trouble."

"Billy owed some people a lot of money," Kael said. "He was in the hole for thousands. He went to the old man but his daddy didn't have that kind of money. Antoinette and I, well we put all our money into running the bar so we sure didn't have it. But Lisa did. She had more than enough. About two months after they met, she came back to Chicago and offered him forty thousand dollars."

Brianna whistled.

"Wait now." Steven put his cup on the table beside the floral centerpiece. "Why would Zoë give Billy that much money?"

"I don't know but if Billy thinks I believe she did it just to be nice, he was crazy. They had something fishy going. People you hardly know don't usually give you thousands of dollars. I asked him why she gave him the money and every time he answered it was a different reason. No telling what he did for that bitch."

"So how long did she know Billy?" Brianna asked.

"Oh man it's been at least a year and a half. And that shit she said about her just coming up here every so often is bullshit. Every time I looked around she was in Chicago. The more I saw her, the more suspicious I got." He shook his head. "Anyway, Billy got the money, blew it and ran off. I guess that's how he ended up in New York. Don't ask me how he knew where she was but obviously he tracked her down."

Antoinette moved her long brown hair out of her cup. "Then the cops started harassing me and Kael."

Steven leaned up. "Cops?"

"Yeah." Antoinette sipped. "They came over here and to the bar. Asking us where Billy was after he left town. We told them we didn't know and they told us to let them know if we hear from him. That wasn't long before he got killed."

Brianna moved her feet from Steven's lap. "Why did the police wanna talk to Billy?"

"They felt he knew some information about this guy, Kenneth Brockman's murder."

"Kenneth Brockman?" Steven gaped.

"Yeah he was some guy who was killed," Antoinette said. "He was shot. They think Billy knew something."

"Bree." Steven batted his eyes.

"Jim Klein." Her hands trembled. "Holy shit."

"This has to be some mistake."

"I don't think so, Steve."

Antoinette put her feet up. "Who's Jim Klein?"

Kael scooted up. "Does Brockman's death mean something to you guys? What does this have to do with Lisa?"

"Not sure." Steven made a fist. "But I'm gonna find out."

CHAPTER THIRTY-TWO

Three Weeks Later

Steven pretended to be asleep when Zoë's cell rang that night. He peeked when she got out of the bed. She stood naked by his dresser with her back turned. She slipped on his shirt. When she looked his way, he closed his eyes.

She told the person on the phone to hold on. Her finger brushed Steven's lips and a light kiss followed.

"*What*?" She spoke to the caller. "No. What do you want? I have nothing to say to you." She sneaked out and closed the door.

Steven put on his pants and tiptoed into the hall. He leaned down on the stairs. Zoë slunk into the kitchen. "Why would you need to talk to me?" She turned on the light and stood by the food cabinet with her hand on her hip. "You've been acting like I don't even exist for weeks."

She walked to the refrigerator with his shirt hugging her ass. Whether she was hiding something or not, he couldn't ignore how much he wanted to throw her down and make her scream the way he had an hour ago.

"Why I'm angry?" Zoë poured a glass of apple juice. "Oh jeez I can't guess why." She put the juice back in the refrigerator.

"How about you betraying me and coming here when I specifically told you not to?" She got a stalk of celery out of the vegetable tray. "Uh-huh. Everything was fine until you showed up." She got the cheese sauce from the cabinet and dipped her celery stick in it. "I just want you to leave. I can handle this."

Steven propped his arms on the railing.

"You love me? Yeah I bet not as much as her huh?" Zoë chomped the celery stick. "You damn right I'm jealous."

Steven sat on the top step of the stairs.

"Let's just be honest okay? I can't compare to her. I never did. I'll always be second best!" She threw the celery in the sink. "Of course I love you. I wanted you to stay away so you wouldn't get hurt." She put the cheese sauce up. "You always say you wanna protect me, well I was trying to do that for you. She'll never accept you in her life. Not the way you want her to."

Steven moved down two steps.

"You know I miss you too. I wanted to come to your hotel but she's always there." She scratched her forehead. "Yeah I know. I'm sorry I spoke to you that way but I just don't understand why you came to Albany. Yeah. I know." She sniffled. "It's been hard for me too."

Steven moved down another step.

"The Daily Inn motel? Well you're right, no one we know would see us there and we do need to talk." She sucked the celery stalk. "I'm sorry I got angry. I'll never love another man the way I love you."

Steven dug his fingernails into the railing.

"Okay, I'll see you in a little while. Bye." Zoë clicked off.

Steven ran to the bedroom, snatched off his pants and hopped into bed.

"Steve?" Zoë rushed in. "Steve?" She poked his chest.

"Hmm?" He faked a yawn and stretched. "Is something wrong?"

"No I just gotta go."

"Go? You gotta be kidding me."

"No something came up." She kissed him. "I'm sorry. I was hoping I could stay over but I got something to do."

"Did I hear your phone or was I dreaming?"

"It wasn't anybody."

"Hey." He pulled her on top of him. "You okay?"

"I'm fine." She got her bra and panties off the floor. "I just gotta go. Can you understand that?" She threw his shirt on the dresser.

"Yeah I guess." He kicked under the covers.

"Don't pout." She fastened her bra. "I'll make it up to you." She zipped her skintight black jeans. "I'll give you a blowjob next time."

"And that would be different from any other time we meet, how?"

She sat beside him with a slick smile. "Okay how about this? Next time I'll let you do anything, anything you want to me in every possible position you can." She sucked his nipple.

He kissed her. "I'm gonna make sure you keep that promise."

"Can I ask you something?"

"A woman as beautiful and sexy as you can ask me anything." He pulled her hair back.

Her fingers crawled down his chest. "How do you feel about me? I mean really?"

"Uh, you know how I feel. I like you a lot. You know that right?"

"Is it just for sex? Because this has been going on a while and I'd like to know."

"No." He scratched his head. "It's not just sex."

"Then how come you've never taken me out on a date? We just meet up for sex and it feels so cheap."

"You didn't used to feel that way."

"Yeah but I do now." She put her hands on his stomach and rested her head.

"Umm I didn't know you felt that way. You should've told me. I would've taken you out. Where do you want to go?"

"I shouldn't have to ask."

"Zoë what's with the attitude? I'm not a damn mind reader. You have to tell me what you want."

"I want us to be a real couple."

"You...uh...you do?" He tried to catch his breath but wasn't sure he had any left.

"I'm not trying to put you on the spot or make any demands but I really care about you. I love the time we spend together. I haven't been this happy in a long time. I want to be your girlfriend. I'm falling in love with you. I know you're surprised and feel like this is coming out of the blue. Maybe it's my fault. I shouldn't have had sex with you so quickly that first time. I regret that now."

He rested on the pillow.

"You don't have to say anything." She put her finger on his lips. "I understand if you're not there yet."

Yet? He wasn't sure if he'd *ever* be there.

"Zoë you mean a lot to me okay? You're a very special person."

"Can I ask you a question?"

"Sure."

"Have we been having sex or making love?"

Why did women always do this? At one point he thought he could learn to love her. But his feelings for her hadn't moved since they had sex on Jasmine's stairs. He cared about her. He wasn't the kind of man who could have sex with someone and not care. But love? He couldn't bring his mouth to say that word around her. He felt obligated but not once had he felt he loved her. He loved Bree.

He'd been so desperate to teach Bree a lesson. He felt if he moved on, it would force Bree to take him back. Shit *that's* what he wanted.

Now he had this gorgeous woman in front of him who'd just spilled her guts. Was he a jerk or just an idiot? Any man would kill to be with a woman like Zoë Peron. But if Brianna gave him one tiny bit of a shot with her he'd drop Zoë on the spot.

Yep he was a jerk.

"I..."

"Shh. You don't have to answer that."

"Well we really haven't known each other all that long right? It takes time."

She caressed his face. "Yeah you're right."

"If we're talking getting serious, we need to know more about each other."

"I think we already do." She went to kiss him but he stopped her.

"Sexually speaking, we know each other very well." He touched the ends of her hair. "But I want to know about you in general."

"I don't understand. What else would you need to know? We've talked about my modeling, where I went to college and me being adopted."

"But you don't talk about your adoptive family. You don't talk about your parents. You don't talk about where you grew up or where you're from. Have you lived in New York all your life? If not, where did you grow up? How many guys have you dated? How many serious relationships? I don't know enough about you, Zoë."

"What's with you lately? How come every time we're together now I only get questions?"

"You're the one who just said you want us to get serious. Well I can't if I don't know you well enough. You know all about my family and past. I've been upfront even about Bree. You haven't shared much of anything. I'm beginning to think you're using sex to divert me from asking about you or something. I care about you and I just wanna know more about you."

"But why all of a sudden you're so anxious to know more? At first just knowing how to make me come was enough for you."

"Is that another diversion? You just asked me how I felt about you and I told you that being in love is part of knowing someone."

"You do know me." She got her barrette off the dresser. "You know what's important."

"What's the matter?"

"I don't like being interrogated all right?" She got her comb from her purse.

"So because I wanna know more about you, it's an interrogation? Why? You got something to hide?" He threw the covers off.

"No. But man you've been a drag lately. Every time we're together it ends up with these questions and I don't like how you look at me lately."

"And how do I look?"

"Like that." She pointed. "Like you're accusing me of something. I don't need this shit, Steven. I like you a lot and it hurts that you seem to be only suspicious of me."

"Wait." He held her. "I just asked some questions. Why are you getting so upset?"

"I'm not upset but I feel like something has changed with you. I hope Bree hasn't been planting things in your head."

"She wouldn't do that."

"Steve." She combed her hair. "You might think you know women but I am one and we're all shady sometimes." She made a tight ponytail and clipped it down with her barrette. "Even Bree's not perfect."

"I never said she was."

"Did she get a bunch of questions after you guys made love or did you save such special treatment for me?"

"I don't understand the attitude at all. You act like I accused you of being with another man or something."

She put on her earrings.

"You're not right?"

"Not what?" She put on her bracelet.

"Seeing someone else?"

"Stop it, Steve. Goddamn it what's going on? Of course I'm not seeing someone else but I don't get you. I ask you if we can be serious, you give me the runaround now you wanna know if I'm with someone else." She got her lipstick and eyebrow pencil out of her purse. "You really don't have the right to ask."

"You're right. I don't."

She painted her eyebrows. "I'm not seeing anyone else. I really, really like you. Don't I show that every time we're together?"

"Yes."

"And I'll share more okay but I'm very private. It's just how I've always been. It takes time for me to open up. But please don't doubt that I want us to be more than just sex. I mean that with all my heart."

"I wasn't trying to make you feel bad."

She threw her arms around him. "I just don't want this to change. You're the only thing in my life that brings me peace."

"Things won't change." He kissed her cheek. "Just know you can come to me if you need to."

"I know." She put on lipstick that made her dark skin sparkle. "I gotta go." She kissed him. "I do trust you. Do you trust me?"

"Why wouldn't I?"

"Goodnight. I'll see myself out." She blew him a kiss and left the bedroom.

"Goodnight my ass."

Steven got dressed.

CHAPTER THIRTY-THREE

Zoë parked behind the building next to the Daily Inn. She sauntered down the connecting sidewalk and went up the outside stairs.

Steven parked behind an overloaded trash bin. Tonight boasted a significant temperature drop from previous nights. The violent chill shot through the car doors.

Zoë stood in front of one of the motel rooms. She kept looking around as if someone might follow her. The door sprung open when she knocked. Steven couldn't see the person from where he sat. Zoë dipped inside. He didn't understand anything about her. His only concern should've been finding out her connection to Billy. That's why he'd led her on all these weeks but personal feelings kept seeping in.

His cock tingled.

Hell he didn't give a shit about her and Billy right now. He wanted to know who'd called her. Who would make her rush out in the middle of the night? Who was that man on the phone that she loved?

He hadn't committed to her but that didn't stop how enraged he got when he thought of her with another man. Maybe it was a man thing but he didn't want to share her no matter how selfish that was.

Ring! Ring!

"Shit." He got his phone from his jeans. He guessed Brianna before seeing the caller ID.

"Yeah, Bree?"

"Hey. You with Zoë?"

"Um, yes and no." He took his keys out the ignition.

"What does that mean?"

"I'm with her but she doesn't know it."

"What?"

He got out the car. "I'm kinda busy here, Bree."

"Just wanted to see if you found out anything yet."

He ducked under the security lights in the lot then stopped at the steps.

"No." He stooped around the corner when a man walked through the lot.

"You said you'd find out something soon and it's been weeks."

"I can't just come out and ask about Billy can I? You think it's so easy why don't you confront her yourself? I feel like shit, sleeping with her only to find out answers."

"But you didn't mind when you were doing it behind my back right?"

"It doesn't feel right. I feel like I'm using her."

"This is serious. I know you don't wanna hurt her but we gotta find out why Zoë lied. I'm beginning to think you're dragging this out on purpose so you can spend more time with her."

"Oh that's bullshit. You know it."

"Do I?"

"I can't get anything out of her, nothing."

"That's a sign that she's well-guarded and she wouldn't be if she wasn't hiding something."

A man and woman came down the stairs. The woman dug underneath her miniskirt and spit gum on the steps. The man shot Steven the "you-don't-know-me-and-you-don't-wanna-know-me-either" look and went to the soda machines. The lady stopped in front of Steven, pushed up her bosom and licked her lips.

"Hey." Her breath smelled like cigarettes and pastrami. "You wanna date, handsome?"

"Steve?" Brianna yelled through the phone.

"Hey, bitch!" The man pulled her away. "I paid for your ass

for the whole night. Bring your ass over here, trick."

She blew a kiss at Steven and followed the man to a black pickup truck.

Steven fanned away the woman's stench. "I gotta go, Bree."

"Where the hell are you?"

"The Daily Inn. I'll call you later."

"Why the hell are you down there?"

"That's what I'm trying to find out."

∞ ∞ ∞ ∞

Steven awoke an hour later to a lady getting in the car beside his. The lady drove off the same time Zoë did. He wasn't leaving until he saw the person Zoë had met.

A man walked out of the room in a baseball cap and jacket.

The man's movements seemed familiar, something about the shuffle in his walk.

"Come on, walk into the light."

The man tilted his cap and looked toward the security lights.

Steven did a double-take. "What the fuck?"

Nick Sebastian strutted from the motel.

∞ ∞ ∞ ∞

Dylan opened the Albany paper the next morning. Bruce's release made headlines.

All Charges Dropped Against Prime Suspect in Kuriakis Murder.

Beside the article sat a picture of Bruce on the county jail steps with Annabelle at his side.

Ballistics had confirmed that the bullet found in Shannon's skull hadn't come from her gun. The police lacked sufficient evidence to keep Bruce in jail for the murder.

Dylan swayed in Jasmine's hammock on the front porch. Thank goodness Bruce wouldn't go to prison for something he didn't do. But she'd give anything to find the killer and put this nightmare to an end.

The birds hopped from one point of the roof to the other. Bruce's release signified the first chance at peace since Nadia's death. She'd thought about him everyday. It became excruciating to think of him in jail no matter how angry she'd been about him sleeping with Shannon.

If she lost Bruce forever she'd deserve it. She loved him but hung onto pride instead of standing by him. All because she wanted to save face and not have to explain herself to Jasmine. But now she didn't give a shit what anyone thought. She might've been alive without Bruce but she wasn't *living*.

A drop of sweat fell down the side of her face. Nothing she'd done helped her to get over him. She'd thrown herself into activities, painted, anything to keep her mind off of him. Spending time with Nick had been amazing but sometimes she wished he'd been Bruce. She'd give up everything if he forgave her. She'd beg and plead. She didn't care how it looked.

No wonder Mr. Swaggert hated her so much. She'd turned Bruce's life upside down and didn't have the nerve to support him in the end. Despite how much he'd done for her.

Bruce always said he didn't deserve her? Bullshit.

She slung her legs off the hammock.

She had to get him back. She'd been a wreck just the short time he'd been in jail. But how could she expect him to forgive her? She couldn't even *think* of forgiving herself.

Bruce once told her that their love could survive anything.

But did he still love her? Was it too late?

CHAPTER THIRTY-FOUR

New York City

"I can't believe we're doing this, Steven." Brianna stood in Zoë's living room doorway. You know the trouble we could get into for this? Captain Jersey would wring our necks."

"She won't know if you keep your mouth shut." He zipped around the room like Spiderman. He searched Zoë's bookshelf and the drawers in her entertainment system. "Instead of just standing there you could be helping." He knelt in front of the computer desk. "We'll get out of here quicker." He shook sweat from his face.

"And since when is breaking and entering something you've ever seen me do?"

He walked across the hallway to Zoë's bedroom.

"Steve this is nuts!" Brianna stomped behind him.

"You're the one who wanted to know more right?" He scooted Zoë's end table from the bed and went through the drawers. "Don't you wanna know what she's hiding once and for all?" He flipped through a notebook then tossed it on the bed. "You gonna help or just bitch? 'Cause I could've come alone."

"You begged me to come."

"I thought you'd help." He pushed the end table in place and started on Zoë's underwear drawer.

"Don't." Brianna slithered between him and Zoë's chest. "You can't search her underwear drawer."

"The hell I can't." He pushed her aside and rummaged the drawers. "Don't pretend you care about Zoë okay? Please." He threw panties and bras over his shoulders.

Brianna scooped up the garments. "And you think she'd hide something in her underwear drawer?"

"Duh, that's why I'm searching it." He hocked a lacy thong over his shoulder.

"You sure could learn something about women. You gotta be one to know where we hide stuff."

"Ah, I don't think so, Bree." He searched the last drawer in the chest.

"Can you tell me why you are so suspicious of Zoë all of a sudden? And why you dragged me here this morning?"

He opened Zoë's double closet doors. "She was with another man last night."

"What?" A part of Brianna wanted to throw a party while the other felt guilty for the desire. "Uh, how do you know?"

"Remember I was at the Daily Inn right? I followed Zoë last night and she met another man." He went through Zoë's clothes.

"I'm sorry but I still don't see why seeing her with another man made you so suspicious now."

"The man was Nick." He pulled out boxes of designer shoes.

"Nick Sebastian?"

He nodded.

"Hold on. Are you sure?"

He looked through a box with a pair of Italian suede heels in it. "And she was in there an hour, Bree. I doubt they were exchanging recipes."

"She's having an affair with Nick?"

He shrugged.

"Do you think they knew each other all along or they hooked up after he got into town?"

"Your guess is...ah..." He crawled into the closet and threw shoes from his path. "As good as mine."

Brianna thumbed through designer suits, mini dresses and pants. "It doesn't make any sense to have this many clothes." She examined tags. "She's only a size *four*?"

He crawled out the closet. "Jealous?"

"No," She lied. "I just didn't know she was that small."

He got boxes off the top shelf.

"Are you mad that Zoë was with another man or that it was Nick?"

"I'm not mad."

"Yes you are." She touched his hand. "You can be honest. Is it that you don't wanna see her with anyone else?"

"I...shit." He threw a box down. "I don't know. What the hell is she doing meeting up with Nick? I just wanna know why." He pulled out a mound of fur. "What the hell is this?"

"It's a shawl."

"Oh." He put it back in the box.

"We need to get out of here."

"Shit." Steven straightened up the closet. "Man I know there's something here." He went to the other side of the bed. "Something about her and Billy and why she gave him that money."

"Look the best bet is to see if you can get something out of her like we planned. Anything else might set her off."

"No. I can't keep pretending with her."

"What?"

"I can't keep being with her knowing she's hiding something. I mean, she gave Billy that money for a reason. Not to mention he's a suspect in Klein's murder."

"Do you think she knew about that?"

"I don't know shit, Bree. But we both know something went on between her and Billy. She gave him that money for a reason."

"Is there another reason why you don't wanna keep doing what you been doing with her?" She sat on the edge of the bed.

"You know it is."

"Do I?"

"It's not fair to you or Zoë. I gotta end it before it gets out of hand."

"But do you wanna end it because she's hiding something or for another reason?"

"Jesus you know why. I don't love Zoë. I never did and I probably never will."

"I thought it was becoming serious."

"Well it wasn't. I'm very, well extremely attracted to Zoë. But as far as love, it's not there for me. I was mainly with her to make you pay attention and I hoped that would..."

"You don't have to say more. I understand."

"I feel horrible about this all around. I used Zoë, lied to you and I played myself. I gotta end it."

"Well." She stood. "We need to split before we end up suspended or arrested."

"Wait."

"What?"

"What's the most obvious hiding place everyone uses but people still never remember to check?"

"Uh..."

Steven dug underneath the bed.

"Steven."

"Bingo." He held up a raggedy black shoebox stuffed with folded up papers and envelopes. "See?" He took the cover off. "Everyone keeps things under the bed."

"Man." Brianna grabbed a stack of photos. "She's got more photos in here than I do in my photo album. Why would she keep photos in a shoebox?"

They flipped through photos of Zoë as a baby. She was just as gorgeous then.

"Aw." Brianna cooed at the photo of baby Zoë reaching toward the camera. "Look at those fat little arms. Hate to admit it but she was a cute baby."

"Adorable." Steven held a photo with Zoë on a tricycle. "It's weird to see these, to see her so innocent you know?"

"Wait." Brianna pointed at the photo of little Zoë sitting with a man and woman in the yard. "Are these her parents?"

The woman had on a straw hat that covered the top of her face and the man wore shades.

"I guess." Steven took the picture.

"So her adoptive parents were white?"

"I guess these are her parents, yeah."

"You didn't know?"

"No how would I?"

"Oh excuse me for thinking that maybe you two actually talked in between all that hot sex."

"I knew she was adopted but she didn't tell me they were white. I guess she didn't think it mattered. You sure those are the parents?"

"I assume so." Brianna separated the pictures in her lap. "Steve."

"What?"

She showed him the picture of the woman in a rocking chair with little Zoë.

"Wait one fuckin' minute here." Steven squinted. "Is that who I think it is?"

"Yes. It's definitely Elle Givens."

They stared at each other for the longest minute Brianna had ever experienced then looked at the picture again.

"She's the daughter, Steve. Zoë is Elle Givens' adopted daughter."

CHAPTER THIRTY-FIVE

"This can't be." He held the photo closer. "How the hell can Zoë be Elle's daughter?"

"Obviously it's possible. That's Elle in the picture and she's holding Zoë."

"Wait. This makes no sense. Maybe the woman just looks like Elle."

"That's *Elle*." Brianna pointed to the woman's face. "You know damn well it is."

Brianna ran through more photos. "It's definitely Elle. Jesus Christ."

"If Zoë is Elle's adopted daughter why the hell didn't she say anything when Jayce mentioned it?"

"Maybe she was surprised Nadia had the clippings." Brianna wasn't convinced of that theory herself but couldn't think of anything else to throw out there.

"I don't believe this. First she's having an affair with Nick, now she's Elle Givens' daughter?"

"Uh, Steve?" Brianna stared at a photo of a dark-haired man holding little Zoë.

"What?"

She wiggled on the bed. "Oh...wow...uh..."

"*What?*"

"Uh, I don't think Zoë and Nick are having an affair. In fact I'm positive they're not."

"What the hell are you talking about?" He snatched the photo. "Oh fuck me. Bree is that..."

"Yes. That's definitely Nick Sebastian in that photo."

∞ ∞ ∞ ∞

Nick escorted Dylan onto his hotel terrace that night.

"Wait here." He dashed inside the room.

Albany had the most beautiful nights. Her gold bracelet shimmered under the moonlight.

Nick had become a great distraction from her problems once again. She'd showed up earlier expecting a shoulder to cry on and he'd whisked her to New York City no questions asked. He doted on her as if it were his only duty in life.

The night started with a trip to a fancy NYC boutique and salon. She'd gotten her hair trimmed even neater and makeup done by a woman who once did the professional makeup for local models and celebrities. From there she had a professional fitting at the boutique and walked out with a satin black dress that made people gaze every time she walked past.

They enjoyed a gourmet meal at a Gordon Ramsey restaurant where she ordered food she couldn't pronounce. They took a horse and carriage ride through Central Park. They caught a live show everyone had been raving about for weeks. They finished the evening at an art exhibit where a local artist showcased his new work. Dylan exchanged info with the man and wowed him with photos of her own artwork.

She maneuvered her curves within the snug gown.

It was as if she'd stepped out of her body and into a whole new world. No one took the time with her that Nick did. No one made her feel so appreciated or so beautiful.

Nick turned the terrace light on. The most unique female voice in the history of music crooned from his stereo. Dylan closed her eyes and swayed to Billie Holiday's Strange Fruit. Billie's low tones guided the rhythm, soothing Dylan's soul.

She'd grown up on Billie's music. She used to play Nadia's collection to drown out the fights between Nadia and Clay. Listening to Billie became a ritual when Dylan couldn't find solace anywhere else.

She glanced inside the room. Nick got two glasses and a bottle of champagne from the fridge. She hadn't told him how much she loved Billie. Yet out of all the music he could've played, he picked Strange Fruit which happened to be her favorite Billie song?

The reason they'd gotten so close so fast had been for their similar tastes. She placed her hand on her flat stomach.

Sometimes she felt Nick knew her better than she knew herself. How could that be possible? *Was* it possible?

He set the glasses on the terrace table and filled them with champagne.

She hadn't had champagne since her cousin's wedding two years ago.

"Here you go." He handed her a glass and sipped from the other.

He'd worn his contacts tonight and she'd seen a glint in his eye that she couldn't shake. Sometimes he'd stare for no reason. As if he had something to say but never got around to it.

He lit the night up with his smile. He'd taken off his tux jacket. She didn't have romantic feelings for him of course but he was a very handsome man. He'd draw any woman in by the attention he paid and how he made you feel like you were the only person in the world.

"Are you all right?" His cologne stole her senses.

"Yes." A tear fell from her eye.

"Then why are you crying?" He caught her tear with his fingertip.

"It's just that no one's ever done for me the things you do. It's overwhelming you know?"

He put his finger on her cheek. "I only want to make you happy. I live for that, Dylan. Nothing else matters to me."

She stared into her glass. "I shouldn't drink. I gotta drive home."

He put his hand over hers. "One sip won't hurt."

He claimed his interest wasn't romantic but wasn't he trying to seduce her now? What caused the hungry look in his eyes?

She looked over the terrace. A man with headphones walked underneath the streetlights.

The champagne trembled in her hand. She just couldn't stop shaking all of a sudden.

"Whoa." He steadied her hand. "You're supposed to sip it, not drop it."

"I know. I..."

"Are you really okay? Something's been bothering you all day."

"Can I be honest?"

"You know you can." He bent over the railing.

"Nick I just..." She caught her breath. "I'm nervous and I don't know but this feels so strange."

"Being alone with me like this?" He sipped.

She shrugged.

"You've been alone with me many times before and you felt fine."

"I know. Tonight feels different. Doesn't it to you?"

"You feel uncomfortable?"

"I'm kind of confused that's all."

"Confused?"

"Nick I'll always be grateful for what you've done. It kills me that I can't give you half of what you've given me."

"You've been giving me all I've ever wanted, Dylan. God you really can't see that?"

She lost herself in Billie's voice.

"What's the matter?" He pulled her close. "Please don't shut me out. If I've done something wrong, let me know."

"You do everything right. That's why this is so hard."

"What's so hard?" He held onto her hand. "What's changed?"

"You're wonderful and I adore being around you but I think it's best if we don't see each other anymore."

CHAPTER THIRTY-SIX

"What?"

"I don't want to hurt you, Nick."

"But you are. You will if you cut me out of your life."

"I don't want to."

"Then don't. Don't shut me out, Dylan. Please."

"Let me go, Nick."

"I can't let you walk out of my life."

"Please." She tried to move her hand. "Nick."

"Honey, you don't understand." His eyes filled with tears. "You just don't understand."

"Please, Nick. I wanna leave."

He let her hand go.

"You will always mean the world to me." She kissed his cheek. "But I think that this isn't a good idea anymore. I can't explain it but that's how I'm feeling now."

"I wanted to make this night perfect for you." He looked into the night. "Guess I failed huh?"

"You're wonderful. Like an angel that has been sent to me. But I feel like there's something you're hiding from me. Something you want to say but you never do."

He clutched his chin.

"Nick, answer me please."

190

"I love you, Dylan."

"I know that. I love you too."

"I'm not talking about as a friend."

"I really think I should go." She set her glass on the table.

"And I don't think you could ever know how much I love you."

"Nick."

"You wanted me to explain? Well maybe that's a good idea. I've been holding this in for too long and I don't think I can do it anymore."

She backed up. "What are you talking about?"

"Come here." He went inside.

She stayed at the doorway.

He turned off the music and got a thin black box from the end table by his bed.

"I got this for you."

She put her hand on her bosom. "What is it?"

He handed it to her. "Open it."

She flipped the box open. She held up a gold necklace with an amethyst dangling from it.

"What's this?"

"It's a present for you." He put the necklace on her neck.

"It's so beautiful." The gold glistened against her skin. "But it's not my birthstone." She faced him.

"Yes it is."

"I was born in June. My birthstone is the pearl."

"No. It's the amethyst."

"Nick I think I know my own birthstone. I was born in June, not February."

"No. You were born in February."

"Nick." She walked to his computer. "Look it's a beautiful necklace and I appreciate it but this is not my birthstone. I think I'd know when I was born."

"You were born in February." He stood behind his bed. His gaze didn't leave her face once. "And amethyst is your birthstone. You just don't know it."

"Okay." She sighed. "Uh, maybe you had a little too much champagne or something but I'm gonna go until..."

He ran to the door. "No."

"Nick."

"You can't leave yet, Dylan."

"Nick please." She backed up toward the bed. "I just wanna

leave okay? I think you're confused about everything."

"No you're the one confused. But I'm gonna help you not be."

"Get out of my way, Nick."

"Are you afraid of me?"

"Yes." She ran across the room. "With the way you're acting now I'm very scared."

"You don't ever have to be afraid of me. You know that."

"Let me leave, Nick."

"I can't until you know the truth. That's what you wanted right?"

"Stop it!" She pushed him but he held onto her. "What's the matter with you?" She hit his chest. "Let me leave! Goddamn it!"

"Listen to me." His grip burned her skin.

"Nick please." She sobbed. "Please just let me go home."

"You are so beautiful. You look just like your mother."

Her heart pounded. "My mother?"

"There was no woman as beautiful as her to me, except you. She was the most beautiful woman I've ever seen in my life."

She stumbled.

"You look just like her. It's like she's right here with me again."

"You knew Nadia? You lied to me."

"I'm not talking about Nadia. I'm talking about your real mother."

"What the fuck are you talking about?"

"Victoria."

"Victoria? What the hell are you talking about?"

"That's your name. Your real name is Victoria."

"Let go of me!"

"Shh."

"You're fuckin' crazy!"

"Honey calm down."

"Let go of me! Help! Someone help me!"

"I'm trying to tell you the truth! Please listen!"

"No!" She slapped him. "You stop this shit right now! I'm not playing this sick game. You're trying to say you knew my real mother? Bullshit!"

"It's the truth."

"There's no way!" She pushed him. "I don't even know my real mother! You're a liar!"

"Dylan listen!"

"You stop these lies! There is no way you could know my mother!"

"There is a way!"

"You're lying there's no way!"

"Listen!"

"You're full of shit! How could you know my real mother? How could you?"

"Because I'm your father!"

She stared at him.

"That's how I know."

CHAPTER THIRTY-SEVEN

Dylan's shoe caught on the carpet when she moved back. "Get away from me."

"Listen to me, sweetheart."

"Get away, Nick."

"I know it seems impossible but it's the truth. I am your father."

"You stop it!" She ran to the door. "This is crazy! I never wanna see you again!"

"Wait!" He held the doorknob. "Please listen to me."

"You're a fuckin' nut aren't you? Aunt Jas was right about you. I should've been cautious. I shouldn't have ever trusted you!"

"I can't let you go now." He took her hand. "I've waited all this time to tell you the truth."

"You're sick. This is totally fucked up." She ran to the other side of the bed. "Why are you doing this?"

He walked toward her.

"No." She raised her purse. "You come near me and I'll hit you. I swear it."

"Okay please just calm down. Dylan? You kept saying you didn't understand the connection we have. Why you trusted me so easily. It was something inside you." He patted his chest.

"And there's a reason."

She shivered over the headboard.

"I know this is the most incredible thing you will ever hear but I wouldn't lie about something like this. You are my daughter."

Dylan doubled over from nausea. "I feel like I've been drugged. Is this even real?"

"It's real."

"It can't be happening." She quivered. "Please, Nick. Whatever you're doing, just stop it now."

"I am your father and I can prove it." He pointed. "Look in that briefcase in the closet."

"No."

"You have to, sweetie."

"No. This isn't true. You can't be my father!"

He slowly approached. "Get the case outta the closet. What are you so afraid of if you think it's not true?"

She held her breath. He couldn't be her father. There was just no way. It wasn't possible.

"Please, Dylan."

She opened the closet. A black suitcase sat by Nick's shiny wingtips.

He stood behind her. "Pick it up."

She reached for it but couldn't control her trembling fingers.

"The last thing I'd ever wanna do is hurt you."

"Then why are you doing this to me?"

"It has to be done. No more secrets will be between us after tonight." She tensed up when he touched her shoulders. "What are you more afraid of? That I am or that I'm not?"

"Okay you wanna do this huh?" She threw the briefcase on the bed. "Wanna play this sick game of yours?"

"Dylan."

"No come on. We'll play it!" She opened the briefcase. Three large photo albums sat on top of each other. She snatched the first one.

"Open it, Dylan." Nick whispered in her ear. "Put me out of my misery."

"No." Her tears dampened the cover.

"Open it."

"I can't." Her fingers trembled beyond control.

"Don't be afraid. This has to be done."

"No." She backed into the dresser. "I can't do this." He stroked her chin as she sobbed.

"If you really care about me than stop this and just leave me alone. Pretend we never met."

"I can't, honey." His tears hit the front of her dress. "I've waited for years to find my little girl. And I promised I wouldn't ever lose you again, Victoria." He turned her toward the mirror. "Look at us. Is it so impossible?"

She lowered her head.

"Look." He shook her. "Look at us, Dylan. We look so much a like."

"No we don't."

"Yes we do. Look at the coloring, the features. You got my nose. Your mother's eyes."

"Stop it!" She broke away. "I'm going to the police!" She got to the door before him this time.

"Dylan you have to let me explain."

"You stay away from me."

"Don't do this sweetheart."

"You're sick and demented. You've got some fixation on me and you've painted these lies from fantasy."

"No."

"Yes you did! You are not my father!"

"I am your father and Elle Givens was your mother!"

"*What*?" She wobbled. "Oh god you are sick. You're completely sick and I'm going to the police."

"I didn't commit any crime. You are my daughter. No matter if you wanna face it or not."

"I wish I never met you."

She yanked the necklace off, threw it on the floor and left.

∞ ∞ ∞ ∞

Bruce barely heard the faint knock at his door. He opened it to Dylan, sitting on his porch with her face in her lap. She wore a stunning black satin dress and looked more beautiful than she did in his dreams. She had her shoes in one hand and sobbed into her arm. She had runs up and down her stockings.

She raised her head to the porch light. She seemed to have been crying a while but her makeup looked like she'd walked off a stage.

"I'm sorry, Bruce."

He knelt down.

"I am so sorry for what I...what I did to you. I am so sorry I didn't stand by you." She swung her shoes. "I know I shouldn't be here and that I'm the last person you wanna see but I had nowhere else to go. No one understands me like you."

"Dylan." He pulled her into his arms.

"Oh Bruce I need you now. I know I wasn't there for you." She cried into his smudgy T-shirt. "But please don't turn your back on me. I have no one. I'm so alone."

"Shh." He hoisted her up. "It's okay, honey. Shh." He took her inside.

"I'm so sorry, Bruce. You have every reason to hate me."

"I couldn't ever hate you, Dylan." He laid her on the couch. "Shh, come on. Dry your eyes." He dried her eyes with a napkin he had from his dinner.

She squirmed. "I..."

"You look so beautiful. Like a princess." He cleaned his oil-stained palms on his jeans. "Shit I'm such a dick, touching your pretty dress with my dirty hands."

She cried into the napkin. "I love your dirty hands. Oh, Bruce. I've made so many mistakes."

"Shh, calm down, honey. What's happened?" He touched her cool face. "You gotta tell me so I can help you."

"So they dropped the charges against you huh? I bet it was rough. I'm so sorry for what you went through."

"Hey I can take care of myself." He rubbed her hair. "The only torture was missing you. I can live with anything but that."

"How can you not hate me after I turned my back on you when you needed me?"

"Hey I wasn't exactly innocent right?" He dabbed the tears she missed. "I love you, Dylan. No matter what happens, that will never change."

"I almost ruined your life. Don't tell me you can forgive that."

"Look you're not responsible for me being in jail. I shouldn't have lied. But I don't give a shit right now, tell me what's wrong."

"I don't do anything but cause problems. I'm no good for anything."

"That's not true. Stop saying that crazy shit."

"I'm gonna go away." She laid her pumps in her lap. "Everyone would be better off then. I'm no good to anyone."

"No." He kissed her. "Don't fuckin' say something like that. I'd die without you. I don't want you to go away, baby." He kissed her cheek. "I don't want you to ever go away. Why are you all dressed up?"

"I went out with Nick again."

"I see." He bit his bottom lip. "So he's still around?"

"I get the feeling you object to our friendship too."

"Well can't say I like having my ex hanging around a man old enough to be her father."

"He took me to New York City and treated me like a queen."

"I bet. Well we all ain't able to do that right?"

"Are you jealous?" She touched his hand. "It's not like that. After tonight I never wanna see Nick Sebastian again."

"Why? Something happened?"

"Everything was wonderful. It was one of the most fascinating evenings of my life. But we got back to his hotel and he started acting crazy."

"Define crazy."

CHAPTER THIRTY-EIGHT

"He started talking crazy and saying stuff that didn't make sense. Then he wouldn't let me leave. I was so scared, Bruce."

"What?"

"I'd never seen him like that. The way he looked at me. I haven't been that afraid since the night I was almost raped."

"Just what the fuck are you saying? Did he put his hands on you?"

"I just wanted to leave." She sat up. "That's all and he wouldn't let me. He kept saying all this stuff. I only went to see him because I was so depressed about you and he whisked me away and made all my dreams come true."

"And tried to seduce you didn't he? Let me guess. He brought you back to his hotel and didn't take no for an answer right?"

"Wait."

"And probably laid on that bullshit that you owed him for all he's done for you right?"

"Wait you don't understand."

"Oh I understand. That son of a bitch put the moves on you didn't he?"

"Bruce." She raised her arm. "Hold on."

"That son of a bitch!" He kicked over the table. "That motherfucker! I'll kill him!"

"No!" She pulled on his arms. "Listen!"

"I knew this would happen! I didn't want you hanging around him." He went to the door.

"Stop, Bruce! Listen to me!"

"I'm gonna kill him."

She blocked the door. "Goddamn it, listen to me! That's your problem you never listen before you fly off the handle. Nick didn't try anything with me. It was nothing like that."

"Then what the hell did he do that has you so upset?"

"He says...he said..."

"What?"

"He says he's my father." She let go of his shirt.

He slumped against the wall. "Say what?"

"Nick says he's my father."

"Wait, your natural father? That's bullshit."

"That's what I told him then he said Elle Givens is my mother. He gave me a necklace and told me I was born in February."

"Who the hell is Elle Givens?"

"Shit." She ran back to the couch and got her shoes. "I gotta go, Bruce."

"What? Wait you're in no shape to drive anywhere."

"I gotta see Detective Matthews. With what Nick said tonight, he might even be involved in my mom's murder."

"You really believe that?"

"I don't know what to believe about Nick anymore." She put her shoes on.

"I'm going with you." He got his keys off the banister.

"No after all I've done to you I don't deserve you being there for me."

"Well I never deserved you in the first place." He kissed her. "So now we're even."

∞ ∞ ∞ ∞

Nick's dream of reuniting with Victoria after all these years hadn't gone as planned.

He'd expected her to be shocked and upset but hadn't intended on angry. He set the briefcase beside his chair in the interrogation room.

Would she ever accept that he was her father? Could he get her to?

Bruce walked in with anger blazing from his eyes and his fists swinging.

Was he *always* angry?

Dylan snuggled with Bruce in the corner. Damn it she was afraid. In all this time Dylan hadn't ever been afraid of Nick and it killed him. He wanted to gather her into his arms and hold her like the night they first met.

Jasmine blew into the room, cursing like a late-night comedian. Jayce tried to hold her back but she knocked him into the table.

Shit.

"Settle down, Ms. Hudson!" Jayce blocked her flying fists. "You gotta control yourself."

"Control myself? He's a big fat liar! This entire thing is ridiculous and we won't entertain this nonsense!"

"It's not nonsense." Nick's throat had grown dry from anxiety. "What I told Dylan is the truth and it's about time everyone knows it."

"You wouldn't know the truth if it bit you on the balls, Nick!"

"Stop it, Ms. Hudson!" Jayce forced her arms to her side. "Now listen. Nick was kind enough to come down here and answer some questions. He didn't have to do that."

"He's completely insane." Jasmine stomped to the back of the room. "For all we know he might be the killer and saying these lies is a part of some fantasy he created to get close to my niece."

Dylan glanced from behind Bruce.

"You need to calm down or I'll have to ask you to leave," Jayce said.

"This is my niece we're talking about. If he can come up with this bullshit then is it impossible to think he killed Nadia?"

Bruce kissed Dylan's forehead. "Just like you knew I killed her, Jasmine?"

She opened her mouth to respond but ignored Bruce.

Jayce sat across from Nick. "My main concern is solving Nadia and Shannon's cases. It's not to intervene in family drama but I have to admit I'm very curious about what Nick has to say myself."

Nick cleared his throat. "I'm sure you are, Detective. And I'm sorry for any inconvenience this might cause. I just want to say I never meant to let things carry on as far as they did."

Jasmine mumbled.

"Dylan the last thing I want to do is hurt you but I can't let you go on not knowing the truth."

She held onto Bruce.

"I love you, sweetie. We both felt a connection when we first met and I guess I hoped you knew what it meant."

"Just please say what you're gonna say," Dylan said. "Get this over with."

"Okay. How about I start with how Elle and I fell in love?"

∞ ∞ ∞ ∞

Nick sipped from a can of Sprite twenty minutes later. He'd shared the details of his romance with Elle. How they'd met in college. How she'd been a sheltered kid and had latched onto Nick for an escape. Dylan's inquisitive expression suggested that she recognized similarities between her and Elle.

Dylan had become everything he pictured her to be. She shared Elle's spunk and Elle's lack of self-confidence in making her own decisions.

But nothing about Dylan reminded him of Elle more than her talent for art.

Her eyes lit up when he spoke about Elle's favorite hobby.

"She was an artist?" She moved away from Bruce for the first time since she got there.

"Yes she was." Nick focused on the soda can. "She was amazing just like you. Don't you see, Dylan? That's where you got your talent from."

"Oh that is pathetic." Jasmine sat at the smaller table in the back. "That doesn't mean anything. Just because people can paint doesn't mean they are related."

"No it doesn't. But Dylan *is* my and Elle's daughter."

"And nothing you've said confirms that does it?"

Jayce watched Jasmine then turned to Nick. "Tell us about the kidnapping."

"I was working as usual that night. There'd been friction between Elle and me. She was upset because I'd started working longer hours. The stress of having a new baby didn't help her either. She kept saying she had no one to turn to and she felt I was abandoning her. She was lonely."

Dylan eased toward him. "And?"

"That's when she met Kate in the park." Nick's stomach twisted. "And it's funny but I was the one who suggested Elle go to the park and see if she could meet a friend. Yeah." He bent the soda can. "I'll never forgive myself for giving her that idea."

"You can't blame yourself. Listen to me okay?" Jayce scooted his chair up. "No matter where Elle went, the same thing would've happened. It's just how things worked out."

"But I feel like it's my fault. I always will."

"What happened then?" Bruce sat on the edge of the table.

"When I got home she told me all about Kate. The next thing I know it's a month later and Elle's running to that park every single day. She's smiling, getting new clothes, starting to lose the baby weight. She's feeling more confident and more independent. That was another thing about Elle. She wasn't very independent "

Dylan sat down. "What did you think of Kate? Didn't you pick up signs at all?"

"I never met her. Elle always invited Kate to dinner with us but she always said she couldn't come. After she kidnapped the baby, I knew it was because she hadn't wanted to come around *me*. Maybe she thought I'd see through the façade and realize something was up with her."

"If my wife got that involved with a woman she'd just met I'd demand to meet her at least," Bruce said.

"It's not a day of my life I don't regret that I didn't ask more questions about Kate or pay more attention. Maybe I was selfish because Elle had finally gotten off my back about spending time with her. I was glad she wasn't depressed and finally had a friend." Nick dropped his arms from the table. "So, one night I was working some overtime and that was the night Kate took the baby. She'd come to our place, lied and said she had some headache or something and Elle went to the store to get her some medicine." Nick dropped his gaze. "She came back and both of them were gone."

CHAPTER THIRTY-NINE

"Nick I sympathize with what you've gone through," Jasmine said. "Believe me I do. But you need help."

"Why do I need help?"

"Because you're crazy if you think my niece is your daughter."

"I love Dylan and I'd never wanna hurt her."

"Then why are you doing this, Nick? How do you expect us to believe such a crazy story?"

"Why is it so crazy unless you just don't wanna face it? You *are* Victoria, Dylan."

"I've had enough of this." She headed for the door.

"Wait."

"Let go of me, Nick."

Bruce pulled Dylan behind him. "How did you find Dylan in the first place? Assuming she really is your daughter."

"I've been keeping tabs on her for a while."

"How long?" Dylan let go of Bruce's waist.

"A couple of years, well, a little longer."

Jasmine gawked. "A couple of *years*?"

"But you told me you just moved to Albany. Was that a lie too?"

"No. I just moved here recently. I couldn't stay away anymore. It was killing me."

"So you've been stalking me from a far?"

"I wasn't stalking you."

"You had someone else do it didn't you?" Dylan moved from Bruce. "Did you have someone watch me and report back to you or something?"

"You make it sound so sleazy."

Jasmine held her waist. "That's exactly what it is."

"So what, did you hire someone to look for your daughter and they found Dylan?" Bruce asked.

"No. Does it matter how I found her? Look at me, Dylan." Nick stooped down to her. "You know the truth in your heart. That's why you didn't want to look at these." He got the briefcase from the side of the table. "Open the briefcase and you'll see proof right here."

Jasmine marched to the table. "I don't care what you've faked to try to say you're Dylan's father. You're obsessed with her and will do anything to stay in her life."

"I don't give a damn what you say or what you think. She is my flesh and blood and no one in here can change that!"

"You're lying!" Jasmine jumped in his face. "You got nothing in that briefcase but lies!"

He opened it. "Can you shut your mouth up long enough to look?"

"Whoo wee! Photo albums!" Jasmine jumped up and down. "Is that supposed to mean anything to us?"

Dylan crept to the table.

Nick spread out pictures of Victoria as a newborn. Jasmine picked up the close up of the baby wrapped in a pink blanket.

"Oh god."

Jayce stood from the table. "You all right, Ms. Hudson?"

"You recognize that baby don't you, Jasmine?" Nick took out more photos. "Don't you?"

"No." She threw it down. "This can't be happening." She walked in circles. "This is not happening. How did you get that picture?"

"I took it when she was born that's how I got it."

Jasmine fell against the table. "This just...it just can't be happening."

"Not enough to convince you?" Nick passed Dylan a thin folder. "Open it."

Her hands trembled as she held up a piece of paper.

"Know what that is?"

She stared at the paper with her mouth opened.

"It's your birth certificate. See the year?" Nick pointed. "Same year you were born. But look at the month. It's February isn't it?"

"So?" Jasmine snatched the birth certificate. "That only proves you're Victoria's father." She threw the certificate at Nick. "It does *not* prove Dylan is Victoria."

"Why is it so impossible to believe? Does me being Dylan's father threaten you somehow?"

"The only thing that threatens me about you is that you're insane. I'm warning you, Nick." Jasmine threw her head back. "Don't mess with my family or you will regret it."

"I'm telling the truth."

She left.

"Dylan?" Nick put his arms around her.

"Don't touch me." She moved. "I don't know what you're up to but I won't fall for your games again."

"I'm telling the truth."

Dylan turned to Bruce. "Can I stay with you tonight?"

"You can stay with me for the rest of your life."

"Fine, let's get outta here."

"Dylan." Nick ran in behind her. "We can take a DNA test. DNA tests don't lie right? That will be the only proof we need."

"No."

"Why not take the test if you don't believe me?"

"I said no. What I want is for you to take your pictures and all your shit and leave. I don't ever wanna see you again."

"Dylan."

She slammed the door in Nick's face. He fell over the table in tears.

"Nick?" Jayce patted his arm. "Calm down okay?"

"I feel like I did when she was first stolen from us! I thought when I told her the truth it would be the happiest day of my life but it's not. She hates me!" He hit the table. "I finally found my little girl and she hates me!"

"It's gonna be okay. She's just confused. You gotta admit this is strange to say the least."

"This was a big mistake." Nick stuffed the photos in the briefcase. "I shouldn't have told her the truth. Everything was fine the way it was. At least she wasn't mad at me."

"You didn't tell the complete truth, Nick."

He squinted through tears. "What?"

"You didn't tell Dylan that Zoë's your adopted daughter."

"What? You know?"

"Morris and Kemp told me. How they found out's not important. It's the truth isn't it? Zoë is the daughter you and Elle adopted after Victoria was kidnapped isn't she?"

"Good lord."

"Why didn't you tell Dylan?"

"It's hard to explain but I promised Zoë I wouldn't say anything. She didn't even want me to be around Dylan."

"Why?"

"It's a long story. Will you just keep this between us? Don't tell them Zoë is my daughter."

"And you really think you can keep that a secret for long?"

"I already hurt one daughter by telling the truth. I won't betray the other."

"Why did you and Elle decide to adopt? Why didn't you just have another baby?"

Nick closed the briefcase. "Elle went through a horrible pregnancy with Victoria. After that the doctor said it would risk her health to have another baby." He headed out.

"Nick?" Jayce pushed the chairs under the table.

"Yes?"

"Don't leave town all right?"

"I didn't kill anyone if that's what you're thinking."

"Oh don't worry." Jayce threw the soda can in the trash. "If you are the killer I'll find out. You can bet on that."

CHAPTER FORTY

"No! Don't touch me." Zoë yanked away from Nick's hands. "How could you do something so fuckin' stupid?"

"Just listen to me, please!"

"Why should I?" She threw her purse on his bed and marched to the terrace. "Hell you did everything tonight without telling me first so why you need me to listen now?"

"I know you're mad but it was time. I had to do it."

"No what you had to do was keep your promise to me. You have no idea how much this could fuck everything up! You should've stayed your ass away like you promised!"

"Well I tried." He felt the back of his neck. "But I'd already been away from her all those years, how could you expect me to stay away the rest of my life?"

"God I knew this would happen." She dabbed her forehead. "Why am I not surprised? Nothing ever goes right for very long does it?"

"Honey I love you. Nothing will ever change that."

"Right." She clutched the railing. "And I am supposed to believe that your real daughter won't impact our relationship at all?"

"You are my real daughter." He shook her. "No one will ever take your place. You're a part of me. You don't have to feel threatened."

"The fuck I don't. You have no idea what you've done. Did you ever once think of me tonight when you were telling everyone the truth? Did I ever cross your mind?"

"Yes! That's why I didn't tell them you were my daughter. I thought it would be better if you told Dylan yourself."

"What?" The ends of her hair tangled in the breeze. "God you are an idiot aren't you, Dad?"

"I know you're angry but I will not condone you speaking to me like this much longer."

"I can speak to you any damn way I like after what you've pulled tonight! I'm not telling Dylan a damn thing and you won't either."

"What the hell is the big deal about telling her the truth? She'll forgive you and get over it. She loves you."

"And what fuckin' planet are you on, Dad? Look from now on you can tell her any damn thing you like but do not tell her I'm your daughter and I mean it. If you do I will never forgive you."

"And how long do you think we can walk around here and she not find out?"

"That's not my problem. If you hadn't opened your big mouth everything would be okay! No scratch that." She flicked her hair out of her face. "If you'd stayed your ass away like I'd told you to, everything would've been okay!"

"You found her, Zoë. You were the one who told me where she was and who she was. Why would you do that if you didn't want me to ever meet her?"

"Because I love you and I felt you were owed to know Victoria was alive and where she was. But you promised me you'd stay away and you couldn't even do that."

"Put yourself in my shoes. If you'd gone through all that pain your mother and I had, would you have stayed away from her?"

"Says you to the substitute."

"You are not a substitute."

"Bullshit, it's all I ever was! You wouldn't have adopted me if Victoria hadn't been kidnapped." She brushed a tear away. "I've been living in her shadow all these years and I guess you expect me to just move aside so you can make room for her?"

"Stop it. This isn't a competition."

"The fuck it's not. That's all it's always been, Dad. Why did you adopt me?"

"What the hell kind of question is that?"

"Answer it. Why did you adopt me?"

"I'm not gonna answer that question."

"I was the one who fixed everything! I was there when you suffered, not her. I was the one who put the pieces together! I'm the one who's done my best to make everything right for you and Mom. How could you do this to me?"

"What do you mean, you've made everything right?"

"Damn it I fixed everything the best I could to show how much I love you and Mom. I did that out of duty and because I wanted to. *I'm* your daughter more than she is."

"Honey."

"She'll never love you like I do. And if they find out I'm your daughter everything will be for nothing."

"Zoë." He looked her straight in the eyes. "Is there something you need to tell me? Is something going on?"

"No."

"You're lying. What did you mean when you said you've made everything right?"

"I gotta get outta here before someone finds out I'm here." She got her purse off the bed.

"Don't go yet, honey. Please."

She dabbed tears. "Right now I'm so mad at you I can't stand to hear your voice."

"Zoë you'll always be my daughter. There is room in my heart for the both of you."

"You always said you'd do anything to make me happy right?"

"Always."

"Then leave Albany and never come back. Just go away like you never found out she was here."

"Honey I can't do that. I can't go off into the shadows again. My heart wouldn't let me."

"And you claim things won't change?"

"They won't, sweetheart."

"Really?" Tears dissolved on her lips. "You just picked the desire to be with her over what I want. I'd say things are changing fast as hell."

∞ ∞ ∞ ∞

"And well, that's it." Jayce put his feet up on Brianna's living room table and flipped through the cable channels. "Ever think of getting Direct TV, Bree?"

"I can't believe this shit." Steven paced with his hands on his waist.

He stopped in front of Brianna as if he expected her to make sense of the situation. Hell she couldn't believe it herself. She'd been on many cases that started out one way and ended up doing a one-eighty in another direction. But never like this.

"I know it's shocking." Jayce stopped on the Home Shopping Network. "Do you know I ordered something from them last year and never got it?" He switched the channel.

"Poor, Dylan." Brianna snuggled in her robe. "Couldn't imagine how she's feeling right now. And I don't even wanna think about how Jasmine acted."

"Shit." Jayce put his arm behind his head. "I'd be locking her up for Nick's murder if she'd gotten her hands on him."

"Fuck, man." Steven paced in front of the window. "I just can't believe this."

"All this about Dylan possibly being Nick's daughter is fascinating but is he connected to the murders? That's the magic question," Brianna said.

"Well I told him not to leave town."

Steven scoffed. "And you think he'll listen?"

"He's not running off believe me." Jayce pulled his feet down. "He wants to get close to Dylan more than anything."

"God I hope he didn't kill Nadia." Brianna scooped up Davis. "But if he cares about Dylan like he seems to, I can't see him doing something so horrible. Or am I just being naïve?"

"I think we're all being naïve when it comes to this case." Jayce laid the remote in his lap.

"He definitely has a motive to kill Nadia." Steven sat on the table. "He could have been angry that Nadia had his daughter and killed her."

"But why would he be angry at Nadia?" Brianna stroked Davis' head. "She only *had* Dylan, she didn't do anything wrong."

"If she knew Dylan had been kidnapped she did." Jayce looked at both of them. "That's a possibility right?"

"Please. Hell no. This woman was a therapist for goodness sakes. She spent her life helping others with their problems. She was a kind person despite what folks have been saying."

"What about how she hated Bruce and all the stuff she did to break him and Dylan up? What about her forcing Dylan to get an abortion? Is that the sign of a kind person or a master manipulator who'd do anything to get what she wanted? I think you're seeing what you want to because she was your friend."

"Jayce I'm not saying she didn't make mistakes but I don't think Nadia would condone kidnapping. Who would do something like that?"

"People do it all the time," Steven said.

"No." Brianna nuzzled Davis. "Look I'll accept the other stuff being said about Nadia but she wouldn't keep a child that had been stolen from her family. She wouldn't."

"Well why did she have those clippings?" Steven asked. "And don't say it's because she was collecting them like the others. We all know we found way more than clippings."

"Okay, what about Zoë? You think Nadia knew she was Elle's daughter?"

"No." Jayce shook his foot.

"What about Jasmine?" Steven shrugged. "Think she knew about this?"

"If she did she deserves an Oscar for how she acted in the station. No I don't think Jasmine knew anything either. She loves Dylan too much to hide something like this."

Steven turned toward Jayce. "Even if Nadia told Jasmine Dylan was kidnapped and made Jasmine promise not to tell?"

"We don't know Nadia even knew Dylan was kidnapped."

"She knew. You can stay in your fantasy land where Nadia is so great if you want, Bree. But if you start looking at this with sense you'd see what Jayce and I do."

Brianna scratched Davis' ear. "Don't talk to me like I'm an idiot."

"Then stop acting like one."

"Hey." Jayce leaned up. "Don't go there, Steve. The last thing we need is to be fighting. We're all on the same side."

"I apologize okay, Bree?" Steven tilted toward her. "But you gotta look at what's going on here. I know it's hard to imagine but you can't ignore it. Nadia knew. I'd bet my life on it."

His scent.

She sniffed several times to make sure her nose wasn't playing tricks on her. Did she smell what she thought she smelled?

"You okay, Bree?"

She sniffed his shirt.

"What?" Jayce raised his hand. "He needs deodorant or something?"

She put Davis down, got on her knees and sniffed Steven harder.

"Bree?" He wiggled. "What the hell are you doing?"

Jayce set the remote on the table. "Uh, you guys want me to leave?"

"Bree you're freaking me out here." Steven held her still. "Wanna tell me why you're sniffing me?"

"Cologne." She pushed her face into his shirt. "What kind is it?"

"I'm not wearing cologne."

"Smell." She pushed Steven's face into his shirt. "You smell that?"

"Oh that? That's Zoë's perfume. I was with her earlier. You should see how many different perfumes she has, like a damn boutique."

"Bree you look like someone hit you over the head again," Jayce said.

That's the smell.

"That's...that's the smell. The smell, the cologne I smelled the night Nadia was murdered."

"What? Wait a minute."

"It is, Jayce."

"You're mistaken, Bree."

"Steven I'd never forget it." She sniffed him again. "No. This is the exact same smell." She inhaled to her stomach. "Zoë was at Nadia's that night. Oh god she was there."

"What the hell are you talking about?" Steven snatched his arm from her.

"You heard me. She was at Nadia's the night she was killed."

"This is fuckin' crazy."

"Is it?" Jayce asked.

"Yes. If Zoë had been at Nadia's the night she was killed she wouldn't have hidden it."

"Like she didn't hide her relationship with Billy Curtis and the fact that she was Nick and Elle's daughter?"

"Stop it, Bree. She would've been honest about something this serious. She wouldn't play with a murder investigation."

"Then ask her about everything straight out." Brianna got up. "See if she for once tells you the truth."

CHAPTER FORTY-ONE

Bruce cleaned his bedroom while Dylan changed in the bathroom. He sprayed some of the old air freshener he hadn't used since she was last there. He hadn't had a woman spend the night in a long time. Of course Dylan wasn't just any woman. He didn't want her smothered by unholy man-funk when she came in.

They'd stopped by Jasmine's for Dylan to get some things. Funny but her overnight bag had turned into two suitcases. Had she planned to stay longer than a night? She even brought her easel and paints. Thank goodness Jasmine hadn't been there. He wasn't ever in the mood for her shit but tonight he probably would've mangled her if she'd said the wrong thing to him.

He threw dirty clothes into the closet and tossed junk into the dresser drawers.

He thought of the last time they made love.

"Snap out of it." His dick pulsated.

Why drive himself crazy with what could have been if it wasn't possible? He got sheets out the linen closet in the hall. Or was it possible? Did Dylan want to be with him again?

He stripped the sheets off the bed and threw them in the corner.

He'd been the first person she ran to tonight. She'd clung onto him at the station. She'd held his hand as if she'd been afraid to walk without him.

Didn't that mean something? Oh god. Did she still love him?

He smoothed the lavender sheet over the mattress. He imagined laying her down on top of it and moving his hands all over her body.

"Shit." He yanked the crotch of his jeans.

The real question wasn't if Dylan still wanted him. It was whether or not he could control himself if she did.

She walked inside. He took one glimpse of her in that flimsy nightgown and his dick sprung up like a sword.

"Jeez." He held the sheet in front of him. He pretended to straighten out the wrinkles long enough to coerce his dick to behave. "Uh, you can sleep in here and I'll take the couch."

"No I couldn't do that. This is your place. I'll be fine on the couch. Besides I don't know if I'll get much sleep in anyway."

"I'm not letting you sleep on that couch. It smells like ass." He slapped the sheet. "You're sleeping in here. Besides I sleep in there sometimes anyway to watch television."

"Oh I was gonna ask you what happened to the TV in here?"

"Took it to the pawnshop."

"Oh. Uh..." She crossed her arms then uncrossed them. "You did?"

She looked like she wanted him to explain but he wasn't about to pile his financial problems on her when she had her own shit to deal with.

Tkk...tkk...tkk...

"God when are you gonna get that faucet fixed?" She propped her supple hip on the dresser. "You think I should take the DNA test?"

"What?" He turned the sheet to her to block his cock.

"Do you think I should take the DNA test?"

"I can't answer that." His dick relaxed against him. Usually he'd be pissed when he lost a hard-on but thankful tonight.

"Come on, Bruce."

He laid the top sheet on the bed. "What the hell do you want me to say? You gotta make that decision. It's your life."

"Don't be an asshole. I need some advice."

"Jeez." He tucked the sheet in the corners. "Take it then."

"Why?" She chewed on her thumbnail. "Why do you say I should?"

"Well hell, then don't take it. Look I don't know." He sat on the bed. "Do you want to know if Nick's your father or not?"

"I know he's not." She looked at her fingers. "I think this is some game he's playing."

"Okay fine well then take it and prove it if that's what you believe."

"You say that like you think he could be my father."

"He could be right? You can't ignore the shit he had at the station."

"So you think I'm Victoria? Is that what you're saying?"

"Hold on okay?" He raised his hands. "You asked for advice now you're charging at me."

"I'm sorry." She played with one of the rubber bands from his dresser. "This is just so painful."

"I know." He went to hold her but backed off. "You can stay as long as you want. You can paint all you want, relax, anything."

"Thanks. Bruce?" She lay on her stomach on the bed and kicked her legs up. "What's it like having a real family?"

"You have a real family."

"No I mean that shares blood." She watched him like a newborn baby. "What's it like?"

"Hell you're closer to your family than I am to mine. Shit you know how it was with my dad." He scooted up in the bed. "Shit we barely got along. Always getting on me about making mistakes but hell they were the same mistakes his ass made."

"What about your momma?" Dylan rolled over and put her arms behind her head. "I know she abandoned you but don't you ever think about her?"

"Shit she left when I was three. I don't even remember her. Wouldn't know her if she walked up to me."

"But didn't you wonder about her at all? I mean you had to."

"No." He scratched his head. "Not really."

"How could that be? I thought about my real parents even though I was happy with my adoptive family."

"I never thought about her much. I mean, sometimes I wonder if she's still living. But other than that I don't care. The bitch left her kid. Why would I wanna know her?"

"Ever wondered if she thought about you? Maybe she wanted to come back."

"Please. That bitch ain't thought about me once." He scratched behind his ear.

"You don't know that."

"Well she's had decades to come see me if she wanted to. She knew where I was. So fuck her."

"See?" She propped up on her elbows. "I wish I could be like you."

"What do you mean?" He took his *Nikes* off.

"You see things so differently than others. You don't brood over the sadness or depression of something that happened. You just go with the flow and cut folks who do you wrong out of your life no questions asked."

He shrugged.

"But me, I'd be sad. Most people would be sad. But you have a different way of looking at things and I admire that. That's what I like about you. It's easy for you to let go."

"Not of everything. Some things I can't begin to see my life without."

"I'm just so tired of all this shit." She closed her eyes. "It's so peaceful here." She propped her leg up and moved her knee from side to side. "I've missed this so much."

Did she miss him in particular or just being able to relax without someone jumping down her throat?

Seemed like it had been a million years since the first time they met. He'd gone to the art museum with another chick on a first date. She'd been an artist too and he'd hoped to impress her with his false knowledge of art so he could fuck her.

But at the museum he'd found the most enchanting piece of art he'd ever seen in his life. It bewitched him at first glance. Michelangelo couldn't have painted something this remarkable. This work of art wasn't hanging on the wall or propped on a platform.

This work of art was just as alive as he was. She walked around the museum with some dude and Bruce forgot about the other chick and why he'd been with her. Once he saw the girl with that short green hair, giant smile and bright eyes it was too late.

Shit he didn't believe in love at first sight but with one look he knew he and Dylan would be together.

He lay back. She hummed beside him.

That day he'd declared his mission of wooing the chick with the short green hair. He vowed to win her heart no matter how hard it would be.

And he had.

∞ ∞ ∞ ∞

Zoë arrived at Steven's five minutes after he called. He didn't speak just gestured for her to come inside. He obviously hadn't invited her over for lovemaking or a glass of wine.

They went into the living room. He didn't take her up to his bedroom or light candles like he had before. He didn't tell her how beautiful she was or that he wanted to make love to her. His eyes didn't hold the passion of an encouraging lover but the glare of a cop.

What was going on?

"How come I get the feeling you didn't invite me over for a little nightcap huh?" The red teddy underneath her dress couldn't have seemed sillier now. "Am I wrong?" She unbuttoned the first two buttons of her dress.

He sat on the arm of the couch. "We need to talk."

"What do you wanna talk about?"

He scratched his arm. "Are you really in love with me?"

"I am falling in love with you, yes."

"And you want this to grow into something more than what it is?"

"I think I've been clear about that." She sat on the table.

"And you trust me right?"

"Of course I do. Steven what's going on?"

"And I assume you want me to trust you too right?"

She kissed him so hard that their lips made a suckling noise when she pulled away.

"Does that answer your question?" She opened another button. "If not then maybe this will."

"No." He laid his hand on her chest. "This isn't happening okay?"

"Did I do something wrong?" She touched his cheek. "I love you, Steven. Nothing else matters."

"I need to know more about you and I mean it."

"I don't get this attitude but I'll play along." She closed her dress halfway. "I've been as honest with you as possible but if you don't believe that then ask away." She crossed her legs.

"I wanna know the truth about you and Billy Curtis."

CHAPTER FORTY-TWO

"I...I told you the truth."

"We both know you didn't."

"I don't know what you mean."

"You remember when I went out of town a few weeks ago?"

"Yes. You went to some law enforcement seminar in Chicago."

"Guess again."

"Well what did you go there for then?"

"Bree and I went to Chicago to find out answers about you and Billy. We spoke to his friend Kael."

"Why would you lie to me?"

"Because I asked you to be honest about Billy and you weren't."

"The fuck I wasn't! I told you he was bothering me and that I didn't want anything to do with him. He tried to rape me and I shot him in self-defense." She touched his knee. "I thought you believed me."

"I did at the time."

"What changed? Oh right." She snapped her fingers. "You said you went to Chicago with *Bree* right?" She got up. "Yeah I see now."

"Zoë."

"Let me guess. This bitch is planting lies about me in your head and you're dumb enough to believe her?"

"This has nothing to do with Bree and I'm not about to play these games with you anymore."

"You're the one playing games. You go off to Chicago behind my back and ask questions about me? How could you?"

"I wanted the truth and obviously you weren't telling it."

"I didn't lie about anything. I thought you were on my side."

"You might as well just admit that you and Billy were more than just drinking buddies."

"I don't have to listen to this." She went to the door. "Call me when you wanna listen to reason and not before then."

He held the door closed. "You're not going anywhere."

"What the hell is the matter with *you*? Why are you treating me like some criminal you hardly know?"

"Just cut the shit okay? It's over, Zoë. You can say what you want but I know you've been lying."

"She's turned you against me hasn't she?" She caressed his cheeks. "This is Brianna's fault. Can't you see she's jealous?"

He knocked her hands down. "Why did you give Billy money?"

Fuck.

"Did Kael tell you that?"

"What do you think?"

"Before I knew how warped Billy was I wanted to help him out. I didn't say anything because I thought if I told I'd given him money that people would try to say his death wasn't self-defense. I thought people would twist things."

He raised an eyebrow. "Why did you go to Chicago in the first place?"

"You mean the very first time?"

"Yep." He kept his spot between her and the door.

"I just like to go places to get away you know? I thought Chicago would be interesting to see. I ended up at Kael's bar and met Billy there. It turned into this other shit and I got in over my head. That's the absolute truth, Steven."

"Hmm well Kael paints you to be some femme fatale who seduced Billy and gave him money to do something for you."

"That's a crock of shit. What the hell does Kael know? He never liked me from the beginning and I don't know why."

"So you gave Billy money to help him out?"

"Yes. That's all it was. He had a ton of bills and was whining about his financial situation. I had the cash and I felt sorry for him that's all. Maybe I shouldn't have done it. It put more ideas in Billy's head about us but I just felt so bad for him."

"And you really expect me to believe this story?"

"It's the truth!"

"I get the feeling you wouldn't know the truth if it were between your legs."

"Oh!" She slapped him. "How dare you speak to me like that? I love you, Steven. Please don't treat me like this."

"Ever heard of Kenneth Brockman?"

She almost threw up over them both. "No."

"Oh well uh, he was believed to be Jim Klein."

"Klein?"

He clapped. "And the Oscar goes to Zoë Peron for Best Actress."

"Stop it! I don't know who you're talking about."

"Oh you know. Jim Klein was the man responsible for Elle Givens' baby being kidnapped. Surely you haven't forgotten those clippings Nadia had of all this."

"What the hell does this have to do with me? You're acting crazy."

"Kael wasn't the only person Bree and I spoke to in Chicago."

She lifted her head.

"We talked to a cop who is investigating Kenneth's, Klein's murder."

"Murder?"

"Oh yeah he's dead. The police believe Billy had something to do with Klein's death."

"Get out of my way!"

"No." He pulled her from the door.

"Let go of me, Steven!"

"I want you to admit it."

"Let me go." She smacked him. "Let me go, Steven!"

"Tell me the truth. Did you have something to do with Klein's murder?"

"God you're crazy."

"Answer me." He pulled her into the living room. "Is that why you gave Billy that money?"

"No! Why would I be involved in something so horrible? I didn't know what Billy was up to."

"Were you at Nadia's the night she died?"

"What? Are you crazy? No."

"You're a liar."

"No."

He held her tighter. "All this time you've lied about everything to everyone but you won't get away with it anymore, Zoë. You were at Nadia's weren't you? Why would you hide that?"

"Steven."

"Answer me damn it. What the hell is going on with you?"

She drifted to that dark horizon in her mind that held her deepest sins and gave her the courage to act them out. That place where vulnerability didn't exist or have power over her.

That place she'd lived all her life.

"Please don't do this, Steven. I care about you so much."

"Then be honest with me. See I know your big secret."

She shivered. "I don't know what you're talking about."

"Your Nick and Elle's adopted daughter aren't you?"

"Oh my god."

"Zoë?" His fingers stiffened on her arms.

"Oh no, no, no." She flattened her hands against his chest. "You know don't you?"

He took a long breath. "Know what?"

A tear fell. "That I'm the killer."

∞ ∞ ∞ ∞

Dylan checked the clock by Bruce's bedroom. She didn't remember dozing off but she'd been asleep for at least twenty minutes.

"Bruce?" She went downstairs. She smelled her paints from the living room.

Bruce stooped in front of her easel shirtless and barefoot. His jeans hugged his tight ass.

He hadn't turned on the overhead light, just the desk lamp on the table in the corner.

A Three Stooges episode ran on the television in mute. Bruce seemed oblivious to everything except the easel.

"Bruce?"

"Shh." He waved a dark-blue palm.

"What are you doing?" She peeked around him. He pushed her back, leaving blue fingerprints on her gown.

"Look what you just did to my gown. What are you doing in my paints?"

"Shh. I got it." His ass moved from side to side as he finger-painted odd shapes on the canvas. He'd mixed several of her paints together to get the unique blue.

"Bruce?" She yanked up one of her brand new paints he'd opened. "How could you?"

222

Stacy-Deanne

He put dots around the edges of the canvas. "What?"

"Oh you know what!" She punched him in the back.

"Oww!"

"You ruined my paint! Look at this!" She seized the bowl of mixed paints. "You got my army green in here with the black? You know how much this stuff costs?"

He dipped his fingers in the white. "You didn't have the blue I wanted."

"Don't dip your fingers in the white when you got blue on your hands!" She dipped blue streaks out of the white paint. "Are you a complete moron?"

"Just go on back to sleep. I was trying to surprise you."

"Oh you surprised me all right." She covered her paints. "You messed up my paint."

"No I didn't."

"Bullshit." She shoved him from the easel. "Just get away from my stuff. This isn't anything to play around with."

"Hold on." He laughed. "I was just trying to do something nice for you."

"Oh this is nice?" She followed him around the room throwing baby punches to his chest.

"Hey, stop." He laughed with his arms up. "Cut it out, Dylan."

"And you think it's funny? You're gonna buy me new paint." She punched his arm. "I don't care what you gotta do."

"I was trying to be nice and paint you something!" He laughed. "I was trying to be nice."

She followed him into the kitchen. "You're an asshole."

"Oh come on." He turned on the sink and poured dishwashing liquid on his hands. "You can't see the compassion in this at all?"

"Well I guess I can't."

"No good deed goes unpunished right?" He washed his hands. "So what do you think of my masterpiece?"

"It's not funny. You're like a big kid sometimes."

"So I opened your brand new paints. Wow." He threw the dishtowel on the counter. "Come on. You're a *little* flattered aren't you?"

She turned so he wouldn't see her smile.

"Hey I really was trying to paint you something. I thought it would get your mind off things you know? I wanted you to wake up and see it."

"Well I'm glad I was asleep already or that thing would've

given me nightmares."

"Fuck you." He threw the towel at her.

She laughed. "Okay I do appreciate the gesture but you still owe me some new paint."

"And you owe me an apology."

"Excuse me?"

"You heard me. Tell me you're sorry or I'll tickle it out of you."

"I don't have anything to apologize for." She stood behind the table. "You should apologize to me."

"No apologize for being a bitch when I was doing something nice." He chased her around the table.

"Stay away from me!" She laughed. "Bruce! Wait!" She zipped from around him and went to the sink.

"Apologize." He wiggled his fingers. "Or I'm gonna tickle it out of you."

"You wouldn't." She waved a wooden spoon. "I'll hit you."

"I don't think so." He threw the spoon in the sink.

"Wait, Bruce!" He tickled her stomach. "Stop!" She fell on the floor. He tickled her underarms. "Ha, ha! Leave me alone!"

"Apologize!" He tickled her sides. "Apologize or I'm gonna tickle you to death."

"Ahh! No!" She tried to keep his hands from under her neck. "Ha, ha, ha! Wait! Stop!"

"Come on."

"Okay!" She coughed. "Stop it!"

"I didn't hear an apology yet."

"I'm sorry okay!"

"For what?" He tickled her waist.

"For...oooh....hoo...hoo!" She crawled up in a ball to combat his hands. "For you being such a...a terrible painter!"

"Oh so that's how it is?" He tickled her feet.

"Ooh!" She giggled. "Okay I'm sorry for being bitchy!" She kicked. "Stop!"

"Yeah that's right." He pulled on her gown. "Where you get off acting that way when someone was trying to be nice?"

"You're still an asshole."

He stared at her with his face titled. "You got the prettiest smile."

She went hot in the face and neck. "I uh, I'm going to bed." She headed for the door. "Goodnight."

He got there before she did. "Uh-uh."

"Please, Bruce." She sweated all over. "I just wanna go to bed."

He pulled her close. "You must be psychic because that's exactly what I had in mind."

"Bruce."

"I want you." He pulled one of the straps of her gown down and fondled her erect nipple. "We gonna really play this game, Dylan?" She tingled from his demanding touch. "When we both know you want me too?"

"I...I'm not ready."

"Well." He picked her up. "You better hurry up and get ready."

Ring! Ring!

Dylan giggled. "I'm saved by the bell."

He put her down. "Shit, man."

They went into the living room.

"I swear phones only ring when it's time to fuck." He answered it. "Hello? Yeah she's here." His face went through a million expressions. He ran his hand through his hair. "Thanks for calling." He blew a big breath and hung up.

"Is something wrong?"

"Dylan."

"What?" Butterflies coiled in her stomach. "You look like someone just died or something."

"Fuck. I don't know how to say this."

"Just tell me. After what happened tonight I'm ready for anything."

"Not this. I don't think you could ever be ready for this."

CHAPTER FORTY-THREE

Dylan charged down the hall of the police station with Bruce by her side. She tried to analyze what Bruce had told her because it couldn't be true.

They made it to the little room the police had Zoë in. Brianna and Steven sat on the bench. They smiled at Dylan in a way that should've been comforting but only made her feel worse.

Sandra and Donna sobbed into tissues.

Jasmine pulled Dylan into a smothering embrace. "Oh, honey." Her tears wet Dylan's cheek. "Oh I'm so sorry, baby."

"Just tell me this isn't true." Dylan looked at the detectives. "Please just tell me it isn't true."

"She confessed, Dylan," Steven said. "I'm so sorry. I know this is hard for you."

"And you guys really expect me to believe that my best friend killed my mother? Bruce?" She ran to him. "It's not true." She pushed her face into his shirt. "Oh please tell me this isn't true!"

"I wish I could." He rocked her.

"She wants to speak to you," Brianna said. "Jayce is in there with her now."

"I don't care what anyone says. Zoë is not a killer and she'd never do anything so horrible. She's like my sister. She'd never hurt me."

"We were just telling your aunt things we've found out," Brianna said.

Sandra and Donna held each other.

"What's she talking about, Aunt Jas?"

"Sit down, honey." Jasmine guided Dylan to the bench. "There are a lot of things about Zoë that you don't know."

∞ ∞ ∞ ∞

Zoë sat in the cold interrogation room. The jumpsuit felt more comfortable than she thought it would be. She knew this day would come for a long time. She just hadn't expected it to be like this. Every time she made an effort to tell the truth the fear had stopped her. So she welcomed being cornered. She couldn't run away or pretend everything would work out on its own.

Things never worked out that way. Plus she'd grown so tired of running, lying and pretending. Even freedom hadn't outweighed the guilt.

Dylan stared at her from the other side of the table. Moments went by. She didn't feel like she was really there. She figured she'd end up telling a cop about what she'd done. Even if it ended up being one she cared about. But telling *Dylan* the truth? No one had invented a way to prepare for something like that.

Dylan was her sister. They couldn't be any closer if they shared the same blood.

As long as Dylan knew Zoë loved her then it hadn't been all for nothing.

"I'm sorry, Dylan. I am so, so, so, so sorry."

Dylan closed her eyes.

"You don't understand the place I've been all my life. The pain I've felt. It just consumes you." Dylan moved her hand when Zoë went to touch her. "It gets inside of you and you can't do anything about it. It just takes over and before you know it, it's all you have."

Dylan covered her eyes.

"I'm the daughter Elle Givens and Nick Sebastian adopted, Dylan." Zoë walked around. "They're watching and listening to us from out there aren't they?"

Dylan laid her head on the table.

"God I love you, Dylan. Whatever you believe, please believe that." She touched Dylan's back. Dylan scooted her chair away.

"I never wanted to hurt you. That's not what I wanted to do. But I just couldn't let it go. For years it had been my mission to make things right. Don't you see?" Zoë knelt beside the table. "Dylan my life with my mother was stolen from me. After you were kidnapped she was just breathing but not living."

Dylan turned away from her.

"Jim Klein had ruined so many lives." She clenched her jumpsuit. "And it made me so incredibly angry and sick that he'd gotten away with it. Someone had to make it right. He stole my mother's happiness." She touched Dylan's hair. "You were her entire world."

Dylan jerked her head.

"She loved you more than anything. She was a shadow without you and I tried to make her happy but I couldn't." Zoë stood in the corner. "I knew I could never replace what she'd lost. Please talk to me."

Dylan played with her mood ring.

"I need you to know I loved you. Whatever lies I told or what I did, our friendship meant more to me than anything, Dylan. You are so important in my life. And I never, ever, ever wanted to hurt you."

"You killed my mother, Zoë. You killed my mother!"

"I'm so sorry."

"But you don't regret it do you?"

"No! She deserved what she got. She bought you, Dylan! She bought you and kept you from your real family. That's why I hated her!" Zoë punched the wall. "Nadia is partly responsible for my mother killing herself. I don't regret what I did and I'd do it again and again and again!"

"You're sick." Dylan went to the door.

"Don't leave!"

Dylan stopped.

"You want to know the truth then know the entire truth. You're only seeing it from one side but Nadia caused more pain than I ever could."

"I doubt that."

"Nadia knew you were kidnapped. She *knew* it, Dylan. That's the secret she was trying to tell you. She was trying to tell you what she'd done. She was sicker than I ever could be."

"You stabbed her in the bathroom like she was a piece of meat and *she's* sick?"

"She was. She was obsessed with you, Dylan. She didn't want

you with anyone but her. Everyone else in your life she wanted to cut out and you know that's true. Nadia paid money for you and didn't give a damn about your real parents. How does that make you feel?"

"You killed Shannon."

"I didn't want to."

"Why did you?"

"Look she just got mixed up in it. I followed her the night of Nadia's funeral. I saw her go to the junkyard and I heard her confront Bruce. When she left I caught up with her. I was just gonna ask her some things."

"Why?"

"Remember earlier that day you said that Nadia might've told Shannon something? I wanted to see if she knew Nadia's secret."

"Even if she did, no one knew who you really were or would've been able to connect anything to you."

"I know but I couldn't take the chance. I had to talk to Shannon to make sure."

"If you only planned to talk to her then why did you bring a gun?"

"Dylan."

"You are nothing but a cold-hearted killer. You *planned* to kill Shannon to set Bruce up."

"That's not true."

"Bullshit. You bitch. If you can plan the other shit you've done then you can plan that. You killed Shannon because you knew the police would think Bruce did it."

"Everything happened so fast. I couldn't get a hold on it."

"And you stood by while Bruce went to jail for something you did."

"I didn't plan it. You gotta believe me."

Dylan nodded. "Come on. Don't chicken out on my now, Zoë. You didn't give a damn about anyone but yourself. Look at the people you hurt! You cared about your vendetta and nothing else. Hell you probably would've killed me if I'd gotten in your way!"

"Don't ever say that. You are my best friend in the entire world. I did what I did for *my* mother and everyone else who'd gone through this pain! I was there when my mother killed herself, Dylan!" Zoë punched the table. "I was fuckin' there! I saw her blow her brains out! Her blood landed on my goddamn clothes! You could never, ever know what pain is until you experience something like that."

"So you wanted to cause me the same pain you'd experienced?"

"It wasn't about you."

"Bullshit!" Dylan pushed her. "One thing you don't get is that your revenge involves more than the people you wanted to hurt. You're a psychopath, Zoë."

"I'm not a psychopath! I didn't just kill people for pleasure or thrills. I did it because it's what they deserved."

"You don't get it do you? The fact that you can justify what you've done is why you're a psychopath." Dylan gripped her head. "I just can't believe this is happening to me. What did I do to deserve this?"

"Dylan I love you so much. Please don't hate me."

"You saw what I was going through. You saw what my aunts were going through after Mom was killed. How could you put on an act like you cared when you'd killed her? How could you play with us like that?"

"I didn't want you to be hurt. Please believe that. I didn't want you going through that pain and I did my best to comfort you."

"Our entire friendship was based on lies. You planned every part of it."

"No it..." Zoë sobbed into her hands. "It's not like you're making it sound."

"What do you want from me huh?" Dylan's faced filled with tears. "What could you possibly want?"

"For you to know that I love you and that I always did. You were living a lie and Nadia had no right to do that to you. I wanted to make things right for all of us, you included."

"Well for some reason that's hard to believe, Zoë. I think there's only one person in this room you really care about and it's not me."

"Please."

"Go to hell."

"Dylan?"

"And say hello to Nadia for me when you get there."

She left.

CHAPTER FORTY-FOUR

"You didn't have to follow me home, Bree." Steven threw his keys on the living room table. "I'm fine."

"Well convince me you're fine because I don't believe that you can be."

He stretched out of his blazer. "It's been a long night and I just wanna go to bed."

As if he could sleep.

"You can't pretend this doesn't affect you."

"What am I pretending huh?" He threw his blazer on the couch. "I just wanna go to bed and get some rest. Would you please leave me alone?"

"No."

He got the remote and sat down. "I'm not in the mood to argue with you."

"Well I'm not leaving until we talk."

"I don't know what you want me to say. Zoë's the killer." He shrugged. "And?"

"And you cared about her."

He flicked through channels.

"Steve." She sat beside him. "I've been through something similar to this myself remember?"

"This is nothing like you and Simon Watts."

"You're right about that." She adjusted the pillow behind her back. "I killed Simon."

He crossed his arms.

"And even though I know it was what I had to do, it doesn't make it any easier to live with. I cared about Simon the same way you care about Zoë. That's what makes it so hard to get over."

"Maybe we'll never get over it."

"Maybe not." She laid her head back. "But one thing we can do is make sure we don't try to do it alone. I'll always be there for you, Steve. We're friends despite anything else."

"It just doesn't even feel real. I know she confessed and I know she's the killer but it just doesn't seem real."

"That's how I felt about Simon."

"I feel so ashamed because I still care about her."

"Of course you do. You can't expect your feelings to just shut off. There's nothing wrong with caring. What would be wrong is you letting this eat you up when it was beyond your control."

"If I feel this bad can you imagine how Dylan's feeling?"

"Ooh." Brianna crossed her legs Indian-style. "She didn't deserve any of this. No one does."

"You know what really bothers me? All this makes me wonder how much we know about our own families." He took off his shoes. "Look at all the shit Nadia was hiding. No one had a clue of what she'd done not even the people closest to her. Can you imagine how Dylan feels? How it would feel to learn that your entire life has been a lie and that your mother could do something so horrendous?" He touched his stomach. "Makes me wanna hurl right here."

"I know I shouldn't feel like this but a part of me believes Nadia got what she deserved. I know that Zoë did a horrible thing but what Nadia did..." Brianna shook her head. "In a way it was worse. She contributed to the pain so many people had gone through for years."

"You think our parents could be hiding stuff from us too?"

She pulled tiny threads off the couch. "Not something like this."

"But how would we know? How do we really know our lives aren't lies too?"

"We just know."

"Like Dylan just knew?"

∞ ∞ ∞ ∞

232

Dylan dotted dark blue paint over the yellow and red stripes on the canvas. She'd been painting since they got back from the station. Her arms should've fallen off by now but she wasn't even sore. She didn't feel *anything*. Numb inside and out.

She wanted to jump into her paint and swim over the canvas. Get lost in something she'd created. Escape.

"Dylan?" Bruce's fingers crawled up her arms. "It's almost four in the morning." He nuzzled his face in the back of her neck. "I thought you'd gone to bed already."

She almost broke her paintbrush in half.

"Talk to me. Tell me how you're feeling."

What did he expect her to say? That she didn't feel like any human would to find out their mother had bought her like a piece of furniture and created some fake existence to protect her disgusting secret?

She trickled brown paint at the bottom of the picture. She did her best work when she wasn't aiming for a specific direction.

"I know this is hard for you but you can get through it."

"I feel like a fool." She dipped her thickest brush in white paint.

"You're not a fool. How the hell could you know about Zoë or Nadia?"

"Others knew. Maybe I just didn't pay attention."

"What are you talking about?" He yawned. "No one else knew until the cops found out."

"I'm talking about what Nadia did." She flicked the thick brush in water. "It hurts to even say it. Remember I always said I couldn't understand why Clay hated me so much?"

"Clay was an abuser and a drunk. He didn't care about anyone but himself."

"That's what I thought." She added purple to the painting. "That's what Mom let me think but she knew the truth. Clay didn't hate me. He hated her for what she did." She glared at the painting. "Clay knew, Bruce. I know he did. She couldn't have held that in from everyone. She didn't tell her family, not even Aunt Jas. But I know Clay knew."

"You don't know that."

"He used to look at me with such disdain and I'd sit around and wonder why. Now I know."

"Okay that's enough." He took the brush. "You can't paint your problems away."

"Sure I can." She picked another brush.

"No you can't." He took the other one. "These issues are gonna still be here for you to deal with. You can't run from everything, Dylan."

She dripped paint on the carpet. "Shit." She sobbed. "I'm sorry."

"You have nothing to be sorry for." He kissed her. "You didn't do anything wrong. No one could've known what Nadia or Zoë did."

"How could they do this to me, Bruce?" She snuggled in his arms. "How could two people I loved so much hurt me like this?"

"Shh." He patted her head. "If I could take it away I would."

"What do I do? How the hell can I go back to living a life after all this? I don't even know who I am now."

"Course you do. You're the same talented, loveable, beautiful and passionate woman you've always been. The woman I love with all my heart."

"I'm not so sure I am."

"You are but you can't run from things anymore. That's all you do."

She sat on the stool by his magazine rack. "You telling me you could deal with this any better? How could you possibly know how this feels?"

"You're right. I have no idea how this feels for you." He swung his arms. "But if you look at it, it's not that bad of a situation."

"Bruce my mother bought me. I was kidnapped and stolen from my parents."

"Yeah but look at the good that came out of it. You got a part of your real history now if Nick's your father. Take the DNA test." He bent in front of her. "You got to if just for closure."

She swung her feet. "So what if Nick is my father? You expect me to fall into his arms and love him with no questions asked?"

"Don't you already love him?"

"It's not that easy."

"Dylan you gotta look at the big picture okay? This will be the chance you get to know your real family. Your blood family and that's a beautiful thing."

"Blood family?"

"Honey it's not just about your real parents. You probably got aunts, uncles, cousins and shit you never even thought of. The situation is fucked up I agree but what you got now is wonderful. It outweighs all of that other shit. This is the biggest opportunity of your life. Can you turn your back on it?"

"Bruce."

"Can you live your life not knowing if Nick is your real father? No one says you have to accept it, just find out for yourself. For your life and your history. Just to know, babe." He kissed her cheek. "Just to know."

"I'm just scared. Can you understand that?"

"I gotta be honest. I'm jealous."

"Jealous?"

"I know my dad and I weren't close but I loved the bastard. If I could have one minute with him I'd take it faster than you could blink. I know you felt the same way about Nadia when she died. You just wanted one more chance to make sure she knew you loved her and to make sure she'd be in peace. Well I wanted that for my dad too. All that arguing and shit was just wasted time. I can never get that back." He kissed her hand. "Don't make the mistake that I did. You have the chance to be with your father if you open your heart." He touched her face. "Take the test, Dylan. Don't lose what I wish I could get back."

CHAPTER FORTY-FIVE

Three Months Later

"Oh Dylan you look beautiful." Sandra stuck the white rose above Dylan's right ear.

"Like a princess." Donna held a tissue to her nose.

"Oh Aunt Donna stop crying." Dylan kissed her cheek. "Please be happy for me."

"I am." She blew her nose. "I just can't believe you're getting married."

"Hmm." Jasmine brushed off Dylan's veil. "That makes two of us."

"Aunt Jas please." Dylan played with her dress in the mirror. "You promised you would behave."

"How can I?" She fumbled with the veil. "You're marrying someone who is gonna ruin your life. Bruce McNamara is not the man for you."

"I think that's her decision, Jasmine." Sandra fastened the back of Dylan's dress.

"Oh come off it." Jasmine plucked the lace on her hat. "You mean to tell me that you and Donna don't have a problem with her marrying Bruce? And having a shotgun wedding at that?"

"It's not a shotgun wedding. Jeez." Dylan snatched her veil.

"It might as well be for the good this is."

"Well if you don't like it then you don't have to stay." Donna helped Dylan with her veil. "You promised me you were gonna trust me from now on."

"I do." Jasmine marched around the bedroom in her blue satin suit. "But I'll never agree with this. Bruce is gonna drag you down."

"How?" Dylan untangled the veil. "He loves me and I love him."

"Well love don't pay the bills."

Sandra combed Dylan's short sides. "It didn't pay the bills for you and Charlie either."

Jasmine sat on the bed. "Excuse me?"

"You heard her." Donna dabbed concealer on Dylan's cheeks. "Charlie was just like Bruce when you first met him."

"That's a lie." Jasmine crossed her legs. "Charlie had a plan for us."

"Really?" Donna smoothed blush into Dylan's cheeks. "So working two jobs that paid below minimum wage and having you guys get clothes and food from church charities for the first five years of marriage was a plan?"

Jasmine huffed. "This isn't about me."

"Yes it is." Sandra spread lotion on Dylan's hands. "You loved Charlie and at first no one thought he was good enough for you but you didn't listen."

"Oh this isn't at all the same thing. Charlie wasn't a brute like Bruce is. He didn't have a record." She scratched underneath her hat. "And that's another thing, Dylan. He won't be able to get a decent job because he's been in prison. Is this who you really wanna start your life with?"

"Yes!" She twirled around. "I love him, the entire package. I want to marry Bruce and whether we have a rough time or not, I'll be happy. I'll be happy because I'll be with him."

"But you're getting married in his backyard by a Justice of the Peace. When you dreamt of getting married I bet this isn't what you had in mind."

"Maybe it wasn't but it's what I want now. I could marry Bruce anywhere and it wouldn't be any less special."

"Oh please, Dylan. Does it have to be Bruce? Of all the men in the world you could be with."

"Yes it has to be Bruce. I love him. How many more times do you have to hear it to understand?"

"I just don't want anything to happen to you. You've been through so much lately. I just think you're rushing into something you can't handle."

"She can handle more than you know," Sandra said. "It's her day, Jasmine. Who are we to take that away from her?"

"Isn't it more important that Dylan be happy?" Donna passed Dylan her shoes. "Isn't that what we've always wanted for her?"

"Okay fine." Jasmine puffed out the front of Dylan's dress. "I don't like it and I don't like Bruce. But I will accept this."

"Thank you so much, Aunt Jas." Dylan hugged her. "That's the best wedding gift anyone could give."

"Okay." Sandra pulled Dylan from Jasmine's hold. "You're gonna start crying and messing up your make-up. Let's give her the gifts." She gave Dylan a tiny black box. "For something borrowed."

"Oh, Aunt Sandra. Your pearl earrings?"

Dylan held one up. "I'm not worthy."

"You've been begging to borrow them forever so now you can."

"Oh thank you so much." Dylan put them on. "They fit my dress perfectly."

"Okay, something blue." Donna took out a gold bracelet with a cluster of sapphires. "Here you go, honey."

"Oh, Aunt Donna." Dylan slipped it on. "It's gorgeous." She hugged her. "Thank you so much."

Jasmine cleared her throat. "I got you something new."

"Aunt Jas you actually got me something?"

"I might not want you to marry Bruce but I wasn't gonna go without getting you something." She took out an envelope. "Open it."

Dylan pulled out two plane tickets to Hawaii.

"Oh my god!" She jumped up and down.

"Oh my god! Oh my god!"

"What?" Sandra laughed. "Tell us!"

"Two tickets to Hawaii!" Dylan danced around the room. "Ahh! I've always wanted to go to Hawaii!"

"I know." Jasmine scrunched her face. "You can go on your... honey...honey..."

"Come on. You can say it." Sandra touched Jasmine's shoulder. "Honeymoon, sis."

"Funny."

"Oh Aunt Jas you're the best!" Dylan hugged her. "Oh I love

you! I can't believe you did this for me."

"You deserve even more than that."

"Oh I love you, Aunt Jas!" Dylan kissed her.

"Okay, okay." Jasmine wiped lipstick off her cheek. "You're gonna mess up your makeup."

"I can't believe Bruce and I will be honeymooning in Hawaii! Owww!"

"Oh that was nice, sis." Donna kissed Jasmine's cheek.

Sandra snapped her fingers. "We need something old now."

"Am I old enough?" Nick walked in.

Sandra nudged Donna.

"Oh uh, hello, Nick."

"Hello, Donna." He kept his hands behind his back. "Is everyone okay?"

"What are you doing here?"

He cleared his throat. "I didn't come to cause trouble, Jasmine. I'm not here to fight."

"Then answer my question." Her satin heels squeaked when she approached him. "I'm pretty sure you didn't receive an invitation."

"Isn't it obvious I came to see Dylan?"

"Why?" She pulled the veil over her face.

"Honey please. You know why I had to see you."

Jasmine slid in front of Dylan. "She told you she needed time and space yet you pop up at the worst times."

"This is the worst time?" He straightened his bowtie. "My daughter's getting married today and I think I have a right to be here."

"Not if she didn't invite you."

"Well the groom invited me."

"What?" Dylan batted underneath the veil.

"I know it's strange but Bruce invited me. He said I should be here. He said he spoke to you about it but you didn't agree."

"It's not that I didn't want you here it's just..."

"Too hard for her. Can't you respect her wishes? You expect Dylan to just accept you as her father because of some DNA test results? She still doesn't know you."

"She knows me well enough. It's not about the time we've been together, it's about our bond. I'm her father and that won't change whether you like it or not."

"This is supposed to be the happiest day of her life! She doesn't need added stress."

"Cool it, Jasmine," Sandra said. "Why don't we leave them alone?"

"Nick I want you out of here."

"Jasmine that shouldn't be your decision."

"Aunt Donna's right. I will be making my own decisions from now on, Aunt Jas. I said it and I meant it. I would like to talk to Nick alone."

"But..."

"You heard her, sis." Donna gave Jasmine the evil eye. "She wants to talk to him. We have no right to butt in."

Sandra got Dylan's bouquet. "I'll take this down for you, sweetie." She kissed Dylan's cheek.

Jasmine stood in the doorway with her arms up. "You sure about this, Dylan?"

She nodded.

Donna swept up the ends of her dress as she went to the door. "Nice to see you again, Nick."

"You too, Donna. You look lovely."

"Thank you."

"Let's go, Jasmine." Sandra flung her out the door.

"Oh and uh, I should warn you guys." Nick lifted a finger. "Mr. Swaggert's out there licking the frosting off the vanilla cupcakes and putting them back on the tray."

"*What?*" Dylan flicked her veil off her face.

"Yeah if I were you I'd get down there before he transports his germs on anything else."

"Oh gross!" Sandra ran out.

"Goodness I swear that man was raised by wolves." Donna shut the door behind her.

"Is that for me?"

"Yeah." Nick passed Dylan the gift-wrapped box. "Do me a favor. Don't open it until after the wedding."

"You didn't have to get me anything." She set it on the dresser.

"You really mean I didn't have to come. Isn't that what you mean?"

"Don't do this."

"How can I not?"

"You said you'd give me space."

"I know but this is so hard for me. I think about you all the time. I want us to have a relationship."

"We had one but it was based on lies."

"Are you gonna hold that against me forever?"

"I don't know. Might."

"You're just like your mother." He touched her cheek.

"Don't."

"You are. Elle was just as stubborn as you. She'd do something just because you told her not to and never do something you tell her she should. But I loved that about her. It's like someone took everything she was and poured it into a bottle and out came you."

"I uh saw they'd interviewed Zoë in the paper the other day."

"Yes."

"So she kills people and they treat her like a celebrity?"

"She didn't wanna do the interview."

"I hope she spends the rest of her life in prison."

"I visited her last week and she told me to tell you she misses you."

"Am I supposed to care?" She put on perfume. "I can't believe you still do."

"She did a horrible thing but she is still my daughter. I can't turn my back on my child no matter what. I'm the only one she has."

"Seeing you has made me more nervous than getting married."

"I'm sorry. I didn't come here to upset you. Are you uh sure you are ready to marry Bruce?"

"That's none of your business."

"Bruce said I could stay for the wedding but I won't if it's gonna bother you. I'll be out of town for a few weeks. I'll be in Atlanta visiting my sister. She isn't doing too well."

"What's wrong with her?"

"She has pneumonia."

"Oh no."

"Yeah she's had respiratory problems all her life. She's usually able to fight them off with her medications but I guess because of her age it's getting harder."

"How old is she?"

"She'll be sixty-eight this November. Yep, my older sister." He smiled. "Should've seen us when we were younger. The hell she put me through."

"I bet you put her through some times too. Little brothers can be hell."

"You ever wanted siblings?"

"Sometimes. I figure I probably would've had more independence or at least not babied so much if I had a brother or sister. But a little of me enjoys being the only child. Uh." She sat on the bed. "I didn't know you had a sister."

"You don't know anything about me. That's the point. But I want you to."

"I bet she's nice, your sister."

"My mom's still living. My dad died ten years ago."

"Have you told your family about me?"

"That I found you? Of course." He moved to the bed. "They wanted to come up here weeks ago. I told them not to because I knew you wouldn't be ready."

"Wow. It's like being in another world. I don't know where I belong right now."

"I told you there was more involved than just the people around here. You've got tons of family that want to know you, Dylan. My family and Elle's. They were there when we went through all that pain and they prayed we'd find you one day."

"This is just so overwhelming." She patted her bosom. "I can't stop shaking."

"Shh." He held her hand. "Don't get upset. Save that until after the wedding."

She laughed. "Well." She moved her hand from his.

"I guess you better get down there huh?" He looked at his watch. "It's ten minutes to two."

"Yeah." She looked in the mirror. "How do I look?" She pulled at the sides of her dress. "Do I look fat?"

"You fat? Look at that waist it's the size of a French fry."

"I guess this dress makes things appear larger."

"You look amazing. Like I knew you would." He dropped his head.

"What's wrong?"

"I've dreamt of this day. Every father does. I just didn't dream it would be this way."

"It's not your fault I was kidnapped. You gotta stop blaming yourself."

"I blame myself every single day. For your kidnapping, Elle's death, what Zoë' did, everything. I should've stopped all of this pain before it reached so many lives."

"Let it go, Nick." She touched his shoulder. "Stop looking at the past. That's what I'm gonna do."

"I just want you to know that I'll always be there for you. I won't pressure you. Just please let me know if you need me."

"I appreciate that."

"I love you so much." He kissed her forehead. "I wish you and Bruce the best and I hope you're very happy."

"Thank you."

He stroked the front of his white tuxedo jacket. "I'll see you when I get back from Atlanta."

"Nick, wait." She held the sides of her dress. "Would you like to escort me?"

"Walk you down the aisle?"

"Well we'll be in the backyard so there's no aisle." She grinned. "But would you just like to walk me out there?"

"Are you sure?"

"Yes."

"Oh." He hugged her. "You don't know how happy this makes me."

"But understand that I still need time. This doesn't mean I can just accept everything."

"Of course." He dabbed his eyes with his handkerchief. "I'm so happy though."

"I thought men didn't cry at weddings." She put her arm in his.

"I don't know about other men but fathers do." He led her into the hall. "Fathers do."

THE END

CPSIA information can be obtained at www.ICGtesting.com
Printed in the USA
LVOW060300280412

279455LV00003B/5/P

9 780985 076306